MORTAL GREEN

THE CONNECTION TRILOGY - BOOK 3

ANITA WALLER

BLOODHOUND
— BOOKS —

www.bloodhoundbooks.com

Print ISBN 978-1-914614-76-7

ALSO BY ANITA WALLER

*For Susan Hunter, for being my friend and
for being such a wonderful supporter of my work.
Thank you, Susan.*

Green is the prime colour of the world, and
that from which its loveliness arises.
— *Pedro Calderon de la Barca, Spanish poet and playwright,*
1600–1681

Green represents the dead image of life.
— *Rudolf Steiner, Austrian philosopher, literary scholar, architect,*
and educator, 1861–1925

PROLOGUE
2ND MARCH 2020

Faith Young pulled on a bobble hat – almost a match in colour for the dark green three-quarter length padded jacket she had opted to wear – and opened the front door. The hat hid most of her short dark hair, and she had added a small amount of lipstick to take away the winter greyness showing in her face. The holiday in Jamaica booked for June was beckoning, but not fast enough.

It wasn't raining, but she could sense impending drops in the cold March air. She hesitated, wondering whether to take her umbrella, but decided it would be one less thing to carry. She hitched on the backpack and closed the door behind her, after automatically patting her jacket pocket to check she had remembered to pick up the key. She walked down the tiny unadopted lane that led to the main road, remembering her arrival, and feeling pleased that her Aygo was a small town car, and not the Range Rover her husband Jack had recently acquired. His would never have squeezed down the track without folding in both wing mirrors.

Will Sandford, the owner of the property she had rented for a month, had given her written instructions for a walk down through Eyam, through a wooded part, then exiting at the top end of the village. He had marked on all the tourist attractions, places she had only seen in books prior to arriving in Eyam two days earlier. She was glad she had thought to put the piece of paper in a plastic sleeve; if the threatened rain did appear at least her instructions wouldn't disintegrate.

She didn't walk at speed. The words at the top of the instructions said approximately three hours, and she knew she would occasionally veer off track to investigate something, then write items into her notebook, so that three hours would probably be a very conservative estimate. She needed some thinking time; her life was on the edge of something new, and she didn't know how to handle what was a potential life-changing decision. She probably needed every minute of that three hours.

She left Leaf Cottage and walked down the main road, stopping to take multiple pictures of the Plague Cottages. These were already in her book, but the reality of seeing them in the flesh blew her away. This was real history. The whole village and the outskirts were real history. She paused a little longer by Rose Cottage, feeling almost a sense of grief for the nine members of the Thorpe family who had all been taken by the plague between September 1665 and May 1666.

She moved on to Plague Cottage where five people had lived. The mother, Mary Hadfield, survived, but her new husband and her two sons, along with an employed hand, had all perished over a period of eleven months. Mary, Faith noted in her book, lost thirteen relatives. Maybe Mary Hadfield could be the centre point Faith was looking for – maybe a descendant? Maybe even bring thirteen into the title? Thirteen Dead...

She felt the enthusiasm grow within her and knew Jack had been right when he had suggested she take off for a month, rent a holiday cottage in Eyam, and concentrate solely on the current book, immerse herself in the real Eyam and not the Eyam anyone could research in books or online.

Already strong ideas were forming, linking Eyam's bleak historical past with the present day and she leaned against a wall while she added something else to her notes. A splodge of rain landed on the paper, and she slipped the small notebook into her pocket.

She took out her instructions and headed towards the stocks. Her brain went into overdrive. Maybe a body discovered in the stocks? She read the words on the information board and saw they had been built for the miners in the lead mining industry who had committed relatively minor offences. She gave a brief smile as she thought of miners committing minor offences, took some pictures and continued on her journey.

Her iPhone worked overtime with the number of pictures taken, and eventually she reached a tea room, where she gratefully found an empty table. She ordered a ham salad sandwich and a pot of tea, and took out her phone to check the pictures. She wrote fresh ideas into her book, feeling exhilarated by how alive this village was making her. She followed up the sandwich with a strawberry tart, telling herself she would walk off the extra calories as she completed the circuit planned out for her.

She paid her bill and thanked the assistant behind the counter. 'You'll see more of me,' Faith said. 'I'm staying in the village for a month, at Leaf Cottage, and I hope to be doing plenty of walking.'

'You'll be very welcome here,' the woman said with a smile. 'Are you writing a guide book of some sort?'

'No, I am a writer but of fiction. I was actually plotting a murder during my lunch.'

'Awesome. I'm Amanda Gilchrist, by the way. If you need anything.'

'Faith. Faith Young. That's very kind.'

'*The* Faith Young? Loads of books? DI Hardcastle series?'

Faith laughed. 'You've read one or two then?'

'I think all of them. Mostly on Kindle, but I have three or four paperbacks. I'm going to bring them in to work, if you wouldn't mind signing them next time you're in?'

'Of course. I always feel quite honoured.'

'I'll bring them in tomorrow, so call in whenever you can. And I apologise for all the banging and drilling. We're having an extension built, so eventually it will be a bistro in the evenings. We have to put up with the noise for the moment.'

Faith laughed. 'No problem. I live with a DIY husband, my life is a noisy one.'

Faith left the tea room and headed towards where the wooded area began. The rain was heavier, and she pulled up the hood of her jacket, more to keep out the cold than the wet. She increased her walking pace in an effort to warm up, and she immediately climbed as she reached the woods. It was dark under the canopy created by the closeness of the trees, and she wondered how many of them had been there since the plague times.

She could see a house in the distance, with white painted walls and green shutters, one of them open at one she presumed was a bedroom window, smoke rising from a chimney, and an end wall covered in what she guessed was an ivy of the darkest green. She took a quick photograph of the building, and dropped her phone back into her pocket. The rain was getting heavier, and she lowered her head to try to shelter her face from the coldness of the water.

Trudging onwards and upwards, the incline grew steeper, but she realised it meant she must be approaching the top end of the village. She stopped and leaned for a moment against a tree, partly to catch her breath and partly so she could study where she was on the hand-drawn map. She reckoned she had about a quarter mile of woodland left to clear, and she would reach the road she was seeking.

She refolded the map and continued to remain by the tree which seemed to be offering her a modicum of shelter from the rain, and also her somewhat erratic thoughts. She tugged her hood tighter around her head and thought about how to describe this situation in the book; her thoughts about her life would have to wait.

It was creepy, almost felt as though it should be four o'clock rather than one, the skies were becoming greyer by the second, and she pulled out her book to jot down the words, knowing she was simply extending her resting pose until her breathing settled to her more normal level. The climb had been steep, but she could tell it was starting to level out.

There were no sounds, no traffic noise, no bird noise, no wind, no leaves to rustle, merely the relentless heavy downpour of rain. She checked her Fitbit and wasn't surprised to see she had already topped her ten thousand steps target by five hundred.

'You'll sleep tonight, Faith,' she muttered to herself. 'And you're going to need a red hot shower to get you warm again, you numpty. Best check the weather forecast next time you fancy a walk.'

She took out her phone, and took pictures of the scene before her, trying to capture the semi-darkness and the miserable weather, knowing she would spend her evening trying to project the scene in words.

The house was in the far distance, and she adjusted the zoom on her phone to bring it nearer. This building would feature in the book, of that she was sure, and she would make it a place of evil. Who would live there? A psychopath for definite.

Or even a wife who was a psychopath with a husband who had no idea he had bodies buried in the back garden...

She laughed aloud at the thought. It was probably a lovely house in the height of the summer with the golden orb of the sun reflecting off its pristine white walls, but currently it looked to be particularly scary. The smoke was grey, the walls in this darker light had a grey tinge, the dark green of the ivy had morphed into black, and still the rain continued to pour.

She took out her notebook once again and jotted down a few leading words that would remind her of this moment, that would bring back to her later how uncomfortably drenched she felt. House. White – grey in rain. Smoke dark grey. Shutters closed. Why? Open earlier. Ivy black not green. No obv people.

Faith glanced at her Fitbit, saw her heartbeat had dropped to a more manageable ninety-two from the racing one hundred and twenty of ten minutes earlier, and she stood up properly.

She shook herself, checked her phone, notebook, pen and her key were still in her pockets, and took down her hood before removing the green hat. It had slipped further and further forward, until the edge of it was slightly in her eye sight. She swivelled it, seeking out the label, and took one last look at the house.

She heard a crack of a twig, and smiled. In her books this would be cue the murderer, creeping up on the unsuspecting victim. In the real world it was probably a fox or a rabbit or something similar trying to find a dry place to get out of the cold rain.

She felt the thud to her head, but nothing else. No more whiteness, no more greyness, no more green, simply black.

1

The sombreness and bleakness encompassed everything about the Connection Detective Agency that dark early March morning. Today was the day they would say goodbye to Doris Lester, albeit from afar, and without Beth, Joel and Luke.

After much discussion and tears from Alistair as he took in what Beth was unselfishly proposing, they had agreed that Doris's final resting place would be in Fréjus, and when it was time for Alistair to join her, they would be together again.

As a result, Beth, Joel and Luke had gone to the South of France to be with the woman they loved so much, on her final journey. Beth had left instructions that Connection was to close its doors for two days, no admittance to the general public, but she had reckoned without the people of Eyam who had come to know Doris so well when she worked at the agency; the front of the offices bore testament to that feeling; it was covered with a mountain of flowers.

Tessa, Fred, Cheryl and Simon had agreed to meet at the office at the time of the funeral, and share memories of her along with a bottle of champagne. Fred, accompanied by Naomi, was the first to arrive, took one look at the flowers that had appeared overnight and were preventing the opening of the shutters, and walked around to the back. He opened up, put lights on to lighten the place, then went back outside to meet the others.

'That's a first,' Cheryl said, taking off her coat when they went inside. 'I've never really used the back door.'

Fred placed the champagne in the fridge, and they moved into Beth's office, setting chairs up around her desk. Cheryl lit a candle and placed it in the centre. She unpacked the huge bag she had brought and put out containers of food. 'Doris was a lovely woman,' she said. 'She deserves a proper wake. When I lost Keith she called to see me and brought me a beautiful lemon cake. I'll never forget her kindness, and I know how much Luke loved her. He would have done anything for her.'

They chatted amongst themselves, talking about their memories of Doris over the previous three years, her kindness, her mentorship of Luke, and then Tessa produced the champagne along with her laptop. Fred filled the glasses and they all looked at the screen, with Cheryl, Fred and Simon seeing the video for the first time – the now-legendary film of Doris battering Ewan Barker, the whole episode caught on CCTV to the point where he virtually crawled out of the office. There was a concerted cheer at the end, and everyone raised their glasses.

'To our lovely Doris,' Tessa said. 'May she rest in peace. We'll never forget her.'

Tessa was alone. The others had gone home, and she had volunteered to tidy Beth's office, explaining she'd like some quiet time to reflect. She locked the back door, and simply sat for a moment staring at the empty containers and equally empty glasses. Losing Hannah and Doris within four months of each other was almost unbearable. Tessa didn't know what she believed, but she hoped they were now together.

Beth, Joel and Luke were due home the following day, sometime after lunch. Their flight from Nice was around ten, and with Joel's car at Manchester airport she knew they wouldn't be late back. The arrangement was that they would stay at Alistair and Doris's home until after the funeral, and they could visit anytime they wanted, the door would always be open to anyone from Connection.

Tessa picked up a napkin and wiped her eyes. The tears were for Doris, but also partly for the world. So many deaths from the virus already, and a government running around like headless chickens wondering what to do about it.

She took a deep breath and stood. The dishes wouldn't wash themselves, and she headed for the kitchen.

Half an hour later, after a quick polish of Beth's desk, she looked around. Everything back to normal, she blew out the candle.

Doris's light went out.

Tessa let herself out of the back door, setting the alarm and locking it. She walked around the building and towards the front door to look at all the flowers. Bending down she moved them around so that access to the shutters would be easier the next day, but there were so many, and she wanted to cry all over again.

Although still officially closed for one more day, Tessa knew they would all drift by the office at some point; they were feeling a little rudderless and touching base at Connection would help.

She read the messages and knew Doris must have affected so many people in some small way. Finally she was happy they would be able to get in using their normal route and she stood for a moment, observing. Beautiful flowers for an exceptional woman.

'You okay, love?' The woman's voice startled her, and she turned to see an elderly lady in a thick navy coat, holding a bouquet of chrysanthemums.

'Not really,' Tessa said. 'It's been a sad day.'

'I've brought these for Doris. We used to swap novels. I met her looking through the second-hand books in the Co-op, and we got chatting about favourite authors, as you do. She came for a cuppa at mine the day after and brought me a box full. We've met up quite a few times since then. I'll miss her.' She bent down and placed the flowers with the others. 'Looks as though a lot of people liked Doris.'

Tessa smiled. 'She was that sort of person. Nothing was ever too much trouble, and she still had years of life left in her.'

The old lady nodded. 'Coronavirus, so I understand. Bit scary.'

'Certainly is. Can I offer you a lift?'

'No, you're fine, love. I'm nipping across to the Co-op, stock up on some bits so I don't have to go out for a few days. I'm only a five-minute walk from home anyway. Now you take care. My condolences to all of you, we've lost a lovely lady.'

Tessa drove home deep in thought. They should do something to keep Doris's memory alive, some sort of permanent 'thing' that people could think about and say oh yes, that's for Doris Lester. The woman had been a force of nature, after all, and should be remembered for the special person she was.

Tessa pulled up outside her home but remained in her car,

leaving the engine running. It was warm, and she knew it wouldn't be inside the house because the heating timer wouldn't have switched on the boiler yet. She stared around her and decided the time had come to seriously think about moving. At this time of year the twenty-five-minute journey wasn't too bad unless it snowed, but in summer she would have tourists to contend with, cows and sheep on roads, and other assorted Derbyshire specialities. She needed to be in Eyam, where she could walk to work, collect her car easily if she needed to go out, and be part of a community she was growing to appreciate. Time to start house-hunting, she decided.

She switched off her engine, locked the car and walked up the garden path. As she had known, the house was cold and she overrode the timer to fire up the boiler. The whoosh it made was a satisfying sound.

She kept on her coat while she switched on the kettle; she wasn't hungry but felt a cup of tea would not only warm her, but it would also comfort her. And today she needed comfort above all else.

Five minutes later, mug of tea in hand, she woke her laptop and searched estate agents' websites for houses for sale in Eyam.

In Fréjus, Luke went to bed before the others. The early start to catch the plane at Nice airport had been his excuse, but he didn't want to talk. He felt angry that Doris was gone, taken way before her time because of this cruel virus that seemed to be killing indiscriminately. The French government didn't seem to be any more effective at controlling it than the British one, and he sensed this was only the beginning. Already it had reached epidemic status, and he was scared. His nan was the same age as Doris – his second 'Nan' – would she succumb to it as well?

His phone pinged, and he saw **Love you xxx** on the screen.

The light in his darkness. He texted back, and for the next half hour he text-chatted with girlfriend Maria until she said it was time to sleep, didn't want him missing the plane.

Alistair drove Beth, Joel and Luke to the airport and watched with sadness as they walked through passport control, and away from his sight. The year, and his life, that had started in such a promising fashion, was now flat and hopeless. He and Doris had had so many plans, plans they had been discussing even when she complained of the sore throat. He had given her a glass of milk to try to soothe it, and she had said she couldn't taste it... three days later she was gone.

Dejected, he turned away and walked back to his car, to return to the home they had both loved. Today he would wait until Beth rang to say they were safely home and then go to Doris's graveside and tell her that.

At various points during the day Cheryl, Fred, Tessa and Simon all dropped in at Connection on the pretext of checking that Oliver was okay and fed and watered. Oliver himself felt he had never had so much attention.

Cheryl had four telephone messages that would all require attention the following day, so put them all on to one email which she sent to each person, and decided they could fight it out between them as to who did what.

When Luke arrived home he arranged to meet Maria from work, so walked down to the office. The shock was evident on his face when he saw the flowers, a complete bank of them.

'My god, Nan, you would have loved this,' he murmured. He took out his phone and videoed the front of the shop, zooming in on several of the cards attached to the bouquets. He sent the video to Alistair along with the words **How am I supposed to get in the door?** Followed by a smiling emoji.

He decided on the easy option and walked around to the back. Oliver miaowed when he saw him, and together they went inside.

'You been fed, Ollie?'

'Miaow.'

'Is that a yes or a no?'

'Miaow.'

'I'll take it that you need some.' He topped up the feed bowl, put down Ollie's third fresh bowl of water of the day, and went up to his office where he sat and stared out of the window.

Since starting at Connection he had been involved in several deaths, some young people, some elderly, but nothing could have prepared him for losing Nan. He sipped at his bottle of water, remembering the many laughs when they had been on surveillance jobs, how much she had taught him, had encouraged him by finding him different courses to take that would advance him in the job. Eventually his smile returned, and he realised that was her legacy to him – his position as a partner in Connection, and she would always make him smile.

'Cheers, Nan,' he said, raising his bottle of water to her, then he stood and headed back to the ground floor. Oliver wanted to go out, so they both exited by the back door, and Luke set the alarm and locked everything up for the night.

It would be a new day with everybody back in work and remembering Doris with gladness rather than sadness.

He walked across the road as Maria was locking up at the vets. They headed home hand in hand, both quiet, knowing the words would come later, because she recognised that much in Luke – he would want to talk out his feelings, make sure she understood how much he had loved Doris, and what losing her meant to him.

Their home was toasty warm, and he held her in his arms for a long time.

'Thank you,' he whispered, 'for being there for me.'

'No problem,' she said. 'Always.'

2

Beth was the first to arrive on that strangely ethereal morning, not sure how she felt. She went and sat in Fred's office for a short while as this, in a pre-refurbishment life, had been her nan's office. She didn't stay long, gave herself enough time to do it and absorb it, then went into her own office. Simon arrived five minutes later, and they immediately put on the amber lights on their phones and began to prioritise who was taking on what file as their permanent work.

Fred and Luke arrived together, pausing for a moment to look at the flowers heaped outside before entering, this time by the front door. With Cheryl's arrival and the subsequent checking of her voicemails, it was decided a meeting was needed, so by eleven everybody was seated in Beth's office.

By twelve all jobs had been allocated and everybody had retired back to their own office to get on the phones and book appointments.

'I'm nipping over to the Co-op.'

Cheryl lifted her head as Luke spoke. 'Okay. No problem. Can you bring us some milk?'

'I can. I'm going for cat food and cat milk. His food seems to be going down extremely fast, has somebody taught Ollie to help himself?'

Cheryl laughed. 'No, I think we've all fed him over the past two days. He's enjoyed himself.'

As Luke turned, the door buzzer sounded. They both looked, and Cheryl pressed for the man standing outside to be able to come in.

'Can I help?' she asked.

'I apologise for treating you like a Tourist Information place, but I've lost a cottage.'

Luke smiled. 'That's not hard in Eyam. We've got some tiny little back alleyways as well as the main road. What cottage have you lost?'

'Leaf Cottage. My wife booked it for a month and arrived last weekend. I don't have the address because the plan was she needed time on her own to complete a book. She switches off her phone when she's writing, but I tried to contact her all last night and couldn't, so here I am looking for a Leaf Cottage and I can't find one.'

'I know it,' Cheryl volunteered. 'Luke, if you go past the little driveway thing that leads to your place, about a hundred yards further on there's another one similar to your access, but quite twisty. There's a tiny plaque on the wall that says Leaf Cottage, but you can't actually see the house until you drive round the twisty bit.'

'I know where you mean. Would you like me to take you?' he asked their visitor.

'Thank you, young man. I would be very grateful.'

'Luke, my name's Luke.'

'Then thank you, Luke. It's pretty urgent I contact her – our daughter is seven months pregnant and went into early labour a couple of days ago. I know Faith will want to make her informed decision on whether to come back home, but she so wanted to steep herself in Eyam for her latest book. This is our first grandchild, and she'd never forgive me if anything bad happened and I hadn't told her, but her phone keeps going to voicemail. I don't know whether to worry about Faith or Helena, but Helena's asked me to let her mum know.'

'Give me a minute to get my coat, and we'll nip up and find out what's going on.' Luke headed towards the lift then went upstairs.

'Your wife has written other books?' Cheryl asked.

'Yes. Her name's Faith Young.'

'Oh my lord. Faith Young's in our village? *The* Faith Young?'

He laughed. 'She is indeed. She sometimes does this when she reaches a tricky part, takes off for a few days, but this time it was the village she needed. She said there's only so much you can get from books, and she wanted to go and see the buildings, really learn the history of the place. But when she goes off, she cuts off communication. I try not to worry, but this time we have a problem. I worry because she likes to walk, and if she has an accident...'

'And you've tried her mobile phone?'

'That's the biggest worry. I've been ringing it for two days, even through the night, but getting nothing.'

The lift door pinged, and Luke walked to the front door. 'Let's go, Mr...?'

'Young. Jack please.'

Cheryl nodded. 'Jack's wife is Faith Young, Luke.'

Luke's eyes opened wide. 'Wait while I tell my mother! She's a massive fan. Come on, let's go find your wife.'

'I'm sure there will be answers at the cottage. Luke will go inside with you. The owner is called Will Sandford, Luke, and he lives in the house on the main road with the tiny plaque on his garden wall. He renovated Leaf Cottage to use it as a holiday let for tourists. It's a lovely little home, he gets a lot of return custom. Once people actually find it, they love it. Try not to worry, I'm sure there's a reasonable explanation.'

The Range Rover managed to get up the narrow road, Jack pulling in the wing mirrors to make it a little easier. He breathed a sigh of relief when he finally used the handbrake outside Leaf Cottage. Faith's Aygo was parked up, and he hoped that was a good sign.

It was a small place which came as no surprise to Jack – he remembered Faith saying it was only one bedroom, but she didn't need more than that. He could imagine the garden being a riot of colour in the summer, it was clearly well cared for even now, with winter pansies bordering the garden path. He and Luke walked up to the front door and tried to open it, to no avail. Jack knocked loudly, but there was still no response.

'I'll go round the back,' Luke said. 'See if that door's open.'

He left Jack peering through the front window and ran around the cottage and into the back garden. This was considerably larger than the front one, complete with a patio and garden furniture. Luke tried the door, but once again it was locked and there was no response to his knocking. He began to feel uncomfortable. Something wasn't right...

'Jack,' he called. 'I'm going down the lane to see if we can borrow the spare key. Won't be a minute.'

. . .

Sandford listened to Luke's explanation and frowned. 'She went for a walk on Monday. Today's Thursday... you're saying her husband hasn't heard from her?'

'He hasn't, but under normal circumstances he wouldn't have. She uses the solitude to get on with her writing, but their daughter is in hospital, and he knows his wife would want to know. He's tried ringing, but no answer, so now he's come to find her.'

'I'll come up with you. I'll go get the key.'

Jack was waiting by his car when Luke and Will walked up the lane. Will immediately unlocked the front door, and Jack shouted Faith's name. There was no response. Jack ran upstairs, but the bedroom and bathroom were empty.

'She's not here,' he said as he came back downstairs. 'Do you know where she was going walking?'

'I know the exact route. I plotted it with her on Sunday night. She told me what she wanted to see, so I drew her a map.' He reached inside his coat and pulled out a scrap of paper. 'This was the original, but I drew it out again for her so that she could read it a bit clearer. My writing can be a bit...'

'Illegible?' Luke picked up the map. 'So she's headed down through the village. Did she say she was calling at the tea rooms?'

'I recommended them, so she probably did.'

'Where would she go from there?'

'Here.' He pointed to the woodland. 'She was going to walk through the woods, then up to the top of the village and back round to here. It's a long walk but she said she does a lot of planning while she's walking.'

'I have to follow this route. She could be lying injured somewhere, and it's been over three days now.'

'We'll all go,' Will said, the concern showing on his face.

'I have to check in, let them know at Connection.' Luke took out his phone and explained to Cheryl exactly what was happening.

'Okay, Luke. Keep us informed.'

They walked down through the village, checking as much as they could. At the tea rooms they had their first success. Amanda confirmed that Faith had called in for some lunch around noon on Monday, but she hadn't been in since. 'I brought my Faith Young books in for her to sign – she said she would next time she was in. So she definitely hasn't called back.'

'Did you see which way she went?'

'No, sorry, I was busy with it being lunchtime.'

'Thanks, Amanda,' Luke said. 'She did have a map with her, so we'll carry on following that.'

They walked across the road and dropped down into a valley, before beginning the climb up through the wooded area. The weather was cold but dry, and the three men made good time, splitting off from each other as they checked undergrowth and different well-worn paths.

Luke felt uneasy. If she had been missing for three days, this might not have a good outcome. He could tell from the other two men's faces that they were thinking the same and there was a sense of urgency to their searching.

Every so often one of them would shout out the missing woman's name, but they had no answering call. Jack and Luke saw the house at the same time and suggested they should head towards it.

'We can do,' Will said, 'but I can't see it helping. It belongs to a family who use it for their sort of summer residence. As you can probably tell, the shutters are all closed, which means there's nobody there. They usually arrive late May and stay till the beginning of October. Maybe we should check it out in case Faith tried to get to it.'

They all veered off to the left and began the long walk across flattened grassland towards the white-walled house. It looked deserted, clearly uninhabited and Luke thought it looked somewhat derelict, as though it needed a fresh coat of paint everywhere, and a bit of TLC. One of the shutters supposedly covering a ground floor window was swaying in the wind, and Luke reached up to it. It slipped into an even more ungainly position, and he sucked in his breath, hoping he hadn't disturbed it enough to make it fall off.

Once again they all called Faith's name, and they spent the next half hour checking the exterior of the building. There was nothing that gave them any hope.

'Come on,' Jack said, 'let's head back to the point where we veered off to come here. We'll rejoin the route Faith was supposed to be taking. If we don't find her though by the time we get back to Leaf Cottage I'm ringing the police. Something's wrong, and it's starting to scare me.'

'Luke?' Will said.

'Don't worry, if we end up needing to report Faith as a missing person, I'll contact DI Heaton. But it's not come to that yet. Onwards and upwards on this hill.'

It was Jack who found the hat. It was almost invisible in the undergrowth, but he picked it up. 'This is Faith's.'

'You're sure?'

'Positive. I was with her in Marks and Spencer's when she bought it. She wanted one to match her new dark green winter coat. Faith!' he called loudly. 'Shout if you can hear us!'

'Jack, try ringing her phone. She may be around here somewhere if the hat is here.'

Jack took out his phone and opened up favourites. He rang Faith's number, and they heard the sound of Take That singing 'The Flood'.

'That's her ringtone,' Jack said and moved towards the noise and vibration.

The phone was lying in a pile of leaves, with no sign of its owner. As he reached it, it died.

3

'Don't touch it,' Luke said quickly. 'Jack, you're sure it's Faith's phone?'

'Positive. She loves Take That. And the screen picture is me.' He looked around wildly. 'Faith!' All three of them called her name, but there was no response.

'Okay,' Luke said. 'We need help. Give me five minutes. In the meantime, spread out and keep looking. Head in different directions but don't go too far. We don't know what's going on. The police will be here shortly.'

DI Carl Heaton arrived with four uniformed officers who were immediately deployed to search the area.

'Let me check I've got this right. Mrs Young hasn't been seen since leaving the tea rooms in the village Monday afternoon?'

Jack nodded. 'That's the situation as far as I'm aware. I personally haven't seen her or spoken to her since Saturday morning, when she drove here from our home in Gloucester. She did send me a text Saturday, late afternoon, to tell me she'd arrived, and the cottage was perfect. And she said she'd ring me every Saturday afternoon before she left to return home in four weeks' time, simply to check in that everything was okay. Unfortunately, everything went pear-shaped, and I needed to contact her, but that hasn't happened.'

'Will? You saw her Monday morning?'

'I did, Carl. Sorry, I mean DI Heaton, but not to speak to, I simply saw her set off. I bumped into her Sunday afternoon, and she said she needed suggestions for a route around Eyam that would give her a feel for the place, plus the ability to see the touristy parts about the plague. I drew her a map, marked everything on it, and took it to her Sunday evening.' He fished his original drawing out of his pocket. 'It was more or less like this. That's how we knew to follow in her footsteps. She called at Amanda's place for a sandwich and a drink, and then headed for the woods.'

'We found her hat first,' Luke said, 'and because of that, Jack rang her phone. None of us have touched that, I knew you'd want to bag it. The hat was handled by all three of us.'

Carl gave a brief nod. 'Will, do you know who owns that house over there?' He pointed towards the white house, looking darker in the encroaching gloom of evening.

'Kind of. I know the owners as Brian and Ella, had a chat with them one night in the pub, and they did tell me their surname, but I can't remember it. It's a summer retreat for them. Apparently Brian works from home so can basically work anywhere, and in the summer they like to be here. Come end of May, stay till October, and the kids join them when they're out of school. They're both in boarding school, Ella told me. And that's all I know about them. Don't even know the kids' names. Sorry I can't be more helpful.'

'It's no problem. I can soon have somebody find out for me. I think we should check it out though. If Faith has managed to get herself some shelter inside, she may need medical help.'

. . .

'Is Luke in?' Tessa asked as she arrived at the Connection office.

Cheryl shook her head. 'He went out to look for a cottage, and for Faith Young, the writer, who should be there but apparently isn't.'

'Really?'

'He's also called DI Heaton into the search, he's informed me, because they've found her hat and phone, but no sign of her. He attracts problems, that boy.'

'Not so much a boy anymore.' Tessa laughed. 'So finding this cottage has morphed into a missing person's enquiry?'

'Seems so. I must admit, there was a degree of concern in his voice. And Carl's taking it seriously enough to organise a full search of the woods.'

'They need help?'

'Luke didn't say they'd asked for volunteers, but if you were to go and join in, I'm pretty sure he wouldn't object.'

'I'll take Fred if he's in. It's a couple of extra hands for Carl to deploy.'

'He's in. His appointments start tomorrow, so he's probably playing Patience.'

Tessa thought it advisable to ring Carl before mentioning anything to Fred – if the woman had been found they could be more of a hindrance than a help.

'You and Fred would be very welcome,' he said. 'I've asked for four more uniforms to join us, I'm conscious that it's getting dark. If you've got torches, bring them. We're about halfway up the hill in the wooded part, as you climb up to the top of the village. You'll see the cars parked at the entrance. And take care, it's not an easy walk.'

.   .   .

Tessa gave both their names to the uniformed officer.

'Thank you, ma'am,' he said. 'DI Heaton says to head up that path there, and he'll be waiting for you. Keep walking till you find him, were his words.'

Tessa smiled at him. 'Thank you. I take it this means they still haven't found Mrs Young?'

'Not yet, ma'am. It seems she's been missing for three days.'

'Then we'll get up there and see if we can help.'

'Take care, ma'am.'

'Not ma'am. I've not been a DI for a couple of months.'

'No, ma'am.'

She heard Fred laugh and turned to him. 'And you shut up. Smirking gets you the job of leading the way.'

The pathway was clear, but quite difficult to traverse. Initially the climb was steep but by the time they could see torch beams it was starting to level off. Tessa could imagine the writer stopping for a breather – Monday afternoon had been a time of extremely heavy rain. Had she leaned against a tree for some shelter and to catch her breath before tackling the rest of the journey up to the road?

They saw Carl looking at a map and headed over towards him.

'Give us some instructions, Carl,' Tessa said quietly.

'Oh good, you're here. Am I right in thinking one or the other of you two can pick locks?'

They answered 'yes' simultaneously, and Carl leaned towards Tessa and whispered, 'Will you teach me some time?'

She laughed. 'What lock do you want picking?'

'See that house over there?' In the darkness it was only vaguely visible, looking grey and haunted.

'Spooky.'

'Only in this light. It's apparently a summer home for some family, and we can't find Faith anywhere in the locality where we recovered her knitted hat, or her phone, so if she realised she needed shelter she may have got herself to that house. We've checked out the outside, but I think we need to get in, double-check she's not there. I'm reluctant to use an enforcer, they make a proper mess of doors as you know, but if we can find a back door that's maybe not got a sophisticated lock on it...'

'You're clutching at straws,' Tessa said. 'But come on, let's go and look.'

Carl spoke into his radio telling PC Ray Charlton what was happening, and the three of them set off across the even-rougher terrain now that there was no obvious path. It took ten minutes of careful walking before they reached the plot of land on which the house had been built.

Tessa walked up to the front door and tried it, but there was no movement. 'We've no chance with this one, it's too heavy a door, and will have a five-lever lock on it. I'm good, but not that good. We either need a window or a smaller door. Let's go round the back.'

The back door was much smaller, painted dark green to match the shutters. Fred handed his set of tools to Tessa and winked at Carl. 'Tessa taught me,' he said.

Tessa laughed, then checked under the large plant pot holding a Fuchsia, standing by the side of the door. 'Simply looking for a spare key first,' she said.

It wasn't easy, even for master criminal Marsden, but eventually she felt the tumblers give, and she opened the door.

She stepped back and Carl eased the door wide. 'Police,' he called. 'Is anyone here?'

They waited, and then all three walked into the kitchen.

'It's empty,' Tessa said. 'You can feel it.' She shivered.

'We have to check. Tess, can you take the bedrooms, and Fred and I will do down here, along with any cellars we can find.'

'Outbuildings?'

'A couple of uniforms have already checked them. There's a shed and a sort of summer house, furniture visible through the window in the summer house, and garden equipment in the shed. Both locked with padlocks.'

'Okay. I'm going upstairs now.' She slipped on her nitrile gloves and left the kitchen.

The family bathroom was clean although not fresh. Tessa guessed it would be getting ready for a spring clean when the family returned in May, but it currently felt stale. She checked everywhere, then left, closing the door behind her, wondering which member of the family had neglected to flush the toilet as they had left at the end of the previous summer.

The second door was obviously the son's bedroom, with blue walls and Marvel pictures on the walls. The bed was stripped, ready for fresh bedding when the boy returned from boarding school. Nothing was out of place, and Tessa moved onto the next room.

It was almost a carbon copy of the boy's room in shape and size, but it was very pink. And very frilly. Again, nothing was out of place with the bed stripped and ready for being made up again. The room felt really dark, as had the boy's room, and Tessa realised she didn't like shutters. They may look good from the outside, but they added so much darkness to a room it became gloomy, even pretty pink rooms.

There was a door at the end of the landing, and she opened

it to reveal an airing cupboard filled with bedding, pillows and cushions. Her glance was perfunctory. Faith Young couldn't be in there.

The next bedroom was much smaller, with a small flowery paper on its walls, set off with white paintwork. It held a double bed, and Tessa suspected it was a guest bedroom. She gave it a quick check, but again nothing was out of the ordinary.

She opened the final door, but didn't enter. She felt it. Something. She carefully looked around the door jamb and spotted the light switch. The instant illumination revealed a king size bed with bedding on it, although rumpled and not tucked under the mattress at any part. The duvet was simply a duvet, no cover, and there were three pillows, also without covers.

She stood for a moment and simply surveyed. Taking out her phone she took photographs still standing in the doorway, absorbing the room into her mind. Clearly somebody had been sleeping in the house but the tidiness of the rest of the house showed this was a stranger and not a family member. It also explained the unflushed toilet; whoever had used this room had, at some point, used the family bathroom. Had they also used the en suite? She was guessing that the door in the room led into a private bathroom.

She stepped back and called Carl's name.

'You found something?'

'You might want to come up here,' Tessa said, her eyes slowly circling the room, taking in as much as she could. This room could be a little gold mine for the forensics team, once they had confirmation from the family that they hadn't left it in its current state. There were a couple of pizza boxes, sandwich boxes, empty cans – whoever had been here hadn't used the rest of the house, only this room.

She heard Carl and Fred's footsteps on the stairs but

remained where she was. 'I suggest we don't go in but having seen the other bedrooms and the way they have been left ready for the owners to return in May, this one doesn't sit right at all.'

She stepped back and the two men looked into the pretty yellow bedroom.

4

By Friday morning it had been established that Faith Young was not at the house, and no trace of her had been found anywhere on the trail she had taken on that Monday.

It had also been established by the owners exactly what the bedroom had looked like on the day they had left, because they had decided to upgrade the room, and had taken pictures of it to have discussions with their decorator who would also be painting the white exterior walls and turning the dark green shutters white.

Brian and Ella Aylward were quite distraught and wanted to return to their summer home immediately, but Carl persuaded them otherwise, saying it was currently a potential crime scene as they still had a missing woman to find, but he would notify them as soon as they could head back to Eyam. He did suggest they might want to update their security.

Tessa, Luke and Fred met up in Luke's office, all looking somewhat bleary-eyed after their late night in the woodlands of Eyam. They knew there would still be a police presence for some time in the area of the white house and the surrounding trees, but they had completed their part in it.

'Thoughts?' Tessa said, handing out mugs of coffee. 'Drink this, we all look as though we need a pick-me-up.'

Luke leaned back in his chair, and held his mug to his lips, without actually drinking from it. His brow creased into a frown. 'I don't know what to think. When the three of us went to look for her we actually expected to find her, probably injured and very cold. There was always the thought she might be dead if she'd had to spend three nights in the open, but we did expect to find her. It now seems she's disappeared, possibly along with somebody who's been living in that house. Do you think whoever that was had been there for some time?'

Tessa shook her head. 'No, they had stuck to that room with the possible exception of one foray into the family bathroom, and I also suspect they had a key. If they'd been there for a long time, there would have been a lot more rubbish lying around. I think we're talking days, rather than weeks. There were no obvious signs of a break-in, and there was a big plant pot by the back door that probably had an emergency key under it. It doesn't now.'

'So if they hadn't been there long, that raises other questions. Let's assume it's a man. Was Faith Young the target, or could it have been anybody passing through those woods at that time? Was she spotted in the tea rooms, when she told Amanda who she was, and then followed? Or did he simply follow her until she was on her own? And why Faith Young? Do authors earn mega bucks?'

'If you're called J K Rowling or Stephen King, yes. But I imagine she did earn quite a bit. She's very well-known and now that detective series of hers has been turned into a TV series, that will be putting her into a high earnings bracket. You're thinking ransom demand?'

'Kind of, it seems to have taken a long time though.'

Fred's head moved between them as he listened to the two of them talk. 'For what it's worth,' he said, 'I don't go with the ransom demand scenario, because I too think it's now four days, and I think the contact would have been made much earlier than this. I feel uneasy about it and can't really see a good ending.'

Cheryl looked up at the sound of the buzzer and pressed the door release.

'Mr Young. What can we do for you?'

'I've popped in to thank you all. Is anybody in?'

'Give me a second while I find out what they're doing.'

She rang Luke's office, and within a minute Luke had joined them in reception. 'Jack! Any news?'

'Not of Faith, no. I only wanted to say thank you...'

'Come upstairs. We're having a coffee to try to wake us up. I imagine you could use one as well.'

Jack followed Luke to his office, and he gratefully accepted the coffee poured by Tessa. 'I had hell of a night,' he said. 'Wasn't asleep at three, wondering where Faith was.'

'You slept at Leaf Cottage?'

'No, Will put me in his spare room. DI Heaton said they would have the forensics team in at the cottage today, and I could stay there from tonight. They aren't expecting anything from looking at the cottage, because obviously Faith was seen after she had left there on Monday, but they have to do it. I had a phone call before seven this morning, and it seems Faith and I are now grandparents to a beautiful baby boy. He's early, and they couldn't stop Helena's labour, so he's here. A little small, and will have to stay in hospital for a few days, but it seems all is good.'

Luke, Fred and Tessa stood and shook his hand in turn. 'Congratulations, Jack. That's wonderful news. Does he have a name yet?'

'I don't think so. My son-in-law sounded shattered and I didn't like to ask. Faith would have, of course...'

'Has DI Heaton contacted you this morning?' Tessa asked.

'He has. There's a forensic team in the white house at the moment, and he's upbeat about getting DNA from the cans, or the rubbish lying around.' Jack hesitated. 'Where is she?'

'Wherever she is, I don't think she's gone there of her own volition,' Tessa said. 'You've said several times this is so out of character, Jack, and it's not as though she's some flighty teenager out to cause trouble. She's a mature career woman with everything to live for, so wherever she is, I'm pretty sure it's not with her agreement.'

'My thoughts on it exactly.' Jack sighed. 'We're close, you know. There's no trouble between us, we're simply... normal.'

Fred frowned as he spoke. 'What I can't see is where she can be. First of all I can't imagine it being a woman who's taken her, because there would be an issue of needing a lot of strength, and secondly she disappeared right from the middle of the woods. Where's he taken her to, hidden her? He can't get a car to that point, that's for sure, so he would have had to carry her or drag her, and there were no drag marks.'

Luke held up a hand. 'Yes, but let's not forget she's been missing four days. I couldn't sleep for thinking about it last night, and I reckon he attacked her and took her back to that house. You can get a car to there, there's that small road leads down from the main road, that finishes at the house. The Aylwards obviously have to use it when they visit their summer home.'

'So you're saying she could be anywhere now?' Jack asked,

fear written on his face. 'We're searching all around those woods and she could be in a bloody different county!'

Jack took his leave and walked up the village towards Leaf Cottage. He hoped it was clear of police officers and the forensic people; he felt as if he needed to sit in a chair and simply close his eyes for a few moments. The previous night spent in a strange bed in a strange house hadn't afforded him much rest, and he thought if he could snatch some sleep maybe it would stop his imagination from working overtime.

He briefly wondered if he should contact Faith's publisher – sooner or later it would make the headlines, and he guessed he should make the call before it became public knowledge.

Later, he thought, as he reached the cottage, *I'll ring them later*. The crime scene tape had been removed, and he entered the tiny hallway, using the key Will had given to him that morning.

'Hello?'

There was no response, and he hoped it meant everything was done with. DI Heaton had explained they didn't expect to find anything, it was more a matter of routine that they checked over the cottage. The receipt on the coffee table told him they had taken her laptop, and Jack's first reaction was that Faith would be furious. It held her new book, and nobody was allowed to see that until after her commissioning editor had given it the go-ahead. He wished his wife were there to be furious...

His mobile phone rang, and Carl Heaton explained the cottage had been cleared and he was free to move in.

'You've found nothing then?'

'No, not a thing. I do realise this laptop is your wife's writing laptop, so I promise we'll take good care of it. We need to check her emails, make sure there is nothing untoward going on there, and then I'll get it back to you. I'm sorry I haven't anything better to tell you, Jack, but I still have men combing those woods. I've given permission for the owners to visit their home, because we don't know it and they do. He may have removed something, damaged something – we're clutching at straws, but the Aylwards are going to know better than us if there's something not right. They're coming tomorrow.'

'Thank you, DI Heaton. I wish there was something I could do. I feel so bloody helpless.'

'You've explained the situation to your daughter?'

'I had no choice. She wanted her mum. She's devastated, and obviously it hasn't helped that the baby is a little premature. I was toying with the idea of ringing Faith's publisher...'

'You should. Does Faith have frequent contact with them?'

'Yes, they're good friends.'

'Then you should definitely give them a call. We're putting Faith's picture on tonight's news asking for people to look out for her. She's so well-known, it'll be on all the front pages tomorrow.'

Jack finally sank down into the chair. The call had been difficult, with Marianne Kingston, Faith's publisher, sobbing through most of it. She had wanted to immediately drive to Eyam, but Jack had talked her out of it, promising to update her every step of the way in the hunt for his wife.

'You find her, Jack. She's very precious.'

'The police are doing all they can. Pray for her, Marianne.'

'Always, Jack. Always.'

. . .

Beth looked tired, as if the light had gone from her eyes. Speaking to Alistair had brought everything back in force, and now she had the issue of the will reading to get through. She imagined it would be pretty straight-forward because there had only been the two of them, and her nan had always told her that Little Mouse Cottage would transfer to her, so she didn't see any reason to have to attend a reading of the will. Couldn't the solicitor have put the details in a letter? Why did she have to go into Sheffield and find out what she already knew?

She'd booked the whole day off, knowing she wouldn't be able to handle work after such a distressing event, and she sank back into her chair, closing her eyes. She needed some time out, and she wanted it to be with Joel. In the Maldives. Or the Canaries. In fact anywhere where there was no rain or wind or snow, simply anywhere.

She picked up the phone. 'Joel? Can we go away?'

5

Saturday morning brought no news, and Fred drove into Bakewell with the missing author still on his mind. His eleven-fifteen appointment was also to discuss a missing wife, although there had been no mention of foul play with this matter.

He pulled up outside the address, double-checking he had the right house before getting out of the car. From the outside it didn't look to be a large house, but it seemed to be immaculately kept. The dark-blue door had brass fittings, all polished to a glowing brilliance. The windows had vertical blinds, and the whole façade of the house was showing that somebody lived there who cared about it.

There was a small brass anchor for a knocker, and Fred quietly rattled the door with it. A man of not inconsiderable height, smartly dressed and with short dark hair, answered.

'Mr Baines?'

'I am. You're Mr Iveson?'

'I am, but please call me Fred.'

'And I'm Cliff. Please, follow me.'

He led Fred down a narrow hallway and through a door that

opened up into a large kitchen. Fred's initial reaction was that the house was much larger than its outside appearance suggested.

'Can I get you a tea? Coffee?'

'A tea would be good, thanks. Milk, no sugar.'

Fred sat at the table and opened his folder. He looked around. 'Nice room, Cliff.'

Cliff smiled, obviously pleased at the compliment. 'It's our main room. It gets the sun most of the day in the summer, so I figured it made sense to have the window taken out and patio doors put in, and to turn it into a living area rather than a dining area. Our lounge is now my office because I have to work from home.' He handed Fred his drink and joined him at the table.

'Thank you. So how can Connection help you? You're hoping to find someone?' He placed the recorder in the middle of the table. 'This is so I don't miss taking anything down on my notepad.'

'That's right, I do need to find someone. I spoke to your receptionist, told her I'd been chatting to Patrick Fletcher, a neighbour of mine who highly recommended your company. He knew of you through something to do with the murder of our librarian.'

Fred smiled. 'I know who you mean. One of our partners met him, they got on really well.'

Cliff gave a quick nod. 'Nice bloke. We've been friends for years.'

'So who do you need help with finding?'

'My wife.'

Fred picked up his pen. 'Her name?'

'Philippa. Normally called Pippa.'

'How long has she been missing?'

'She walked out on us fifteen years ago.'

'And she's still your wife? No divorce?'

39

'No, which is rather strange as she walked out on us to go with somebody else.'

'Us?'

'Yes, sorry. I live here with my son, Ethan. He was six when she left. Let me give you the full story, then you can decide if you can help us. Pippa and I had to get married when we were both twenty, because she was pregnant. Don't get me wrong, we loved each other, were actually engaged, but we brought the wedding forward a couple of years because of the pregnancy. We had Ethan, and were told almost immediately that he was a Down's Syndrome baby.'

Cliff paused for a moment, his thoughts clearly going back to that time twenty-one years earlier.

'We coped. Pippa didn't return to work, but I was earning a good wage working for an estate agency selling higher-end homes. Everything was fine once we'd got over the shock, although Pippa suffered with post-natal depression for quite a long time. We had a lot of support from Pippa's parents, but when Ethan was four we lost both of them. Her mother died of breast cancer, and her father couldn't live without her, so he connected a pipe to the car exhaust. Pippa found him. From that moment on, she changed. It was too soon after her recovery from her depression and it knocked her straight back down. Financially things were good because she inherited from her parents, but she started going out more without me, because one of us had to look after Ethan, and that usually fell to me. My own parents live on the south coast of Spain so we could never ring them up and ask if they could babysit.' He laughed.

Fred was rapidly making notes, thankful the recorder was backing him up. He took a moment of quiet to grab a sip of his tea.

'Okay,' he said. 'I'm caught up. Did she tell you she was leaving?'

'No. Ethan, at six, was in a special school, and every Friday I would finish early and go and pick him up instead of him being dropped off by the school bus. We always went for a McDonald's, and if it wasn't raining, a game of football. When we got home that particular Friday her car wasn't there. I put Ethan to bed around seven, and waited for her to come in. I've been waiting fifteen years so far.'

'You told the police?'

He shook his head. 'No, because Patrick watched her get into a blue car, accompanied by a man, who gave her a kiss before they pulled away. She took two suitcases with her. The following Friday, exactly a week of turmoil later, I received a letter from her saying she wouldn't be back. It was only then I thought to check our bank. She had taken fifty thousand pounds. That's all she ever took, she left the rest for Ethan and me. What hurt the most was she didn't send her son her love. It was a cold letter, one I immediately screwed up in a temper and threw away. The one thing I remember is that it was postmarked Lincoln, but that doesn't mean a thing, does it? It only means she was standing by a Lincoln post box when she posted it. Or her feller was. After a few months Ethan stopped asking where she was, and we've muddled along together ever since.'

'Is Ethan here?'

'No, I'll come to that in a bit. I've been practising what to say to you so I don't miss anything.' He smiled. 'About two years later I started to struggle with juggling my workload, so I left, found some premises and set up my own estate agency.'

Fred looked up, recognition dawning. 'Baines and Son! You're Baines and Son! My colleague is looking at a couple of your properties this weekend, one in Eyam, one in Stoney Middleton.'

'That's good.' He laughed. 'It's what I like to hear. I must admit, it took off pretty quickly, the business, and I've never looked back. Once I employed my own staff it freed me up to deal with any issues that arose with Ethan's care. The first two years were hard work, but from then onwards Ethan has been a delight. We have no idea where Pippa is, so it won't be easy for you, if you decide to take this on.'

'Well I'll certainly look forward to meeting Ethan. Is it urgent that you track down your wife?'

'Pretty urgent, and it's not for the reason you're thinking. I'm not looking to divorce her because I want to remarry, it's nothing like that. If only... No, it's about Ethan. Six months or so ago he complained of pains in his stomach. He's had lots of tests, cursed me for making him have them, but we've got through it together. He was there for the diagnosis of pancreatic cancer. It's also in his lungs and liver. At the moment he's having a week's respite in the hospice, but it seems...' Cliff faltered, unable to go on, and Fred waited.

'It's terminal?' Fred asked gently.

Cliff nodded. 'At the most he will have four months.'

'And he wants to see his mum?'

'He does. I've promised him I'll pull out all the stops, so basically, Fred, whatever it costs, whatever it takes, I need to do it.'

'Does Philippa have a middle name?'

'She does. Lynne. Her mother was called Lynne.'

'And that's all the information we have? Do you have a photograph?'

'It is pretty much all I have, but I'll go through all the pictures and see what I have re one of her. It will be at least fifteen years old. I know this won't be easy, and it may all fizzle out because fifteen years is a long time. I'm only asking that you do your best.'

Fred nodded. 'And I will. I'll make our contact number your mobile if that's okay, and then if I have anything to ask or to tell,

I won't be intruding on your work. You're happy for us to take this on?'

'More than happy. Connection has an excellent reputation. Do you need me to sign anything?'

'I do.' Fred took out some paperwork and passed it across to Cliff. 'It's a pretty standard contract setting out our terms and telling you what to expect in return. I will need a deposit retainer, either by bank transfer or cheque, or you can call in on Monday and pay our receptionist. Whatever's the easiest for you.'

'A cheque?'

'Fine.' He reached across and switched off the recorder, putting it back into his briefcase. 'I'll transcribe this and let you have a copy. In the meantime, if something comes to mind that you haven't told me, please ring me. I don't have much to go on initially, and the slightest memory could be a starting point. As this is urgent, I'm going to take it to the team for thoughts, because there's always somebody who'll have a bright idea. My very best wishes to your lad, Cliff, and hopefully he'll be back home next time I see you.'

Cliff escorted Fred to the front door. 'Thank you for doing this, Fred, I think I chose wisely.'

Fred looked back at him. 'It's an honour, Cliff, an honour.'

Luke was surprised to see Beth at his door. He held the door open, suddenly aware how close to tears she was.

'What's wrong?' he asked and hugged her.

'Don't be nice to me, I'll cry.' Her words were muffled as she spoke into his shoulder.

'Cry if you want. Where's Joel?'

'Gone to buy a suitcase. The handle fell off his.'

'And that's made you cry?'

43

'No, Nan's made me cry. It's rubbish knowing she's not here. And in her will she said how much she loved me.'

'Come and sit down. Maria's in the lounge, or do you need to talk?'

'No, the lounge is fine. I want to tell you what I'm doing, and it suddenly overwhelmed me as I got out the car. Sorry for being a big girl's blouse. I'm not normally like that.'

The three of them sat by the fire, and Beth leaned back. 'I can't tell all of you because it's a Saturday – Tess is out looking at houses, Fred's out meeting a new client, Simon's jogging up a mountain, and Cheryl has taken the kids into Sheffield, so that leaves you to pass this on to the others. I'm off to Manchester at four, staying in an airport hotel tonight and flying to Florida tomorrow at six. We've booked for two weeks, and I know it's scary with this Covid situation, but I promise to be careful. We're not going for the theme parks, we're going to explore Florida, go on an airboat, see the alligators, that sort of thing. I need to go, Luke.'

He reached for her hand. 'I know you do. Don't worry, we'll look after things, and if you need more time when you get back, you take it. Simon knows what he's doing?'

'He does. Ring if anything urgent does crop up, but I won't come back.' She smiled, the tears having dried up.

'It's not us minions you have to worry about, I hope you've left a comprehensive note for Cheryl telling her exactly where you're going to be for the foreseeable. You know what she's like!'

'Cover for me,' she said with a grin. 'Like you usually do for Tessa.'

6

———

The plane took off on time, and Beth leaned back in her seat with a sigh. 'I feel better already.'

'Good. That was my intention. And I will be spoiling you rotten, so I want no arguments about costs or anything like that. You had any thoughts about what you want to do?'

'I have. Maria told me about a place called Blue Springs State Park. It's where the manatees go to over winter because the river is a constant temperature, and I've never seen a manatee. Can we go there? She said that of all the places her family visited in the Orlando area, that was her favourite. There's lots of alligators in the river and on the banksides, and you can apparently swim in a natural pool, but there's a sign saying get out if you see an alligator and notify a warden. I'm not convinced I'd need a sign to tell me that...'

Joel laughed. 'Me neither. Then that shall be our first place to visit, on our first ever holiday together.'

The seat belt light went off, and they unbuckled. Immediately the stewardesses moved around, checking everyone was okay. Joel reached to put the flight path on the small screens in front of them, and Beth smiled. 'That's brilliant. You knew I wouldn't want to watch a movie, didn't you?'

'I did. I also knew you'd find this map far more interesting. Now settle back and enjoy the ride.'

Sunday afternoon saw Luke and Maria walk down through the village and head towards the police tape. They asked if DI Heaton was there and offered their services if the search was still ongoing. The PC at the entrance to the search site rang through and they were directed to where Carl was.

He waved at them as he saw them trudging up the incline, and they reached him with the intention of asking for instructions.

'Thanks for offering,' he said. 'We're all hanging back for a bit because we have two cadaver dogs doing what they do best, and we don't want to muddy any traces for them.'

'You've found nothing?' Luke asked.

'Nothing at all. We only have her phone and hat, both of which I'm assuming she lost in the process of being grabbed. The Aylwards are supposed to be arriving later today to go over their house, so fingers crossed that will give us some small hint of what has happened, but I'm not holding my breath.'

His radio crackled and he responded immediately. 'Thanks, Phil, I'll walk over there now.' He turned to Luke and Maria. 'If you head up to the right, you'll see Ray Charlton. He knows you're helping. I've to head over to that house, it seems the Aylwards have arrived.'

The Aylwards were inside the house when Carl reached them. He explained that Forensics had checked out their bedroom and the en suite, along with the family bathroom. Fingerprints had been found, but he needed their prints for elimination purposes.

They immediately agreed and asked if they could go to look at their room. Carl accompanied them, knowing they wouldn't be happy when they saw the unkempt state of it, but he remained silent. He didn't want to influence their thoughts as they saw it for the first time.

Brian Aylward looked around, taking in the general mess, but Ella drew in her breath with a hiss. 'When you catch him, DI Heaton, can I have first dibs at hammering him?'

He smiled at her. 'Unfortunately not. We're not allowed to hammer our suspects, or indeed do anything to them. But I know exactly how you feel. The rest of your home is clean and tidy, waiting for you to come back to it. It was obvious as soon as we saw this room that you hadn't left it in that state. I have to ask you to leave it for a couple more days before doing anything to it, in case we need to revisit. However, we do need to know if anything's missing, anything's here that shouldn't be, that sort of thing.'

'It seems he's used our bedding from the airing cupboard – we stripped all the beds before we closed it down for the winter, and in April we actually have decorators coming in to change this room. Can we still go ahead with that?'

Carl gave a slight nod. 'I would think so. We've searched the property for the missing lady, and don't think she was ever brought here. We don't even have any proof that whoever was hiding in your home is the person who took Faith Young. Whoever he is, he's disappeared now, and hasn't been back in the house. We've had somebody on constant watch. This could be two separate crimes, one a breaking and entering, the other a kidnap.'

'You think she's still alive?' Ella asked.

'I'm open-minded about it. We haven't found a body despite

extensive searches, we have two cadaver dogs working the woods today so please don't venture over there, and so far there's no trace of her.'

All three of them stepped out of the room. 'I'll go in later and do a bit of an inventory check,' Ella said. 'Glancing around, I can't see that anything's missing, and the stuff that's added is our stuff anyway. We'll sleep in our guest bedroom for the duration of our stay, but I feel as though I want to scrub every part of the house. Thank goodness we've booked this revamp of our room. I might have to extend that to the whole building.'

Brian groaned. 'How did I know that was coming?'

'It's a woman thing, Brian,' Carl said with a laugh. 'It would be my wife's reaction, if that makes you feel any better.'

Sunday evening was quiet in the Taylor household. Geraldine and Naomi were reading, having decided in Geraldine's words, 'There's naff all on TV', and Fred was sitting with his laptop pulled towards him, balancing a little precariously on a small coffee table.

Naomi lifted her head and watched as a frown creased his forehead. 'Problems?'

He nodded. 'The chap I went to see yesterday has asked me to find his wife. It's urgent, and the only information I have is her name and she once posted a letter in Lincoln fifteen years ago.'

'She's been missing fifteen years and he's only now decided he wants her back?'

Fred laughed. 'No, it's not like that. I'm pretty sure he doesn't ever want to see her again, but they have a son, now twenty-one, who has a terminal diagnosis and who wants to see his mum.'

Naomi sucked in her breath. 'That's awful. Sorry I made light of it. Is it cancer?'

'It is. I haven't met the lad yet, but he's a Down's Syndrome adult, and is currently in a hospice, partly to give his dad some respite, but partly to rest him. He was six when she walked away with another feller, so it's possible she uses his name. I'm prioritising this case, so I can see it being a week of computers. I'm going to ask for a meeting tomorrow morning with the others, get their thoughts on it, because of the urgency. Maybe Beth can work her magic, and Tessa is bound to have some out-of-the-box idea. Luke's pretty smart too...'

'Luke's very smart,' his mother responded. 'Except when he's being a bit dim.'

Fred closed down his laptop and leaned back. 'I'll leave it till the morning. Sunday night is for watching TV, not working. What's on?'

'Nothing,' the two women said in chorus.

He stood. 'Anybody want a cup of tea?'

'Might do,' Geraldine said without lifting her eyes from the book. She was getting used to having this man around the place and blessed the meeting that had brought him into her daughter's life. Besides, he usually did the late evening cuppa, and always brought them something nice to eat...

Fred read her thoughts and planted a swift kiss on the top of her head as he went by her chair. 'Anybody fancy a vanilla slice?' he called from the kitchen.

Once again they spoke together. 'Yes please!'

Tessa looked through the details of the cottage in Eyam once again. It was perfect – so perfect she had discounted the cottage at Stoney Middleton without even going to see it. She had pitched her offer five thousand pounds below the asking price but was quite prepared to pay the full price if that was needed. Her own place was sold; after speaking to her neighbours to tell

49

them she was looking for a new home, their daughter had been there within the hour offering her the full asking price if she took it off the market.

Tessa felt it was all happening very fast, and her evening conversation with Hannah's picture mentioned that small fact. She could almost hear Hannah saying *That's the best way, go for it, Tess.*

The back garden of the cottage she had viewed was long, and she knew she would be adding a conservatory. The cottage needed a degree of modernisation, a kitchen and bathroom being priorities. The current owners had moved out to live with their son and his family, and she had been able to explore every nook and cranny.

That it was perfect she was in no doubt; she simply needed to hear that the vendors had accepted her offer.

Maria stood at the lounge window looking out over their tiny patch of garden. The moon was bright, casting an ethereal glow over the mini landscape, and she hugged her dressing gown tighter around her.

Luke would be asleep, she reckoned, he had looked exhausted when they had returned from searching the woods. She felt he had become personally involved in the case, even though it was a police matter and not a Connection job. Following on from his trip to France to say his goodbyes to Doris, and now this conundrum of the disappearing author, he was starting to look wan, worn out.

Maybe they should book a weekend away or something, anything to lighten the load he was obviously carrying. She gave a deep sigh, closed the curtains and picked up her Kindle. *Only one more chapter,* she promised herself.

Luke wasn't asleep.

'I've been thinking.'

She waited.

'Shall we have a weekend away or something? I've checked the calendar and you're off next weekend. We could maybe go to York or somewhere like that, and forget about the rest of this skanky world.'

'Skanky world? I'd been thinking the exact same thing, about having a weekend away. And I love York, so yes, let's go there.'

'I'll book us somewhere tomorrow. Fancy a hot chocolate or something?'

'What's the something?'

He smiled at her. 'Put down your Kindle, and I'll show you.'

The centre of Eyam, the plague cottages, the stocks, the museum, the tea rooms, were all lit by the same shafts of moonlight, creating a breathless quality that impressed all who looked out on it that night. The police constable on overnight duty at the entrance to the woods sat in her car and gazed around intermittently. She occasionally walked towards the entrance where the path began, then walked back again.

Her partner, on the other hand, preferred to play some game on his phone, lifting his head occasionally to pay lip service to his watchman duties.

She walked back to get in the car, and he jumped out of the passenger side.

'Need a piss.'

'Too much information,' she said drily. 'Get far enough away so I can't hear you.'

. . .

Danny Haynes chuckled and walked through the narrow entrance and onto the path. He climbed a short distance up the incline and figured she'd have to have supersonic hearing to hear a trickle of water from this point. He unzipped his trousers, feeling relief as the flow started. He was mid-flow when he heard the scream.

7

PC Danny Haynes ran back down the hill, urine flowing down his legs as he desperately attempted to zip up his trousers.

'Ails,' he called, 'you okay?'

He burst out of the narrow entrance and for a moment his world rocked. He sprinted across to the car and saw the blood, pooling around Aileen's head. He knelt down but could find no pulse, then realised the blood wasn't from a head wound, but her throat. He ran around to the passenger side of the car and threw himself in, keeping low.

'Officer down! Officer down! Ambulance required. Eyam overnight surveillance point.'

There was a crackle, then a voice asked for details, reassuring the obviously scared man that help was on its way. 'She's dead. Aileen's dead, I'm sure. Her throat's been cut.'

'DI Heaton will be there shortly. Hang on, Danny, and stay in the car till help gets there.'

. . .

Carl was the first on scene, still rubbing his eyes as he tried to wake himself. He'd only been in bed an hour when the call had come through.

He left his car some distance from the scene knowing there would be other cars and emergency vehicles arriving, and he ran across to the patrol car that looked empty.

Danny was almost lying across the front seats but sat up as his door opened and Carl spoke.

'Danny, come on, lad. They'll not be back now. You can hear the sirens.' He walked around to the other side and knelt to check for a pulse in the young PC's neck, but he could tell by looking that it was a futile exercise.

'You saw nothing?' he asked the grey-faced officer.

'I'd gone into the woods for a piss... sorry, sir, to urinate... when I heard Aileen scream. I came running back here and saw the blood so called it in straight away.'

'What did you see?'

'Nothing. Nobody about, it's after midnight. Even the dog walkers tend to stop around eleven. I saw nothing.'

Two patrol cars pulled up, spilling out their occupants. 'Ambulance on its way, ETA two minutes, sir,' one of the PCs said.

Carl sighed. 'There's no rush. I reckon she was dead within the first minute. Okay, lads,' he called, and was instantly surrounded. 'I want you in these woods in pairs and find me the bastard who did this. That's where he has to be, PC Haynes would have seen someone going in any other direction. And he's not gone through the gap that leads to the path, he's gone through the overgrown part.' He turned away as they paired up and left at a run to start the search. He switched on his radio. 'I need the dogs here asap.'

· · ·

Carl wanted to cry. He watched as the ambulance pulled away carrying the covered body of PC Aileen Chatterton, twenty-two, a slim, very pretty blonde-haired girl with her life still in front of her at midnight, and now gone. The ambulance had no need of sirens and flashing blue lights.

He turned his attention back to the wooded area. Nobody had returned, they were still searching, and had been joined by the dog handlers. These weren't the cadaver dogs, these two had been trained in finding people who were hidden; people exuding the smell of fear, the smell of sweat produced during headlong flight.

It was going to be a long night.

Carl was sitting outside Connection the following morning when Luke pulled up. Luke got out of his car, waved across the road to Maria, and walked towards Carl's car.

'You've found her?'

Carl shook his head, weariness etched into his face. 'No, nothing. We lost a colleague last night, on watch duty at the entrance to the woods.'

Luke hesitated. He felt like a child again who simply didn't know what to do or say. In the end he found some words. 'You'd best come in and have some coffee.'

Luke handed Carl a coffee. 'Can you talk about it?'

'Her name was PC Aileen Chatterton, and she was only twenty-two. Whoever did this, cut her throat.'

Luke gasped. 'She was on her own?'

'Temporarily. Her partner had gone into the woods to relieve himself. The killer must have been watching them, waiting to see if one would be left alone. In the couple of minutes she was on her own, he struck. We've been all night in the woods because he had to have escaped that way. There was nobody around when Danny Haynes ran to the car. He heard her scream, so he was back like a whippet. We even had the search dogs called in, but nothing.'

'You're linking it to Faith Young's disappearance?'

'God knows. We have no body for Faith, so technically she's still alive. And why kill a policewoman? Why? She was no threat. She was on watch, surveillance, that's all. We simply didn't want anyone walking around in the woods.'

There was a knock on Luke's door, and when opened it revealed Fred. 'Oh! Sorry, didn't think we'd have visitors so early. Hi, DI Heaton.'

'Carl, Fred, it's Carl now.'

'I keep forgetting. Once a DI, always a DI, I suppose. You okay?'

'Not really. We lost a colleague last night, throat slashed while on surveillance duties.'

'Here?'

Carl nodded. 'Yes, by the entrance to the woods. She was there with a male colleague, but she was the unlucky one who died.'

'I'm so sorry. Can we do anything?'

'No, I needed to talk it out of my system before heading home to Kat and Martha. Luke made us a drink.'

'Did he now? Any left?'

Luke stood and filled a third mug before handing it over to Fred.

'Should we be worried?'

'What?' Carl looked surprised by the question.

'Two women in a short space of time. I think we're all fooling ourselves if we think Faith Young is going to turn up alive and well, and it's all happening in Eyam.'

Carl sighed. 'You're right, of course you are. Everyone has to be on their guard now. There was no reason to kill Aileen, no reason at all. And the reason for the disappearance of Faith completely baffles me. There's no body, no ransom demand, nothing.'

The door opened again, and Tessa looked in. 'Can anybody come to this coffee morning?'

Carl left half an hour later, and Fred, Tessa and Luke remained in Luke's office at Fred's request.

'I really need Beth on the Baines case as well, but I'll talk to her later when she gets in.'

Luke frowned. 'Oops. Carl being here completely wiped this from my thoughts. Beth's in Florida.'

Fred and Tessa looked at him. 'Florida? That's a bit far to go on a case.' Tessa laughed.

'She called in Saturday afternoon to ours to tell me. Sudden desire to go on holiday, so they went. I think it means Simon will be in if anybody needs anything financial sorting.'

'Bugger,' Fred said.

'Problem?'

'Not sure, but I thought Beth was the most likely person to help.'

He spent the next ten minutes explaining the issue with Cliff and Ethan Baines, and the urgency of digging up the information.

'I have many contacts in the force,' Tessa said quietly. 'I'm sure between us we can come up with something. Beth needs this time to grieve, and Joel will help her through it.' She glanced at her phone for the second time in as many minutes. 'Sorry, I'm not fixated on my phone, I'm willing it to ring. I put an offer in on a cottage in Eyam, absolutely fell in love with the place, and now I'm on tenterhooks until I hear whether it's been accepted or not.'

'So, have you made any sort of a start on it, Fred?'

'Only a basic internet search.'

Tessa's phone rang and she stared at it before grabbing it up and answering. 'Tessa Marsden.'

She listened to the voice at the other end, and the smile crept across her face. 'That's wonderful. I'm delighted. You'll confirm?'

She spoke for a minute longer, then disconnected.

'It's mine. It's mine! It seems that being a cash buyer swung it, and it's now off the market.'

'So where is it?' Luke wished he had a photo of the smile plastered across her face.

'A little higher up the village than your place, it has a long rear garden that backs onto the grassed area top end of the woods. Very rural, quite old-fashioned décor but its current owners are an elderly couple. I'll need a new kitchen and bathroom, but nothing's urgent. I'm going to add a conservatory to this massive garden, which will cut down a bit on the grass mowing, and there's an old shed that I didn't bother looking at, because I reckon it's a haven for spiders. That can go and I'll have a summer house or something to replace it.'

Fred and Luke raised their mugs. 'Many congratulations, Tessa. We're really chuffed for you,' Fred said.

'You want to take ten minutes to show me this place?' Luke asked.

'Indeed I do. Fred? You coming?'

Fred shook his head. 'Not today. I'm going to get my head down on this case, see if I can get any sort of clues as to where this woman is. I'll hold the fort here, as we seem to be short of an operative.' He smiled.

· · ·

Luke drove, and he pulled up outside the cottage. The For Sale sign had long ago given up the ghost and was lying behind the privet hedge surrounding the small front garden. Baines and Son.

'Baines? Isn't that the name of Fred's client?'

'It is. It didn't click when we were listening to him, but I was feeling really nervous about my phone call, so I probably missed the connection. Did he say what the chap did for a living?'

'I'll ask him.' He sent off a quick text to Fred, and received an immediate reply confirming they were indeed one and the same.

'Small world,' Luke said, and closed the front gate behind him. 'That needs fixing. This window is the lounge?'

'It is, and the one at the other side is a sort of second lounge. I'm not sure how I'll configure them yet, maybe use one of them as an office.'

Luke held up his hand to his forehead as he leaned to look in the window. 'Wow, decent-sized room.' He tried the front door as they walked past it. 'Locked,' he pointed out.

'Yep, they took the keys back with them.'

The garden down the side of the house was a little overgrown, and they tramped through it exactly as Tessa had previously. The size of the garden overwhelmed Luke.

'You'll need a gardener. It goes for miles.'

'There's a kind of road, a mud path almost, that goes the other side of that hedge. Not sure why really, unless it's to separate the gardens from the field, a sort of boundary line.'

They went to the kitchen window and peered through. 'Serviceable,' Luke said, 'but you'll want a new one.'

'A white one.'

Luke tried the back door. 'Locked.' He bent down and lifted the pot by the back door that held some sort of sorry-looking plant that hadn't started springing into life. He picked up a key and waved it.

'Good lord. Well I'm not leaving it here. I don't want to have to make my first job having to get rid of squatters.'

Luke unlocked the back door, and they stepped into the kitchen. 'Bit of a musty smell, but nothing some fresh air won't solve.'

8

Patio doors led out from the adjoining room, which they both guessed would have been used as a dining room.

'Eventually I'll make this one room, and the patio doors will lead into my conservatory. I was so excited, Luke, when I saw this on Saturday. I could imagine it in a year's time, everything changed, everything shiny new yet retaining the charm that hit me when we came through that front door for the first time.'

They climbed the stairs and checked out the three bedrooms, the largest one being at the back of the cottage with a spectacular view down the full length of the garden and across the fields beyond. 'This will be mine,' she said. 'I'm going to have an en-suite, because the bathroom needs a complete makeover. I'll have all the plumbing work done at the same time, and that'll be a priority because there's no shower in the bathroom.'

Luke was still staring across the fields, lost in the view. 'It's stunning, Tess. I can see why it grabbed you, and if you knock down that shed and replace it with a summer house, you can build a barbecue area to the side of it. Let's have a walk down to the shed and see what sort of support it has underneath it.'

'Spiders probably. A great heaving mass of webs is probably supporting the floor. I hate sheds, especially old ones.'

He laughed at her face. 'Then I'll see to this for you. You choose your summer house, but you're going to have to have a small shed as well for the lawnmower and spades and stuff. I'll see to the erection of it all. Maria's pretty handy with a hammer as well.'

'I'll feed you,' Tessa said with a laugh. 'We'd best go now and do the day job.'

Tessa locked the back door and dropped the key into her bag. 'I'll tell the estate agents I've got this.'

'Okay. Come on, let's check out the base of that shed.'

'Not an earthly. I'll wait here.'

'Coward,' he said, and headed down the garden. The flagged path led directly to the door of the shed and must have been laid by somebody skilled, because there were no uneven flags and no signs of any cracked ones. He guessed the owners kept their garden tools in the six feet by eight feet little box of a shed. The door had a padlock, but the padlock was open.

He held the lock in his hand and gave the door a good tug. It opened easily, much to his surprise. Obviously not all garden sheds were like his mum's. He placed one foot inside and stopped. Taking a couple of deep breaths, he stepped back out and turned to where he knew Tessa was waiting for him to finish his spidery task.

'What's wrong? Too many spiders even for you?' she called from the other end of the garden.

'Ring Carl,' Luke shouted. 'Ring him now. Tell him I think we've found Faith Young.'

Carl stared at the body of the woman who had taken up so much of his thoughts and time over the past week. The amount of blood indicated she had been killed in the shed, and he doubted she had gone there voluntarily. Her killer would have had to transport her from where they assumed she had been taken – the spot where they had found her hat and mobile phone.

'And now I have to tell her husband,' he said quietly.

'A shitty job,' Tessa responded.

'I think he's almost expecting it. It's been too long...'

'Is he at the cottage?'

'I imagine so. He said he wasn't going anywhere in case she returned to the cottage.'

'We okay to go back to work now? You know where we are when you want our statements.'

'Yeah, Tess. This isn't the outcome any of us wanted, but I think it's the one I expected.'

Luke was standing talking to one of the PCs and reacted instantly when Tessa walked towards him. 'Can we go?'

'We can. Carl will get our statements later.'

They walked to the car, and eased in, grateful to be sitting down. 'Let's get that heater going, it's bloody cold,' Tessa grumbled.

'You okay?'

'I'm fine. Seeing bodies is never easy, but it's not the first one I've had to deal with. Jack Young is going to be devastated.'

'Let's go. See if Fred's managed to come up with anything for his missing lady.'

Fred hadn't, but he'd made an appointment to go to talk to Cliff Baines again the following morning. 'I didn't manage to track her down, but I did manage to produce some questions, so I thought I'd nip out and see him, and see the neighbour who saw her drive off fifteen years ago.'

'He's a smart man, is my Patrick. Very observant. And it's actually lovely of him to pass on our name to his neighbour.' Tessa smiled.

'So, you two have had a busy time then?'

'We have. The cottage is perfect for me, but the first thing that will happen is that shed will be demolished. Luke went down to it more on a spider hunt than anything, but he looked grey when he shouted up to me to get Carl.'

'All that talent,' Fred mused. 'Wiped out in one stroke. I'm assuming that was the cause of death, the slash across the throat?'

'Not confirmed when we came away, obviously, but Carl and the pathologist said it appeared to be.'

'The same as the policewoman...' Luke muttered.

'Exactly. Scary thought, isn't it,' Tessa replied. 'Don't let Maria go out on her own until they've caught this killer.'

'You think it's random women being targeted? No connection between them?'

Tessa nodded. 'It's what I'm afraid of. There's no logic behind the attacks. But we've stepped into this accidentally, it's not our case. We've other problems to be sorting out, and I'm beginning to think Beth was pretty smart to swan off to Florida at a moment's notice.'

Jack stared at Carl. 'Dead? Faith's dead?'

'I'm afraid so, Jack. I'm very sorry for your loss...'

'It's not only my loss, DI Heaton, it's the world's loss. She still had so much to give.' He turned away and grabbed a tissue from a box. He held the tissue to his eyes as if trying to stem tears before they started, but it didn't work. Sinking on to the sofa he let the grief pour from him.

'Our new baby will never know his wonderful nan, and I don't know how to tell Helena.'

Carl nodded towards the PC he had taken with him, and she disappeared into the kitchen to return with a glass of water.

'Drink this,' she said. 'Would you like a cup of tea?'

Jack sipped at the water, then placed it on the coffee table. 'No, I'll be fine with this, thank you. What do I do now?'

'We'll need you to come in and identify Faith, but that won't be for a couple of days. I'll contact you with a time, and we'll send a car for you. Is there anybody you'd like us to ring?'

Jack shook his head. 'No, I guess it's down to me to sort things now. I need to ring Faith's publisher as a priority, but that will be after I've spoken to Helena.'

Everyone's head turned at the knock on the door, and Carl indicated the PC should answer it.

A moment later Will Sandford was in the room. 'I saw the squad car...'

'They've found her, Will.' Jack hadn't really needed to say anything, his face told the whole story.

'Oh, God, Jack, I'm so sorry. Can I do anything?'

'There's nothing to do, now. Thanks for being there for me, you've been a big support, but now I guess I see about going home in a few days. I talked her into coming here, to being part of Eyam for a month, and now I've lost her.' He made no effort to hide his tears this time.

Carl went back up to the scene of the crime and stayed to watch the forensic team. They all wore the same intense expression, each one acknowledging he was there, but keen to get on with their work.

He left them to it and walked away from the shed until he reached the hedge behind it, and the field beyond it. The beech hedge was incomplete, with gaps in it that would easily accommodate a person wishing to enter the garden without walking all the way round to the front gate.

He slipped through and for the second time wandered around, looking for tyre tracks. It was possible that the killer had made Faith Young walk to the shed, but Carl got the feeling that when the autopsy was complete, it would show the blow to the head would have been sufficient to render her unconscious.

His eyes remained firmly on the ground, the ground that was starting to leave its winter state and come into a spring state. Was it soft enough to show tyre tracks? He thought not. Could the killer have carried Faith Young without being seen by anybody? Again he thought not.

So how the hell had the body, most likely unconscious, travelled between the wooded area lower down the valley and this cottage at the top end of the village? And how many people had known the cottage was no longer occupied?

He shook his head as if trying to clear it of all the questions that were pouring through his brain. The one thing that stood out most of all was the emptiness of the property. The body could have remained here for so much longer if Luke Taylor hadn't decided he wanted to investigate the shed with a view to knocking it down and building Tessa a summer house.

And did this mean that if you brought common sense into the equation, whoever had been sleeping at the white house in the woods was probably not the killer, because surely he would have taken advantage of a killing site being part of an empty property, and stayed there instead?

Frustration was building inside Carl as he sought answers to all his questions. Hopefully there would be some DNA results from the white house bedroom and bathroom by the following day, and maybe, just maybe, a name would be revealed.

Carl headed back into the garden and saw that the forensics

examination of the shed was almost complete. The crime scene tape was being placed securely around the shed, then extended around the entire cottage.

'We're going in the house tomorrow, sir,' one of the team members explained. 'We need daylight, so we've arranged that you leave two officers outside for the night. They'll only be needed for the one night. That okay with you?'

'It's fine, it was my next job to get that organised. Thank you for what you've done today.'

'No problem, sir. Results as soon as we can get them. We realise the press will be hovering with this one, she was pretty famous.'

'And strangely enough,' Carl said, 'the manner of her death will make her even more so.'

Carl contacted the Baines and Son Estate Agency, explained the situation, and said they would require a key by eight the following morning.

There was a gasp of surprise at the agency end of the line, followed by 'But it was only this morning we had an offer on the place!'

'That won't change. I spoke to the lady who made the offer, and she wants me to reassure you that nothing has changed.'

Carl could almost sense the relief as the voice said he would be at the cottage by eight, with a key for the forensics people.

'Thank you,' Carl said. 'I'll make sure it's safely returned to you when we're finished.'

9

Fred pulled up outside Cliff Baines' house and walked up the small front path. He knocked and waited, looking around him. It was quiet, and he guessed it was because of the torrential rain tippling down over all of the Peak District, and probably half the country.

'Come in, Fred,' Cliff said, and opened the door wide. 'Can I make you a drink?'

'No thanks, Cliff, had one before I set off. I've some questions I could do with answering, and I'm here to have a chat with your neighbour as well. I'm trying to get a feel for your wife, but I know nothing about her, and that's not a good place to start any sort of investigation. First of all, do you have a photograph?' He placed the recorder on the table to save taking notes.

'I do but it's fifteen or so years old. I didn't give it to you, because I figured she'll have changed plenty in that time.' He stood and walked out of the room, returning a couple of minutes later with the picture.

'That's her, that's Ethan's mother, Pippa Baines. Philippa Baines. Née Pippa Evans. I didn't tell you that either, did I?'

Fred smiled at Cliff. 'No, you didn't, but I didn't ask. I got kind of wrapped up in the tragedy of the whole situation, I think, and it was only when I was driving home things began to occur to me. I tried answering them on Facebook and the internet, but found nothing, so I decided the sensible thing to do was come back here and really get to the bottom of who she is.'

'And of course we're connected in another way now, aren't we? You've apparently found a body in the shed of one of the properties on our books.'

'Tessa's cottage. Don't you be letting anybody gazump her on it, Cliff. She's really set her heart on it, bodies, spiders and everything that goes with it.'

Cliff smiled. 'So I understand. No, the property is hers, and the owners have agreed to it being taken off the market in return for speedy conveyancing. One of my top colleagues is dealing with it, and he rang me last night to tell me of the developments. I said give the police whatever assistance they need.'

'Did he say who the body was?'

'No, I think he was a bit concerned by it all. Said several times he had to be at the cottage by eight – I suspect he's normally only getting out of bed at that time.'

'Well, I don't want it coming as a shock to you – the deceased is Faith Young, the author.'

Cliff's eyes widened. 'Bloody hell. No, he didn't mention that. I saw on the news she was missing, but I didn't connect the body with her. Bit slow of me, I suppose. I take it she didn't simply wander into the shed and have a heart attack or something?'

Fred shook his head. 'A gash across her throat.'

He picked up the picture Cliff had given him and studied it closely. Pippa Baines had been a beautiful woman in her late twenties, with shoulder-length blonde hair that to Fred's eyes was naturally curly, although he admitted to himself that he wouldn't recognise naturally curly hair from the tonged variety. On the photograph her eyes could almost be described as lavender, although he knew he was being fanciful. Could eyes be lavender? He would have to check out the actual colour when he eventually found her.

In the picture she was leaning against a garden wall with one hand on a pushchair; Fred imagined her son was the unseen child. She was slim and wearing a short skirt that showed off her long tanned legs to perfection. He looked at it for several minutes, imprinting it on his mind.

He put it in his briefcase. 'I'll return this when I've found her,' he said.

Cliff nodded. 'Thank you. It's the only one I kept, and I really kept it for Ethan. I destroyed all the others in a temper one day.'

'No problem. I only need one. How is Ethan?'

'He's coming home at the weekend, but I saw him last night and he was very quiet. I think they've had to up his pain relief. One half of me wants it all to be over because I can't bear to think of my son in pain, and the other half wants him with me always. Have you got kids, Fred?'

Fred shook his head. 'No. We'd spoken about it, and we both wanted children, but then she was killed in the twin towers attacks in New York, and from then until a month or so ago, I'd never looked at another woman. I've now met somebody else who makes me very happy, but we're both a little old for having babies.' He laughed.

Cliff's face became serious. 'I wouldn't change anything about Ethan, you know. I love him so much, always have from the second he entered our world, but I can't say that Pippa felt the same. It was like a shutter coming down on her feelings when Down's Syndrome was mentioned. Our friends were wonderful, rallied round us, gave us support when we needed it most, but it wasn't enough for her. I have a friend, Ivor, Ivor Needham, who has been a constant since Ethan's birth. He doesn't even live around here any longer, lives on the south coast, but he rings every week to see how we're doing, how Ethan is, to offer us his help if we need it.'

'Take my advice, Cliff, make sure your friend is fully conversant with Ethan's prognosis, you're going to need him. He does know?'

Cliff shook his head. 'Not of the terminal diagnosis. I only told him Ethan had a bowel problem, and I think he supposed it was yet another quirk of this syndrome. Telling him, my best mate, would make it unbearable. No, there's time left yet before I have to tell him. And when the time comes, he'll support me through it. It's what we do.'

'Right, I'll keep in touch. I'm going to see your neighbour now, see if I can tease anything out of that sharp brain of his, then I'm heading back to the office. Ring me anytime, you understand what I'm saying?'

'I do. And please tell your colleague not to worry, the cottage is definitely hers.'

Fred laughed. 'She's bouncing about it. All sorts of plans for what she's going to do with it, and of course it's right where she wants to be, in Eyam.' He shook Cliff's hand, and headed back outside, turning right to go to Patrick Fletcher's home.

Patrick welcomed him, offered him a drink which once again Fred refused, and led Fred through into the lounge.

'It's warmer in here,' Patrick explained. 'I hate miserable days like this. I could do with going to the library, but it'll have to dry up a bit before I even consider it.'

'It's awful,' Fred agreed, 'I'd about got dry in Cliff's house, then had to come out again. Never mind, it's only rain water. Do you mind if I record our conversation?' He waved his recorder around.

'Not at all, that's what your Tessa did when we were talking about the murders over at the library. I enjoyed that.'

Fred smiled. He liked this man. 'Is enjoyed the right word?'

'Definitely. Now, how can I help you?'

'I need you to think back fifteen years.'

'No problem. If you'd been asking me about something a few days ago, I'd have struggled, but fifteen years is easy.'

'That's a relief. I want you to think back to the day when Pippa Baines walked out on Cliff and Ethan. I understand you saw her go away with a man.'

Patrick sighed. 'I thought he was over her long ago. He shouldn't be raking this up again.'

Fred waited.

'I can see it clear as day. Ethan was in school, Pippa was in the house and Cliff was at work. He didn't have his own business then, that came later, so he kept pretty regular hours, picked Ethan up from school every Friday afternoon without fail, and they would go play football, or for a McDonald's, or to the bowling alley. Ethan loved bowling. The day she went was a Friday, she had it planned perfectly.'

'Did she know you could see her?'

'No. I was decorating our bedroom, the missus wanted it changing to lemon instead of blue, and I'd been at it a couple of days because it took about four coats of paint. The bedroom window was open, but that was nothing unusual. The blue car pulled up, the one with the twin exhaust or whatever it was, noisy bugger. Pippa came out pulling a suitcase, and he jumped out of the car and lifted the case into the boot, while she went back inside for a second suitcase. By this time I'd figured she wasn't taking stuff to the charity shop, so I stopped the painting to watch. He put the second suitcase in the boot, then he grabbed hold of her arse and leaned her over the car to kiss her. Lasted a while that kiss, then she stroked his face, smiling all the time, and went round to get in the passenger seat. The car growled its way down the road, and she's never been back since.'

'I don't suppose...'

'Nay, Fred, I didn't get the number plate, but the car had been at that house before. I remember the sound, real throaty. Don't quote me on this, because I'm not too good with car makes. Perhaps a Mazda. But really, it could as easily have been a Ford, so maybe ignore that. Lovely colour though, even if it was noisy. Metallic look about it, and a deepish blue, bit lighter than royal blue.'

'You're a star, Patrick Fletcher. Tessa said you were, and now I know it. All these little details give me something to work on.'

'He wants her to come and see Ethan doesn't he?'

Fred felt lost for words.

'Don't worry, we've talked long into the night about Ethan and what's happening to him. He said Ethan wanted to see his mum before...'

Fred nodded. 'He does. I'll move heaven and earth to find her. I'm hoping to meet Ethan next week, Cliff's expecting him home at the weekend.'

'He's a lovely lad. The world will be a worse place when he passes. You want any more help, Fred, you ring me or call round.'

Fred stood and picked up his recorder. 'Thank you for the information. Do I have your permission for Cliff to hear it?'

There was a brief moment of hesitation from Patrick. 'It's something he'll be hearing for the first time. I only said a man had picked her up. He didn't know anything about seeing the car here before. At first I hoped it would all blow over and she'd come home, so I kept quiet. By the time it was clear she wasn't coming back, it was too late to give him the details, so you may get some sort of reaction when he does hear what I have to say.'

'Don't worry, he'll understand your reasons behind saying

nothing. Thank you for your company, Patrick, I'll no doubt be speaking to you soon.'

Patrick opened his front door to allow Fred to go out. 'You'd best run. This bloody rain's getting heavier. The library's definitely going to have to wait, I'm not venturing out in this.'

Fred jumped in the car and shook his head. Raindrops scattered around him, and he put the heater onto full, directing the flow of air onto the screen. He drove away, looking forward to getting back to the office and re-starting his research.

10

I t rained heavily all day. Carl Heaton attended the post-mortem on Faith Young, and was told the blow to the head was severe enough to keep her unconscious for a long time, and she would definitely have still been in that state when her throat was cut.

Carl felt somewhat grateful for that news because he couldn't help but imagine how it would have been to be awake and scared witless, and then seeing the knife that was going to end your life.

It was confirmed that the same knife had been used on both Faith and Aileen Chatterton; Carl had already linked them in his mind, so wasn't surprised by that information. Of the two women, Faith had been the first to die. Carl hoped with all his heart that the two murders hadn't led the killer to wanting more.

He felt the killer had to be local, with both deaths happening in Eyam, and without any sort of evidence, he also knew it had to be a man. Faith Young had had to be carried – intensive searches of the woods hadn't identified any tracks that suggested someone having been dragged. He doubted a woman would have had the physical strength to carry an unconscious body very far. The killing site was easily half a mile from what they believed to be the abduction site.

The worst part about being given the evidence from the post-mortem was that he couldn't help but reflect that possibly the two killings, although linked to the same killer, were unplanned as to the person, merely opportunistic. It could have been anybody walking in those woods. Had he seen the author leave the tea rooms and follow the path down to the entrance to the woods? And Aileen – had he simply been watching the police car, then spotted Danny Haynes heading off to the woods alone? Opportunistic. Not necessary. Unless the desire to kill had been awakened and had to be fulfilled. Then it became necessary. To the killer.

Fred opened up Facebook and typed in the name Pippa Evans. Several options appeared, and he scrolled through them all, trying to match up what little information he had with the on-screen photographs. There was nothing to help him, so he cancelled Pippa and typed in Philippa. Again, he found nothing to indicate a direction in which he should be travelling, so he repeated the first two names with Baines as a surname, although he had already tried that and found nothing of any help.

He shook his head, wishing he could simply nip into Beth's office and give her the names – she would produce something, he was sure. He abandoned the Facebook idea and moved onto the ancestry sites. He spent a considerable amount of time on them because he kept getting side-tracked by the wealth of information, but still he didn't find the woman he was seeking. He was beginning to slowly accept that she had probably changed her name completely, and was probably using the surname of the man she had driven away with.

He picked up the phone and rang Cliff.

'Did you have absolutely no idea Pippa was seeing somebody else?'

'No idea at all. She changed so much after Ethan was born, kind of retreated inside herself, and that's how she remained. The bright and bubbly woman I'd married disappeared. She became withdrawn, looked after Ethan but never really bonded with him, and life became quiet. It never occurred to me she was withdrawing from me as well, I always thought it was the shock of having a Down's Syndrome child that turned her inwards. And then she disappeared, and it seemed I'd got it all wrong. She simply wanted out of our little family. And she found somebody to help her with that objective.'

'Somebody with a blue car,' Fred said. 'I don't hold out much hope of tracking her by following the blue car clue. Okay, thanks, Cliff. I was simply clutching at straws.'

'No problem, Fred. I'll give you a ring if anything should occur to me, but so far it's all like a big dark hole I can't get out of.'

'Understandable. Is Ethan still coming home at the weekend?'

'He is. And he seemed brighter today, so maybe he's getting used to the new meds.'

They disconnected and Fred leaned back in his chair. He needed help. They all had their own areas of expertise, and Beth had the one he currently needed.

He opened his emails and began to type.

Beth was sitting on the bed in their room. They had been out for breakfast to the Ponderosa, and she felt stuffed. She had tried to convince both herself and Joel that 'all you can eat' doesn't literally mean that, to little avail. She loved going out for every meal and figured the Americans had got it right with their system of "room only" accommodation. But at the moment, the breakfast felt like a killer meal. Joel was changing his T-shirt after dropping maple syrup down the front of the first one, and she heard her phone ping.

Fred. Her heart gave a quick lurch. She knew he wouldn't contact her unless it was urgent. The message merely said **Email sent. Sorry. Hope it's sunnier where you are than it is in Eyam.**

'Problem?' Joel asked.

'Don't know yet.' She frowned. 'Fred's sent me an email. Out of everybody, I would have said he would be the one least likely to contact me, so I have a feeling this is a last resort sort of email.'

She stood and removed her laptop from the safe.

Fred's email explained in detail the case he had taken on, and the difficulties he was having not knowing which name she was using, and not even knowing if she was still living in the UK. He asked for ideas.

'Can you give me half an hour?' she asked Joel.

He kissed her. 'We're getting on a bus for NASA at ten, is that long enough?'

'Thank you, my love,' she said, and blew him a kiss in return.

Fred heard the ping, and it was with a feeling of trepidation that he opened his emails.

He quickly read through it, and as quickly sent back an answer.

```
You're such a superstar, Beth Walters, and I
think I love you. Promise no more queries,
enjoy the rest of your holiday.
```

He printed off the email and placed a copy in the folder he

was using to gather information for Cliff Baines. It already held the transcript of each meeting Fred had had with his client, plus the transcript of the talk enjoyed with Patrick Fletcher. Information was rolling in – all he had to do was find the woman. Cliff had specified he would like Fred to contact her rather than himself, if at all possible.

He looked at the name that had surfaced for the woman who had left as Pippa Baines and had morphed as if by magic into Julie Ann Needham. It seemed her home was now in Brighton – far enough away to stop Cliff and Ethan from simply dropping in out of the blue to visit his friend Ivor, yet still remaining in the UK.

It was all very well asking him to go and see her, to explain the situation, but the hardest part would be explaining to Cliff exactly who it was he was going to see. He was sure he remembered Cliff saying his friend Ivor rang most weeks to see how they were managing – the words two-faced sprang into Fred's mind.

He pulled the transcript from the folder and checked Cliff's words. Best mate. Lives on south coast. Rings every week. Support.

Cliff was going to have a lot to contend with in the coming months – and it wouldn't only be the loss of his son. Fred stood and walked through to reception. Cheryl and Simon were sharing a joke, with Simon almost doubled up with laughter.

'Care to share?' Fred asked.

Cheryl turned to him. 'Oh, it's nothing, a daft Facebook post. Out of all the millions posted every day, you sometimes see a little gem that really tickles you. Can I help?'

'I'm checking nothing new has come in today that I need to deal with before Friday. I have to go to the seaside tomorrow.'

'That's nice. Any particular seaside?'

'Brighton. I'll fill in the online diary with the address and any other details you might need.'

'You taking Naomi?'

'If only. I suspect she'll be working.'

'She's not working Thursday. Or so she said last night, when we had a bit of a catch-up. It's another shift swap with somebody who has a hospital check-up on Friday, when Naomi should have been off. I don't know how she copes with sorting out the staff rota over there. She might be able to do yet another rota swap and get tomorrow off as well. Worth asking.'

'Certainly is. Back in a minute.'

He ran across the road, dodging the ever-increasing traffic flow through the village as the year headed towards spring, and felt huge disappointment as he realised Naomi wasn't on checkout duties.

'Naomi in?' he asked the young girl sitting patiently waiting for her next customer.

'She's taking some time to catch up on paperwork. She's in the office.'

'Thanks. I'll find her.'

Naomi looked up, then a smile appeared as she saw Fred. 'A welcome sight,' she said. 'Want a cuppa?'

'No thanks, I'm good. Don't think too much about this, simply answer yes. Can you get tomorrow off?'

'Yes.'

'You can?'

'I don't know, but you told me to answer yes. Want to tell me why?'

'I have to go to Brighton, leaving early tomorrow, but I'll be staying over and travelling home Thursday. Cheryl said you'd got Saturday off anyway, so I thought...'

'Leave it with me. How can a girl turn down a couple of days in Brighton in early March, in the freezing cold.' She laughed. 'One thing I'll say about you, Fred Iveson, is you're never boring. Windsor, Brighton, what next? Matlock Bath?'

'We can do Matlock Bath at the weekend. Take the girls and Geraldine, they'll love it.'

'Get out of here. Leave me to sort this. As soon as I know if I can do it, I'll text you. That okay?'

He punched the air. 'Yes! Beth Walters has trumped me on this one, she's off to NASA today, but we've got Brighton's seafront to enjoy.'

Cheryl looked up as he walked back through reception. He merely held up crossed fingers and she smiled. Her glass of wine with Naomi the previous evening had shown her how much her friend felt about this man, and there was no way Naomi was going to give up on the opportunity for a couple of days away with him, even if it was for his job.

She felt she was really getting to know everybody, and she had taken a particular liking to Simon, Beth's new sidekick. Since joining Connection he had spent a lot of time learning what was required of him; much of his time given to shadowing Joel who forwarded various sorts of work in Beth's direction, but Simon had also been by Beth's side when they had discovered the massive fraud in the North East. Since holding the fort following Doris's death, he had grown in Cheryl's eyes.

She smiled as she thought of the laughter shared earlier, and then suddenly heard Fred call out, 'Yes!!'

Naomi had worked her magic on the rota sheet, Cheryl guessed. One text successfully delivered.

11

Carl was sitting at his desk by seven. He had delivered Martha to her grandparents the previous evening, ready for a day trip to a zoo, and he had decided to leave Kat to have a long lie-in after a disturbed night.

Collecting the largest Costa latte he could, he headed towards his office, pleasantly surprised to see several members of his team already at their desks. Losing Aileen Chatterton had been a huge blow to them, and they were clearly overturning every stone.

He felt at a loss. They had nothing to go on with either murder, and he was starting to feel as if he was floundering. There had proved to be no forensic evidence as to the identity of the killer, not even a tiny little hook they could latch on to and follow up.

The picture was firmly fixed in his mind of his first sight of Faith Young in that garden shed. Everything seemed green, from the paint colour carelessly applied to the outside of the small wooden hut, to Faith's coat, to the lawnmower upended in a corner. Green, darkest green. Even the days old blood had darkened, taking on the hue of the coat it spilled down.

The initial sight of her had been shocking, made so much worse by the knowledge that life had been extinct for some time. But even if they had found her within a minute, nothing could have saved her. The slash across the throat had been clean. Deep. Deadly.

He left his office carrying his coffee and walked into the briefing room to stare at the murder board. Two dead women, one missing killer. And Carl felt there was no connection between any of them. The killer simply wanted to kill. Carl shivered as he admitted to himself that there would be more. Two women within a few days of each other, where would he go next? Would he stay in Eyam? Or venture further afield. If his theory was right that the killings were opportunistic, he could travel anywhere and kill again. On a whim.

He. Carl was aware he had discounted the killer being a woman, purely because Faith Young had had to be transported, and it was an uphill journey between the abduction site and the kill site. Could a woman have done it? He doubted it. He thought it would have been heavy work even for a man.

He leaned against a desk and continued to stare at the board. Nothing, absolutely nothing, was telling him that something was out of kilter. He sipped at his coffee, deep in thought, then stood abruptly.

A germ of an idea – had the killer killed before? These two deaths seemed to be pretty efficient as far as he could see. Had the killer already practised? He moved quickly back to his office and pulled his keyboard towards him. Using the email address that was the one generated for sending to every force in the country, he gave details of the case, stressing no forensic evidence left by the killer, but the same method used for both murders. He asked for help – if anyone had unsolved crimes matching the MO of his two murders, he would appreciate further details. Clicking SEND, he sat back, recognising he was clutching at straws. He didn't know which fingers to cross.

Naomi waited for Fred to finish manoeuvring around a complicated roundabout, then said, 'You spoke to your client then?'

'I did. I didn't know what to say. As soon as I said I thought I'd found her, he jumped in straight away with he didn't want any details, he wanted me to pass on the information to his wife of the situation concerning her son. I suppose I could have done it over the phone, but he wanted the news delivering in person and a full report back on how she had taken it. Hence our trip to Brighton.'

'So he doesn't know what her name is now, or that she's possibly living with his best mate?'

'Not yet, but when he gets the full report from Connection, he'll know. I'm not God, I can't make decisions about what he can know and what he can't. He pays us for a thorough job, and that's what he'll get. You think maybe he's guessed but doesn't want to know?'

'I've no idea. But you don't have a choice, so don't beat yourself up about it if this all goes pear-shaped. It's not your fault, Fred. He's the one burying his head, isn't he?'

'He is. I suspect he feels he's got enough on his plate without the added stress of knowing who his wife left him for, fifteen years ago.'

Naomi stared out of the window at the grey skies. 'Think it'll be sunny in Brighton?'

'Nope.' He grinned at her. 'We'll have to snuggle up to keep warm.'

She leaned over and squeezed his hand. 'I'm up for that.'

'I need to talk to you, because something's bothering me.'

'Me? Am I bothering you?'

Fred laughed. 'In a way. It's this Covid thing. I went for a walk through the village yesterday and saw two cottages with notices in the window saying ISOLATING. Now I don't want to be a scaremonger, but I think within the next month we're all going to be imprisoned in our homes.'

Naomi looked at him in horror. 'Imprisoned?'

He turned towards her, aware of the shock written on her face. 'Well, okay, maybe I used the wrong word.' He returned to face the road. 'But I certainly don't think the government will have much choice. I think it's going to be a complete lockdown, while they try to work out what to do about things. It's a killer, Naomi, the deaths are rising daily, and it's going to be a long time before they get an effective vaccination for it. And the thing is, if that happens, I won't be able to see you. Or your family. It's killing the elderly, for sure.'

'They'll not separate families?'

'No, they can't do that, but think about it. There are ways around protecting Geraldine. You're going to have to stay in. Maybe have groceries delivered. Your job will change, because I can't see how they can close food shops, but you'll certainly need some sort of protection so you're not bringing the virus back home with you.'

Naomi stared out of the window, as if taking in what he was saying. 'Fred, there's a services coming up. Can we stop for a coffee?'

'We can. I'm sorry if I've upset you, but I had to make sure you understood the implications of everything. It's important we protect our lovely Geraldine.'

He put on his indicator, and they headed up the slip road, did a tour of the car park as they looked for a parking space, then headed into the food area.

· · ·

Fred collected two cinnamon buns and two coffees, and carried the tray back to where Naomi sat.

'That's not all, is it?' she said, as he sat down.

'What?'

'Your concerns about Covid.'

'No, it's not.' He took a deep breath. 'I think you know how I feel about you, Naomi Taylor. Everything feels right when I'm with you, I love how we enjoy the same sort of stuff, how we can talk about anything, the cuddles and stuff in bed...'

'And stuff?' she asked, eyes twinkling.

'And stuff.' He grinned at her. 'If we do have to go into any form of lockdown, I won't be able to see you. I can see my job being a working-from-home situation, as will all of us, of course. It will, of necessity, limit the types of jobs we can take. Surveillance won't be an issue, but what we're doing today wouldn't be allowed under lockdown rules, I'm sure.'

'Fred, do you love me?'

'I...' He looked at her. 'Very much.'

'Go on. Say it.'

'I love you, Naomi Taylor.'

'Okay, that's good. I love you too, Fred Iveson. Now, will that make it easier for this lockdown that may or may not happen, if I suggest you move in?'

He broke off a piece of his cinnamon bun. 'Well, that was pretty easy, wasn't it?'

'Nope. I need the permission of Rosie, Imogen and Mum. I'm the easy one.'

'Think a stick of Brighton rock will pave the way?'

'Might do. We could try it. Seriously, Fred, you really want to move in with my madcap family?'

'I don't only love you, silly woman, I love the whole lot of you. Even Luke! I'm so happy these days, I even smile.'

'Wow. Fred Iveson, smiling. But on to a more serious note, if

I'm going to be the one who puts Mum in danger of catching this thing, then I have to seriously consider leaving the Co-op.'

'You know I'll back you if you decide to do that. Let's wait and see what government advice is before making a decision on that, but I think we have to move quickly on getting the permission of my other Taylor girls, because once government gives the instruction, I won't be able to move.'

She nodded. 'I know. I'll talk to them tomorrow, but I know what they'll say. However, don't let them bribe you into saying they can have a dog.'

'I like dogs.'

'Dear gods. I'm lost.'

They reached the car, and headed back towards the motorway, holding hands at odd moments as they thought of the uncertain future that faced everyone.

It took Fred and Naomi slightly over six hours to reach Brighton; the M25 had almost broken their spirits, but eventually they reached the seafront and parked the car.

'Okay, partner, do you want me to face this woman with you?'

'No, I don't want you to hear me swear.'

Naomi laughed. 'Hear you swear? That's a joke, right? I'm more likely to swear than you. Seriously, do you need my support? You can always introduce me as a work colleague, she won't know.'

Fred sighed. 'Suppose one of them is starting with Covid.'

'I'll wait here.'

'Thought you might. This is how we have to think now, I'm afraid.' Fred reached across to the glovebox and took out a mask. 'If one of them so much as coughs, I'm putting this on.'

'You've bought some already?'

'Managed to get them before all the shops ran out.'

'So where is this house?'

Fred pointed, the blue mask still in his hand. 'That road there. It's number twenty-six, so I'll leave the car here as it's a nice place to park, and you can sit and survey the sea. I'll go and tell them what I have to tell them, then make my way back to you. We'll go and check in at our hotel after that and have an early meal. That okay?'

'It is. I'll ring Mum while I'm waiting, talk to her about what we've discussed, and ask her to broach the subject with the girls. You know what, Fred Iveson, you've lightened my heart.'

He leaned across and kissed her. 'And you lightened mine the very first time I saw you. Talk to your girls.'

He climbed out, collected his briefcase from the boot, and headed towards the road he needed, hoping the numbers started at the seafront end of the road, and not the opposite end.

12

———

Number twenty-six was a large, double aspect, bay-windowed property, with a small front garden to the right of the central garden path. It was a mass of springtime flowers – bluebells, winter pansies, tiny daffodils, huge daffodils – and Fred paused for a moment to look at them. He reckoned this garden was a good two weeks in advance of his own, and it brought a smile to his face.

To the left of the path was a paved area, on which was parked a silver Lexus. He hoped this meant someone was at home. Preferably the elusive Pippa. He took a quick shot of the house and forwarded the picture to Naomi. He captioned it *nice house* and walked up the path to the door.

The doorbell pealed melodically, and he waited. He spotted the twitch of the curtain but didn't acknowledge he had seen it. He wanted someone answering the door, not taking a glimpse and deciding he was a salesman of some description.

He waited an extra minute, then rang the bell, this time pressing it twice.

The door opened with a chain in place.

'Yes?' He could see her eyes, and the fringe of dark hair, but that was all.

'Ms Needham?'

She said nothing.

'My name is Frederick Iveson, and I work for the Connection Detective Agency in Eyam.' He handed her his card, and waved his ID tag at her, holding it in front of her face long enough for her to read it. He had heard the sharp intake of breath when he had mentioned Eyam.

'I'd like a quick word with you, if that's okay. I can wait while you verify my identity by ringing our office number on my card.'

The door was closed, but this time it was opened without the security chain.

'I don't need to do that,' she said. 'My husband is in the house. Please wait in the hall while I go and get him.'

It was Ivor who made the drinks; it seemed Julie was inwardly collapsing at the thought that someone from Derbyshire was sitting in her kitchen, about to have a cup of tea.

'Thank you for the drink,' Fred said. 'I do have things to tell you, so please forgive me for intruding.'

'You're from Eyam?' Julie said.

'I am, or at least I work out of Eyam. I have been employed by your husband, Cliff, to find you. He has no interest in causing you any disruption to the life you have chosen to follow, but I do have to tell you that when I present my findings and report fully to him, he will know where you live, and who you are living with. Your husband is my client, primarily, and this information is what he is paying for. However, part of what he is paying for involves me meeting with you personally and explaining the situation with your husband and your son.'

Suddenly Fred felt it was Pippa staring at him with the eyes he could confirm were lavender coloured, and not Julie. She spoke quietly. 'He wants a divorce, doesn't he?'

'I don't know. If he does, that isn't the reason I'm here.' He picked up his mug and sipped at the hot tea.

Ivor took hold of Julie's hand. 'Let's listen, sweetheart, and let's find out what Cliff wants from us.' He turned to Fred. 'I guess this means I've lost my best mate?'

Fred wanted to punch him in the mouth, but simply said, 'I expect so, Mr Needham.'

'So, what does he want?' Pippa had disappeared, and Julie was back.

'It concerns your son, Ethan.'

She said nothing, merely stared at Fred and waited for him to continue.

Ivor, however, sat up a little straighter, and put down his mug of tea. 'Ethan? Is he okay?'

'Ms Needham, I'm sorry to be the bearer of such news, but Ethan is very much not okay. He was diagnosed with pancreatic cancer a few months ago, and while everything has been done that could possibly be done, it has spread.'

'Cancer? He's never said a word, I swear, Julie.' There was shock in Ivor Needham's voice.

'Mr Baines chose not to disclose Ethan's condition while there was hope, but the prognosis is it's now terminal, and Ethan has, at the most, four months of life left. Ethan wants to see his mother before he dies. He is aware of his condition, was present at the meeting with his specialist when the terminal diagnosis was revealed.'

There was silence around the kitchen table; Fred waited patiently for one of them to make some comment. Eventually Julie spoke.

'Is he at home now?'

'He is in a hospice at the moment. They have been regulating his medication, and Mr Baines believes his son is returning home this weekend. Mr Needham, I understand you are in regular contact, so I suggest Mrs Baines should be the next person to ring him. I am staying in Brighton tonight and will be heading home at some point tomorrow. Friday I will be reporting to Mr Baines, so you maybe need to think about how much you will be telling your husband, Mrs Baines.'

'My name is Julie Ann Needham, Mr Iveson. I changed it by deed poll. I haven't been Mrs Baines for a long time now. I will ring Cliff tomorrow, and I don't doubt it will be a difficult conversation.'

'And Ethan?'

'Ivor and I will discuss how we handle that. Can I clarify something – is it Ethan who has asked to see me, or is it Cliff instructing me to visit?'

'The request has come directly from Ethan. I don't believe it ever occurred to Mr Baines that you would be the slightest bit interested in seeing your son again, as you haven't made contact in fifteen years. He doesn't know, of course, that you have been via Mr Needham.'

'Will you be telling him Friday morning?'

'I will.'

'Then I'm going to take the coward's way out, and ring him Friday afternoon. In the meantime, Ivor and I will make plans for a visit to Bakewell.'

'I can report you'll be visiting Ethan?'

'Of course. I'm not a monster, Mr Iveson. And please don't ever doubt I love my son. I proved that by leaving him with the best parent of the two of us. If I hadn't suffered with severe post-natal depression after Ethan was born, a condition that stayed with me for nearly three years, I could possibly have bonded with him, and when I left Cliff, I would have brought Ethan with me, but I saw their amazing relationship so I left my son in

Derbyshire. Love helped me give up my son, Mr Iveson, not selfishness.'

Fred finished his drink and stood. 'If you need to speak with me before I return to Derbyshire tomorrow, please do so. My mobile number is on my card. When I have spoken with Cliff, maybe you would appreciate a text?'

'Thank you.' Julie picked up her phone. She rang Fred's number, and then disconnected. 'That's my number. And thank you for understanding. I'm now going to digest what we've heard and work out what will happen next. Is my... husband... handling it okay?'

'As well as can be expected.' Fred shook hands with both and moved towards the door.

'How did you trace us?' Julie asked as he was stepping into the hall.

Fred turned and tapped the side of his nose. 'The clue's in the title. I'm a detective.'

Naomi was leaning against the sea wall, watching the sea, taking in deep breaths of the ozone. There was nothing like this in Eyam, she decided, enjoying the moment. She jumped when she felt Fred's arm go around her.

'You're back!'

'I am, and they didn't try to kill me. They'd mellowed a bit by the end of the conversation, but it was a bit fraught at the beginning. I've passed on everything I felt it reasonable to tell them, and I've assured them Cliff will know by Friday morning who his wife is living with and has been for fifteen years. She's going to ring him Friday afternoon after I've messaged her to let her know my report's been given.'

'That's one of the reasons I love you, Fred Iveson,' Naomi said, her eyes fixed firmly on the shoreline. 'You're a softie, really, going above and beyond to make sure people are hurt as little as possible.'

'I'll never hurt you,' he said quietly. 'Know that.'

'I do,' she said equally quietly. 'Now can we go and check in, I could eat a horse.'

'Not sure horse is on the menu, but the hotel is called A Room with a View, so I'm hopeful it'll be pretty special. Have you ever been to Brighton before?'

'No, but this hotel sounds impressive with a name like that. It doesn't matter about the horse, I'll settle for steak from a cow.'

They crossed the road and climbed back into the car. Fred turned up the heater; early March in Brighton was no warmer than early March in Eyam he decided.

Their room was spectacular with a view that was captured several times on Naomi's phone. 'I'll remember this always,' she said, holding the glass of wine to her lips as she watched the waves that had increased in strength from earlier. 'Thank you, Fred. This is a beautiful hotel, and completely unnecessary. I know you're not claiming this on expenses, and we should have stayed in the Premier Inn.'

'My finger slipped off the Premier Inn and on to this one. I don't know how it happened. Shut up, woman, and enjoy it. We have something to celebrate, and we'll celebrate in style.'

'I have something to tell you. I spoke to Mum who said she'd be delighted to have a feller living with us who would take out the wheelie bins, and when she mentioned to the girls that you would be moving in with us, they both cheered and asked if they could have a dog. So it's a thumbs-up from the Taylor family.'

Fred's smile lit up the room. 'Seriously? They've not thrown a wobbly about it?'

'Of course they haven't. For some strange reason, they like you. We've only got Luke to tell now...'

'He'll say it's too soon. It won't work. The girls don't need a father figure. Geraldine won't be happy. I can hear all his arguments now. It'll eventually dawn on him that if it's too soon for us, then it was too soon for him and Maria.'

'Fred,' Naomi said, walking towards him. 'We have to forget everybody else. This is about us. We're getting older and I thought I'd never meet anybody I felt I could trust, but then you arrived. You fill me with happiness. The days when I don't see you become lengthy days that depress me, even Mum keeps out of my way on those days. I knew from the start you were special, and you are. This is our time and we deserve each other.'

'Let's drink to that. To each other.' Fred raised his glass. 'To Naomi Taylor and Fred Iveson, long may they live together and love each other.'

Naomi laughed. 'Love you, Iveson, and welcome to my somewhat crazy world. Have you thought when you might be joining us?'

'Is tomorrow too early?'

'Not at all. Tomorrow night it won't be wine, we'll pop open the champagne.'

'And can we have a dog?'

13

Brian Aylward sounded frantic on the phone.

'Ella went out around seven for her morning run, and she's always back by around half past eight. That's when we have breakfast together. It's now eleven and she's not back. She's not answering her phone, but she always runs with it on silent – I need help, DI Heaton.'

Carl felt sick and hoped his voice didn't reflect that. 'Calm down, Brian. She may have simply fallen over and hurt herself. I'll have men with you in fifteen minutes, and I'll arrive shortly after that. Whoever I put in charge until I get there will make himself known to you, and I'll put the search dogs on standby. Tell my officer what clothes she was wearing.'

Carl put down the receiver and stared at the pictures of Faith Young and Aileen Chatterton. He had to believe what he had said to Brian Aylward, he had to. The unthinkable was that it was unbelievable...

Carl arranged extra resources and despatched them quickly to Eyam, telling them to begin their search as soon as they arrived at the entrance to the woods. He had a quiet word with Ray Charlton, telling him to go directly to the Aylward house, to try to stop Brian Aylward from tearing his hair out, and to take details of exact times Ella had left for her run, what she was wearing, what her normal route would have been.

Once organised, Carl sprinted upstairs to fill in his boss on the happenings of the morning. Sort it, he was told, and sort it bloody quick. And get the Eyam women stopped from going out on their own until we catch this lunatic.

Carl reached the Aylward home – which he discovered was actually called Woodlands, according to the small wooden sign at the end of the lane – and saw that Ray Charlton and Brian Aylward were deep in conversation.

'Nothing yet?' Carl asked, and Ray shook his head.

'Not so far, sir.'

'Does she take the same route every day, Brian?'

Carl felt a sickening thud in his stomach when Brian said that she did. 'She times herself, tries to do it a bit faster every day, so she takes exactly the same route.'

'Do you know it?'

'More or less, but it's only through listening to her. I've never run it, I don't run anywhere.'

'I've passed as much information as we could get from Brian on to the lads, sir. They're out there now. Nobody's called anything in so far.'

Brian's phone rang and he checked the screen, then shook his head at the two officers, indicating that it wasn't his wife. 'I have to take this,' he said, and moved away from them.

Carl spoke quietly. 'Has somebody been sent to check the shed where we found Faith Young?'

'First thing I did, sir. She's not there.'

'She's a sitting duck, isn't she? Takes the same route every day. I've left one of the young PCs putting together a leaflet. We need to get it into every home in Eyam, warning them not to go out on their own, to vary routes even if it's only walking to the shops. We need officers going round the entire village making sure we visit every home. We can leave a leaflet even if we can't catch everybody in, and do return calls on a different day, but I've a bad feeling about this one.'

'Me too. She's normally out for about ninety minutes, definitely never as long as this. She likes to get back, have a shower and put her face on. According to Brian, nobody ever sees her a mess.'

'Let's hope she's not a mess now, and has simply fallen over and broken a leg or something.'

'Brian says she always carries her phone. Got like a little harness thing that goes round her upper arm. She's not answering it, but she has it on silent when she's running so she's not tempted to answer it and spoil her timing of the run.'

'We checked all the buildings here?'

'I've done them. The outside ones, anyway. I decided to wait for you to go inside the house.'

'Any reason?'

'Only being careful.'

Carl stared at Ray. 'Why?'

'Don't like him. Didn't like his attitude when he found out we'd already been in his house, and he's not been out looking for her. It's not as though he's to stay here because of the kids, they're not here, they're at school. I decided to wait till there were two of us, and then go in.'

Carl nodded. 'We'll go in when he comes off the phone.'

· · ·

'This is what she's wearing,' Brian said, lifting a pale blue running outfit out of the wardrobe. 'She bought four identical ones, chucks them straight into the washing basket when she gets back, and gets a clean one out the next day.'

'So not only does she never vary her route, but she also wears exactly the same running gear every day?'

Brian thought about it for a moment or two, then sat down heavily on the bed. 'Shit. She's a target waiting to be hit, isn't she? We've always felt so safe here.'

'Brian, you're isolated. You're nowhere near any neighbours...'

'But we have security. CCTV is everywhere, good locks on the doors...'

'And a back door that can be opened by picking the lock.'

Brian sighed. 'We have demanding jobs, both of us. This property was ideal as an escape every summer, and we've loved it from first seeing it. It only needed cosmetic stuff doing to it, and we've done a bit at a time since we bought it – hence the plans to paint the outside this summer. We never saw it as a project to spend all summer every summer on. It was our bedroom for the internal bit and the outside for the external part this year. Find her, DI Heaton, find her.'

The woods were alive with police officers, and the dogs placed on standby had been called in. They had been given the previous day's running outfit to get the scent, and they had led their handlers in different directions. Nothing had been reported in.

Carl and Ray had joined the teams doing the searching but had returned to the house. They were standing in the kitchen, staring out of the window and cradling hot drinks.

'Once we're satisfied there's no sign of her in the woods, I want every officer out with a bundle of the leaflets, talking to residents.' Carl took a sip of the hot tea. 'They're all printed and ready to go, but we need the friendly local bobbies to emphasise the importance of staying safe, not going out on their own. Had a thought, and I know it's probably going to lead nowhere, but are there any other empty properties in Eyam at the moment?'

'Probably not ones that are for sale. DI Marsden bagged herself a cracker with that one.'

'She's not DI Marsden any longer.' Carl laughed. 'Simply Tessa now. But you're right, I know they go as soon as they're on the market here. That's why I was asking.'

'But there are various empty properties, ones that aren't up for sale. Faith Young was renting a holiday let. There are others. You think he's pulled the same trick again?'

'It's possible. The dogs haven't picked up any scent beyond the beginning of the trail she follows every day, so what's happened after that point we've no idea. There's no sign of a scuffle, certainly no blood, according to the handlers the dogs simply stopped. They're walking them through the entire trail to make sure, but nothing's obvious. If he took her at the point where the dogs lost the scent, what the hell has he done with her?'

'You're assuming she hasn't simply fallen?' Ray looked at his boss.

'We already have two dead women. You bet your bottom dollar I'm assuming that. How do we get a list of empty holiday lets in Eyam?'

Ray frowned, thinking. 'Give me five minutes, boss. We've got some youngsters with nifty fingers on a keyboard back in the office. They know their way around Google, we'll have some answers soon. I'll make the call outside.'

Carl nodded, aware of their host in the lounge on yet another work-related phone call. He wondered how much of a holiday the Aylwards' annual summer break at Woodlands ever proved to be, as Brian had answered three work-related calls in a matter of ten minutes.

Carl saw Ray walk over by one of the outbuildings and have a conversation with his 'nifty fingers' of choice, before walking back to resume drinking his tea.

'Getting colder out there,' he said. 'They'll have some answers for us as soon as possible. I've asked them to check with all estate agents in Derbyshire, and the bigger ones in the Sheffield area for properties available to let or for sale in Eyam. You're thinking he's following the pattern he started with Faith Young?'

'I've no idea, Ray. My thoughts are all over the place. We need to know of any newcomers into the village over, say, the past year, because why now? What's sparked this off? Was Faith Young random or targeted? Did he kill her, and find out he liked it, so killed our lass? Or has he been practising with the first two, and the real target is Ella Aylward? Too many questions in this, Ray, far too many.'

'And not one answer.'

Slowly, in pairs, the officers that had been drafted in to take part in the search returned to the house where they were given drinks to warm them. The temperature was dropping dramatically, and yet after such a thorough search of the woodland area, Carl didn't think for one minute the cold would be affecting Ella Aylward.

The sinking feeling in his stomach was there because he believed she was dead. Even if she was lying somewhere injured, she could call out for help. There had been enough officers working their way through the winter leaves covering the ground and making new paths through the trees that had shed those leaves the previous autumn.

Gradually they reached the point where the woods had been fully covered, and the anguish was written on Brian's face for everybody to see.

'Okay.' Carl spoke to his team. 'I want everybody back to the church hall. We've been given use of that as a temporary waystation, and you'll be given further instructions once we're assembled there. Most of you are due to go off duty, but don't do that until you've been to the church hall.'

There was a general hubbub as cups were returned to the kitchen at Woodlands, and Brian looked bewildered. 'You're calling off the search?'

'Brian, it's dark. We have to call it off until tomorrow. Please stay here, and if your wife does manage to contact you, you have to let me know immediately. I'll be having a talk with everybody down at the church, and we'll resume the search at first light, I promise you.'

The church hall had been commandeered by the police, and the vicar had been more than happy to help. He had ladies, he said, who would all volunteer to help feed and provide hot drinks for anyone requiring it as they continued their work around Eyam.

Carl spoke to everyone, asked them to come directly to the church hall for instructions the next morning, and sent them home to their families, all of them vowing to wear extra clothing the following day.

Ray stayed until the room was empty of police personnel. 'She's dead, isn't she?'

'I hope not, but I fear so,' Carl responded with a huge sigh. 'It's hard keeping positive for Brian, but we've no choice. Tomorrow I want all results from Google searches and whatever else has been going on back at the station, it's time to start visiting the residents and empty properties of Eyam.'

14

Fred and Naomi arrived home to a full house; Luke and Maria had persuaded Geraldine to make a curry for all of them, and the air was redolent with spices that made both of them smile.

'We're back,' Naomi called as they opened the door. 'Whatever is cooking, smells delicious.'

Luke walked towards them and kissed her. 'Welcome home. Good journey?'

Naomi put down her weekend bag and hung up her jacket. 'Excellent, despite the M25. Brighton's lovely, and before you ask, yes I have brought some Brighton rock.'

Fred came through the door, trying to get two larger suitcases and himself in all at the same time.

'You have news for us, I understand,' Luke said.

'We do,' Naomi said. 'Fred is moving in here, as of now.'

'Wow! You're not hanging about then?'

'It's called forward planning. This coronavirus thing is escalating rapidly, and it's looking very much as if the government is going to have to close down the country.'

'Close down the country?' Luke looked startled. 'How can you close down a country?'

'By shutting everything. Food shops will have to remain open, but basically that will be it. I don't want Fred to be on his own, and he definitely doesn't want us to be away from him. So, it's Operation Protect Nan, I'm afraid. Luke, you above anybody else here should know what this thing can do. You've already lost somebody you cared about, and now it seems the elderly are the vulnerable ones. We'll have a bit of a family pow-wow after we've eaten, because things are going to have to change.'

Luke and Maria walked home along roads mainly lit by moonlight; it was a full moon whose brilliance far outshone the streetlights.

'Beautiful night,' Maria said, linking her arm through Luke's.

'Cold,' he responded. 'I wonder where she is.'

'The woman from the spooky house?'

'Her name's Ella. Carl's had his team out all day looking for her. He called in about five, a few minutes before I went home, to say they're going to be all around the village tomorrow, delivering leaflets warning people not to go out on their own, specifically women. You won't, will you?'

He felt Maria's hesitation. 'I can't always avoid it. Sometimes we have to go out individually. I deal with animals, you know, not humans.'

'The vets will be getting a leaflet and a visit from a PC, I don't doubt, so make sure everybody sees it. There's something or somebody not right in Eyam at the moment. So what do you think to Fred moving in with Mum?'

'I'm pleased. They get on so well, and she watches him with that look.'

'What look?'

'She's fallen for him big style. It's like I used to look at you when we were at school, but you never noticed.'

He laughed. 'I must have been really thick. I'm glad you collared me when you did.'

'Oh good.' She giggled as they turned up the small driveway leading to their home.

The body lay undiscovered all through the moonlit night. Hidden beneath pallets that had been originally intended for use as fencing and discarded because it was too much trouble taking them apart, they had been pushed to one side while the dead weight was dumped unceremoniously on the ground, and the pallets were then heaved quietly back over the black plastic that now covered the body. The hiding place was between a shed and an overgrown hedge, hidden from view, in a rear garden that hadn't seen any attention in years. The house belonged to an infirm elderly man, who rarely moved beyond his front door. His rheumy eyes saw very little of happenings in the outside world. He was waiting to die but his alert brain wouldn't let him.

Maria and Luke set up Code Blue, the PS4 game they enjoyed so much, but didn't play for long. Luke's heart wasn't in it. He had taken on a strange case that involved dogs dying unexpectedly, confirmed by a veterinarian practice in Youlgreave. Two consecutive autopsies showed that poison had been used.

His task for the following morning was to go to Youlgreave, talk to the vets there and decide whether it was something Connection could help with. Maria had confirmed her own vet's practice had received notification of the incidents, and that it was serious, so he was trying to keep an open mind.

'You tired?' Maria asked.

'Thinking about tomorrow.'

'The woman who wants to employ you lost both her dogs on the same day. She requested autopsies, because they were only young. Three years old, I think. Two days earlier they'd had another dog in who was seriously ill, but he was also quite elderly. The owner didn't want an autopsy, she asked that they cremate him, so they can't tell anything in that case, but seeing the two younger animals made them realise the symptoms were the same. The woman with the two pets is your prospective client – she knows Connection from some time ago.'

'I spoke to her briefly earlier, and I'm going to see her after I've been to the vets. Strange affair, isn't it? Why would somebody want to poison dogs?'

'It's more a question of *how* they did it. It's easy enough to stick something in some food, but it's finding out how the dogs were fed it, I think. They'll explain all this tomorrow, I'm sure.'

Friday morning began early for Carl's team. They were in the briefing room by seven, and he had pinned the map of the woods on the board.

'Thank you for the efforts that were made yesterday. We covered the whole of this area to no avail, so now we start on the village itself. Please bear in mind that he hid the body of Faith Young in a shed, so I want every shed, every outbuilding of any sort, checking today. However, I also want you to bear in mind that the route that Ella Aylward took for her run passed very close by the main road, and he could very easily have had a car nearby, ready to dispose of her. I'm not sure what he hopes to gain by hiding them away, because he certainly didn't get the chance to hide Aileen's body, but if he follows his actions with Faith Young, this one will be hidden.'

'Maybe it's his way of testing us, playing with us, sir,' Ray

Charlton volunteered. 'He's going to love it today when he sees a village full of officers, talking to everybody. That will feed his ego nicely.'

Carl nodded, his face grim. 'My thoughts exactly, but it has to be done. Now when you speak to everybody, and I mean everybody, keep a list of anyone who isn't answering the door, we want to know where they were around one on Monday the second of March, when Faith Young decided to walk through those woods, and around midnight on Monday the ninth of March when he caught Aileen on her own. We need to know if they saw anyone, anyone at all. This now also goes for yesterday, Thursday the twelfth of March, between seven and half past eight. I want answers from every resident of this village to those three alibi-providing questions. Where they were and who they saw. Before you leave the premises, you get permission to enter their sheds. No excuses, we're not looking for somebody growing a bit of weed, or brewing a bit of whisky, we're looking for a body.'

There were several nods from around the room.

Carl continued. 'Ray has been up half the night dividing up the village and allocating who goes where. We don't want duplicated visits by different teams. It's important,' Carl paused and glared around the room, 'that you make a note of any address with no response. We have to follow up on those properties. We have a list of known holiday let properties so they may be empty anyway, but you still need to check outbuildings, and have a look through windows if you can.'

Again, he paused, staring round the room. 'At no time are you to be unaccompanied, and this isn't being sexist but it applies particularly to female officers. This man isn't targeting men, he's targeting women. And he's targeting women in Eyam. Every household, whether they're in or not, needs to have one of these leaflets through their letterbox.' Carl waved an A4 sheet of paper. 'It spells out precautions to take, advises no woman to go out alone until the killer is apprehended, and I hope the wording is forceful enough to scare them. It leaves our helpline number for them to call if they suspect anything untoward is going on, or if they simply feel scared. It's an excellent leaflet, let's use it. And well done, Nathan, for producing it, and producing it fast.'

Nathan shrugged, as if a little embarrassed by being singled out. 'Aileen was a friend, sir.'

Carl gave a slight nod in acknowledgement. 'So, are there any questions? Don't start knocking on doors till nine, most people don't utter their first words of the day until that time, but I expect to be deafened by the sound of doorknockers at nine o'clock dead on.'

A hand shot up at the back. 'Has Connection been checked, sir? I'm thinking about that place round the back of the office where a body had been stored.'

'I'll be calling in today, so I'll do a thorough check, but that old empty outhouse is now a brightly lit, white-walled stationery cupboard, no spiders in sight, and very smart. It's a bit different to how we first saw it. But it will be checked, and as most of the staff live in Eyam I'll be interviewing them. Oh, and one thing... I don't know who's got the section where I live, but I suggest you take my home off your list. You wake Kat up from her anytime nap, and you run the risk of being vomited on. This baby can't come quick enough, so I'm warning everybody, don't disturb her. I've already checked our outbuildings, and the riverbank that runs behind our property, and I'll go through the questions with my wife later. The church hall is our go-to point for toilets and drinks, and I think the lovely vicar was arranging for refreshments made by 'his ladies' as he calls them. I've also arranged for the tea rooms to make available their toilets, as it's a fair trek through the village if you're working the tea rooms end.

They sell delicious scones... just saying. It's going to be a long day, that may well spill over into tomorrow, so I hope your shoes are comfortable, and that it doesn't rain. Historical sites are out of bounds unless we need to go in them following information received. The museum people have volunteered to check them very carefully and report on anything that may have changed, or been damaged, or anything like that. I think that's it unless there's anything else anyone wants to ask?'

Some distant voice from the back of the room called out, 'Bacon sandwiches on you, boss?' and Carl laughed. 'In your dreams, whoever said that. In your dreams. Okay, let's get this show started, sort out the leaflets and get your rounds, then go and grab a drink or whatever before you go out and harass our residents. And if anybody says no to you going in their shed, tell them we'll get a warrant, but we'll have to leave an officer on duty at the shed until we get the warrant. That usually shuts them up nicely, and they'll let you in.'

There was a general murmur of movement, and Ray pinned up his list of which officers were together. All the women were paired with a man. He was taking no chances.

15

The navy-blue army of police officers arrived in Eyam in sundry vehicles and were all in place by quarter to nine. There was much shuffling of feet and rubbing together of hands as they realised quite how cold it was, but Carl had already checked out the church hall and knew drinks were available to all of them whenever they needed them. A lady called Nora had been in charge, and he had briefly wondered if she could be the Nosey Nora spoken of by Hattie Pearson while she was being questioned in relation to the murder of her daughter Evelyn. He didn't have the guts to ask her, so let the thought drift away.

He wandered around speaking with officers, and at five to nine they began to disperse, each aware of the importance of that day's work.

Ray Charlton was to be inside the church hall, kept suitably fed and watered by 'the ladies'. He had taken each individual helper on one side, asked them the relevant questions and issued them with a leaflet. He then moved to the kitchen area to speak collectively. 'Nobody,' he said, deliberately making his voice as stern as he could, 'is to go home from here tonight on their own. If necessary, an officer will accompany you. We have no clue as to who this killer is, and we don't want you finding out.'

There were one or two sounds of laughter and he glared at them. 'You won't be able to laugh when there's a slash across your throat. We have close on sixty men and women going through this village today with a fine-tooth comb, looking for anything and most of all talking to everybody. This is how serious this is. Eyam is almost in a state of being under attack, and we want no more deaths. So do I have your word you'll all take this seriously?'

Even Nora nodded.

'Okay, you may still get a visit from an officer, but you can tell them you've spoken to me already. Make sure you show them the leaflet, then they'll know. And make sure everybody in your household realises how serious this is. Make it as scary as you can because I'd rather have everybody scared and on their guard than dead in the woods somewhere. Grass should be dark green, not blood red.'

'You want a scone now?' Nora asked, and he sighed. 'Yes please, love.' He could only hope and pray they'd all listened to him.

Carl walked into Connection as Fred was leaving and Luke was entering.

'Fred, can you spare ten minutes before you go?'

'Certainly. I was going to collect a coffee before heading to Bakewell anyway.'

Cheryl looked up. 'You want all of us, DI Heaton?'

'I do. Is Tessa here?'

'She's upstairs in her office nursing one heck of a cold. She's trying to avoid us, doing some work on her computer and not going out, she says.'

'I really need everybody except Oliver, so shall we use Beth's office?'

Cheryl quickly convened everyone, and Tessa sat in a corner as far away as possible. Luke made drinks, and Carl spoke.

'Okay, don't shoot the messenger, because in this case it's me, and I'm one of the good guys. I need you all to tell me where you were at three specific times. I also need to know if you've noticed anything out of the ordinary going on, people in the wrong place, someone where they shouldn't be, that sort of thing. All of you are trained in recognising odd behaviour, so come on, give me some.'

They looked at each other, and Tessa sneezed. 'Sorry,' she said. 'The only thing I've noticed that was a bit odd was the dead body in the shed of the house I'd recently been told I could buy.' Her head dropped as if it wouldn't hold up any longer. 'Sorry, I'm being facetious. I feel rubbish, and I can't think straight.'

'Tess, go home,' Luke said with a smile. 'You're probably infecting us all, so go home, take some medication and go to bed. You want anything, ring me.'

'Answer my questions first,' Carl said, laughing at his long-time friend.

'You're a slave driver, Carl Heaton,' she grumbled and reached across to pick up the piece of paper he'd placed on the desk. 'The first time I was here, I had an appointment for half past twelve, and it ran over till about two ish, the second one I was in bed, nobody to confirm that, and the third one, at that early hour, I was also in bed, nobody to confirm that either. Arrest me now.' She held out her wrists for the handcuffs.

'Not bloody likely,' Carl said. 'I don't want what you've got. Arrest yourself, Marsden.'

· · ·

The meeting finished in laughter, and Carl thanked them all before going outside to check the small area of garden and the newly spruced up outhouse. The last time he had been in it, the space had been taken up by the remains of Evelyn Pearson who had occupied the tiny building for twenty-five years, and as he opened the door he shivered, immediately switching on the bright light that now lit up the space. It occurred to him there was no longer enough room for a body, so he switched off the light and locked the door. He stroked Oliver who was sitting quietly watching him from the top of his cat shelter.

It hit Carl suddenly how much they all missed Tessa Marsden. If she had remained with the police she would have been in charge of this investigation, and he tried to imagine what she would have done next. He realised with something of a jolt that she would also have flooded the village with officers; most of all she would have had them searching outbuildings, no matter the size.

Cheryl was back on reception, and he handed her the key to the outhouse. 'Thank you, cooperative as always. Tessa really does need to go home.'

'I told her that when she first arrived, but she said she wanted to finish something she started yesterday. It's Saturday tomorrow, so she said she's spending the weekend in bed. I've been across the road and stocked her up with medication, so hopefully by Monday she'll be feeling much better.'

'Good. I'm off now to check on the troops, make sure they've all had hot drinks, it's damn cold out there. There's a possibility we'll be working all weekend if we don't find Ella Aylward today. Gut instinct's telling me she's close by, but it's not telling me where.'

'You're thinking she's in a shed again?'

'Logic says it's a strong possibility.'

'She's not in mine.'

'You've checked?'

'Checked yesterday. Checked the entire garden to make sure. I also think it's a strong possibility. The policewoman was a random. You're sure it's the same killer?'

He nodded. 'Same knife, but I haven't told you that. '

'Understood. You think he simply saw an opportunity with PC Chatterton?'

'I do. I suspect he's planned this, the ones he's hiding, but she was an opportunity to taunt us. When it was Faith Young, and we didn't have a second death to factor in, it occurred to me it could be a disgruntled fan she'd managed to upset. Authors can get quite a bit of backlash, especially authors who sell a lot of books, and that was always at the front of my mind, but now it isn't. We can't see a connection between the two women at all. Like you, I believe Aileen was opportunistic, but I don't believe that of Faith Young and Ella Aylward. The connection between them is Eyam.'

'You think he lives in Eyam?' For a brief moment, worry flashed across Cheryl's face.

'I'm sure of it. He knows it very well, knows back ways out of the village, knows where the hiding places are – it was sheer bad luck for him that Tessa and Luke went to that property that day, and it really wouldn't have happened if Tessa hadn't been so excited about having had her offer accepted.'

'So he's not bothered about them being found?' A frown crossed Cheryl's face. 'It's personal, isn't it? He wants to kill them. What happens after that is irrelevant, and he doesn't want them found. It's enough for him to know they're dead.'

'Spot on. That's the conclusion I reached about three o'clock this morning. Which tells me we're missing something. There must be a link between these two women. I'm discounting Aileen, but if we're thinking the finding of the bodies doesn't matter, maybe we're wrong to discount her. Right, I'd best get up to the church hall, check on what's been reported, if anything. Thank you for this morning, but it seems I don't have anybody here I can justifiably arrest.'

'Well definitely not me anyway,' Cheryl said with a laugh. 'I'm not tall enough to reach up and slash anybody's throat. Is this why you're set on it being a man?'

'That, and the strength issue. Two of the bodies – and we're assuming it's not going to be a good outcome for Ella Aylward – would have had to be transported, and would that be possible for a woman?'

He zipped up his jacket as he prepared to leave. 'I'll be in touch,' he said, and quietly closed the door behind him.

The church hall was a hive of industry as officers were returning for drinks and food after a morning of interviewing residents. All the officers had call-back lists, and all had frozen hands.

Carl walked amongst them, asking questions and receiving shakes of the head in most cases. It was an ever-changing crowd – officers left to return to their lists feeling warmed and refreshed, and officers came in ready to feel some warmth.

PC Keith Dukes and PC Janet Grayson left together, shivering as soon as they stepped outside.

Janet was tired and looking forward to going home. Her baby daughter wasn't well and had been up three times the previous night. She was grateful that her mother would be having her for the night, at least she would be able to catch up on some sleep. Her thoughts were very much on the baby; teething problems had left her with a runny nose and a bad attitude. She was thinking about anything but the job they had been tasked with as she followed Keith down the rutted road that led to Appletree Cottage.

Her first sight of it was that the name was prettier than the building. Keith knocked on the door, and they waited. Janet took out a leaflet and opened up her notebook ready for writing down whatever the occupant had to tell them.

They heard 'I'm coming, I'm coming,' from inside the cottage, and smiled at each other. They had come across several elderly residents, who had all struggled to answer the door, and they were getting very used to patiently waiting.

George Mitchell opened the door. 'I'm sorry,' he said. 'I can't move very fast. Please, come in, it's cold outside.'

'Thank you, sir, but you really should leave your chain on,' Keith said with a smile.

'Knew you were coming. We've a jungle drum system in Eyam. If anything happens, we all get to hear of it very fast.'

He led them down the hallway and through to the kitchen, which faced his back garden.

'Would you like a cup of tea?'

'No thank you, sir. We've recently left the church hall, and you're our first visit, so we're fine at the moment. We have some questions to ask you though, so if we could sit at the table?'

'No problem, young lady. But first of all there's something I have to show you. Come and look out the window.'

They followed him to the kitchen window and looked out at his garden.

16

Fred pulled up outside the home of Cliff Baines and sat for a moment. Naomi had offered to accompany him, even if only to sit in the car and wait, but he'd reluctantly said no, unsure exactly how long he would be at the property.

He'd given her a kiss, telling her he would return to his own home after the Baines visit, and pack some 'stuff' to add to the 'stuff' he had already brought to Eyam. He would organise the rest of his belongings to go into storage until they were more organised.

He felt happy, not quite believing how much his own life had changed in a short three months, and suddenly the happiness disappeared as he remembered what he was about to tell Cliff Baines.

With a deep sigh, Fred opened his car door. Walking up the path felt never-ending, and when Cliff opened the door Fred struggled to raise a smile.

'Morning, Fred. I take it you're escaping Eyam. I've heard there's lots of police activity there this morning.'

'Overrun with them. They're visiting every home, checking every shed, leaving leaflets advising not to go out unaccompanied, especially if you're a woman. They still haven't found Ella Aylward.'

'We've no more empty properties in Eyam, so there shouldn't be a repeat of what happened with Faith Young. I rang your Tessa Marsden yesterday, reassured her that it made absolutely no difference to her purchase of the cottage, the price was agreed, and the vendors were perfectly happy with it. I'm going to do what I can to expedite the sale. She coughed and sneezed through the entire conversation, sounded rough.'

Fred laughed. 'She's in a bit of a state. She was in for this morning's meeting, but she's heading home to bed now.'

Cliff handed him a mug of tea, and they sat at the kitchen table.

'When does Ethan get home?'

'He's seeing the doctor tomorrow morning, so hopefully I can collect him tomorrow afternoon. We watch football every Saturday afternoon, and it's a Manchester United match on tomorrow, so he'll want to be home for that. I've bought him a new shirt from the Man U shop, it arrived this morning. He'll love it. All he wants really is Ronaldo to come back to Man U, and he'll be a happy lad. He's convinced he will one day, but I keep saying he's too old to make moves like that, he'll stay with Juventus until he finishes.'

'Smart lad. If Ronaldo came back, it would solve all Man U's problems.' Fred reached down to his briefcase and took out his folder.

'You've found her and spoken to her?'

'I have. She's going to ring you this afternoon. I told her I would text her as soon as I had spoken to you.'

'She still remembers our phone number, does she?' The sarcasm was evident in Cliff's voice.

And here it starts, Fred thought. 'Your wife has been getting information on Ethan via the phone every week since she left.'

Cliff frowned. 'I don't understand...'

Fred waited a moment. 'Your wife has changed her name from Philippa to Julie Ann. Julie Ann Needham.'

'Needham? She chose Ivor's name?' Cliff looked bewildered.

'She chose Ivor.'

Cliff's chair crashed backwards to the floor as he realised what Fred was telling him. He leaned his fists on the table, needing support, and Fred half stood.

'You okay, Cliff?'

It seemed an eternity before Cliff turned and righted the chair. 'Fifteen years, Fred. Fifteen years Ivor's been the long-distance rock in my life. He's visited us a few times as well. Was she with him on those trips?'

'I don't know, I didn't ask. But she has been kept fully informed about her son – and you – all the time she has been gone. She told me you were a better parent than she could ever hope to be, she loved Ethan, but knew you would give him a better life.'

'I had no idea...'

'I think they planned it well, so that you wouldn't know. It was a real shock when I appeared on the scene. I don't know how you'll handle it personally, but I'm sure that for Ethan's sake it's for the best that he sees his mother.'

'Ivor. I'm struggling to take it in. He was so supportive when Pippa first left. He'd already gone to live in Brighton. Is that where they are now? He's never said he's left there.'

Fred nodded. 'They are. I don't know if it's the same house, but it's in Brighton.' He handed a photograph to Cliff. 'That's the house. A minute's walk from the seafront.'

'Do they have kids?'

'None visible, no photographs of children except one of Ethan, and they didn't speak of children.'

'Pippa always said she wouldn't have any more. I assumed

she meant with me, but obviously she meant with anybody. I'm glad you've told me all of this, Fred, because I have time to digest it. Do me a favour and don't text Pippa until three this afternoon, then I've a bit more time to get my head around how to be with her. I don't want to antagonise, I need her here for Ethan, but if I spoke to her right at this minute, it could be quite caustic.'

'I take my instructions from you, Cliff, not from your wife. If she does take it into her head to ring you before that, it won't be because I've told her. I don't agree with what she did, I think it was a cowardly way to end her relationship with you, but she did do it, and leaving you didn't stop her love for Ethan. However, this is all about Ethan now. You're going to have to watch what you say, probably have to bite your tongue several times, but Ethan wants to see his mum, and that's the priority.'

'I know.' Cliff sighed. 'No wonder I couldn't find her. And no wonder Connection came so highly recommended.'

Fred stood. 'Keep in touch. And when things have settled, I'd like to meet Ethan, if that's okay.'

'You're welcome here anytime. I'll let you know the outcome of this afternoon's conversation.'

They shook hands and Fred walked back to his car. He waved at Patrick Fletcher who was in his front garden putting out seed on the bird table, then Fred set off for home. It was time to sort out his own life.

His house felt cold, and Fred walked through it laying ghosts to rest. He still had a few items of Jane's that he hadn't felt able to let go, but now he knew it was time. He could almost hear her laughter, her words. *Time to move on, Fred Iveson.*

He hunted out a cardboard box and began to pack things in it that could go to the charity shop. His own clothes he packed into a suitcase. Another suitcase held bedding and cushions, and suddenly he sat on the sofa, clutching on to a cushion that bore the word cwtch. He had bought two of them in Wales, and one had ended up outside on his garden furniture. A couple of heavy rainfalls had soon taken care of that, but this one had stayed inside. He had bought them to give him comfort when he missed Jane the most, and he hoped that whoever bought it from the charity shop would understand that cwtch meant hug. He carried it to the charity shop box and dropped it in.

Downstairs he knew exactly what he intended doing. The large frame dominated the hallway and was a talking point when anyone visited. He had spent a most stressful hour on an internet auction site praying he would win the bidding that had been ongoing for a week, and when he did he remembered the feeling that had given him a few days of euphoria. To save damage he had arranged with the vendor that he would collect it, and it had meant a long journey to Edinburgh, but it had been worth it.

The signed shirt of Ronaldo came fully authenticated, and Fred knew exactly what he was going to do with it. It was time for somebody else to feel that feeling of euphoria. It was from Ronaldo's time at Real Madrid, and as Fred lifted it down he smiled. Needed a bit of a dusting, and maybe the wall could now do with a coat of paint, but he knew one young man who would cherish the picture for however long he had left.

Fred found some brown wrapping paper and a ball of string, and carefully wrapped it. He would put it in the boot of his car, and as soon as he could visit the Baines he would go and hand it into their safekeeping.

With the frame in the boot and back seats full of suitcases, Fred returned to Eyam. Police officers were everywhere, and he glanced at his dashboard clock. A couple of minutes after three.

He sent a text to Julie Needham and one to Cliff Baines, crossed his fingers and prayed for the best outcome.

He pulled up outside Connection and went in to complete the paperwork on this difficult case. He was grateful to Beth for having found Ethan's mother, but it was definitely going to be difficult mentally for their client. He wondered how Cliff was feeling, what answers he would get to his questions that would inevitably pour from his lips as he tried to understand the actions of his wife and his best friend fifteen years earlier.

'Sorted?' Cheryl asked.

'So far so good,' he said. 'I'm going to finalise the invoice, then head off home. I'm collecting Naomi when she finishes work, I don't want her walking home alone. You came in your car?'

'I did. Much to the kids' disgust, I took them to school. And I shall carry on taking them and collecting them when necessary until they've caught this man. They've both got four o'clock finishes today, so I'll be on my way in a few minutes.'

'Shout out if you need help with it. Now it's official I live next door, I guess we're proper neighbours.'

'Congratulations. I picked up on bits with you and Luke, but I haven't had chance for a proper chat with Naomi. Somebody whisked her away for a night in Brighton, so I believe.'

'Nice place.' He grinned. 'Well worth the long journey.'

17

PC Keith Dukes and PC Janet Grayson stood either side of George Mitchell as they looked out of his kitchen window.

'What can you see?' George asked.

Keith spoke first. 'A garden that needs some work, a table and two chairs, big tree at the bottom of the garden and a shed.'

'Exactly,' George said. 'The big tree is an apple tree, hence the name of the cottage. Now look at the shed again. What else can you see?'

Janet leaned closer to the window. 'Some wood, possibly pallets, at the back of the shed.'

'That's right. Been there ten years or so. I was, at one time, going to take out that bottom hedge and put up a fence. The thing is, until this morning I couldn't see those pallets. They were well hidden behind the shed. Now they're not.'

Janet and Keith locked eyes, and Janet spoke into her radio. She relayed the information to Ray, who told her to check it out, but carefully.

'Only one of you,' Ray said. 'Preserve the scene. It may be nothing, the pallets may have only fallen over, but don't take chances.'

'I'll go,' Janet said. 'Keith, make George a drink will you?'

Janet headed down the garden, keeping to the central concrete path. She reached the shed and stepped cautiously onto the grass. Underneath the pallets, she could clearly see black plastic. Fresh black plastic. She put on nitrile gloves and leaned over, holding on to a pallet to maintain her balance. She lifted the black plastic and saw a flash of a pale blue fabric.

She withdrew quickly and immediately contacted Ray. 'We need DI Heaton urgently. I can see what I think is a leg, and it appears to be clad in pale blue.'

'He's on his way. Exit the scene, let's preserve as much as possible.'

'I'm going back in the house. The owner is an old man, quite wobbly on his legs, but bright as a button. He knew exactly what it meant, so sat back and waited for us to call. I need to make sure he's okay because I don't doubt he's been watching me. I left Keith making him a drink, but I'll go check everything's okay while I wait for DI Heaton.'

'Is there a side path to the back garden?'

'Yes.'

'Then meet DI Heaton at the front and take him down that way. Let's not disturb the gentleman any more than we have to. When DI Heaton gets there, go back inside as soon as you can and talk to this witness. He may have seen something he's not aware of.'

'He was aware that yesterday he couldn't see the edge of these pallets, and today he could. Don't underestimate him, his body's a bit frail but his mind isn't. I'll go talk to him.'

'Thanks, Janet. The DI's out front, go and get him.'

. . .

So much blood on the clothing, but none on the ground. He didn't need anyone from the forensic team to tell him she hadn't been killed there. Carl watched as photographs were taken prior to the body being moved – there was no way a tent could be erected round the back of the shed, the gap between the wooden hut and the overgrown hedge was about four feet wide, and even if a tent could be put in place, nobody could have got inside it to do any sort of work. The decision was taken to extensively photograph the scene, then get the body moved out to where a tent could be placed, leaving the area where she had been dumped available for a more thorough inspection.

Carl stayed until the body of Ella Aylward had been moved inside the tent, and knew his primary concern now was to visit Woodlands, to tell Brian they had found his wife.

Carl went inside Appletree Cottage, with the intention of saying thank you to George Mitchell, but a cup of tea was waiting for him, and he accepted it with some gratitude. His hands were numb with cold.

'I'm here to collect Janet,' he explained. 'We have to go and tell the lady's husband the sad news. When did you realise things didn't look right in your garden?'

'As I was getting my lunch ready. I guessed you'd be turning up here before long, and I think I knew there would be no hope if it was the lady who was missing.'

'And prior to that, you'd seen nothing?'

'No and heard nothing either. If he brought her during the night, I wouldn't hear. My bedroom is what used to be my lounge, and it's at the front of the cottage. I mainly live downstairs, because by the end of the day I struggle to get upstairs. I always look out at my back garden though, remembering what it used to be like when I could actually do it.

That's how I know the lady must have been brought here last night, because it's only today that my view changed.'

Carl finished his drink. 'Look, I have to go to tell Mr Aylward before the Eyam jungle drums get to him first. Tomorrow I'm going to send someone to take your statement, we won't trouble you to come into the station. Is that okay? Simply keep remembering what you saw, when you saw it. Can a car get down to the back of your garden?'

'For sure. A small truck delivered my shed ten years ago, and that's where they brought it to. The hedge wasn't overgrown then, of course, I used to keep it well cut back. If a car came down these days I wouldn't even see it. And I'm sure I didn't hear one. I got the pallets about a month after the shed was delivered, intending to replace that hedge with a fence, make one less job for me to have to do, but then I lost my wife, and it sort of got put on a back burner. Then I became a bit more doddery, so there the pallets stayed. How did he know it was a suitable dump site?'

Carl sighed. 'The million-dollar question, George. I don't know. I believe he – or she – is local, so maybe that's the answer. Maybe they've lived here a long time. Your home is pretty close to the house where Faith Young was found, so it's somebody who's made sure he knows suitable places.'

'Motive?'

Carl stared at him. 'You're ex-copper?'

George smiled. 'Sorry, can't help it. Stick DCI in front of Mitchell. I finished twenty-five years ago, but it never goes, I can assure you.'

'Then it's a double pleasure to meet you, sir.'

'It was George a minute ago.'

'Not anymore, it isn't,' Carl said. 'The job might have finished, but you'll always merit the respect.'

. . .

ANITA WALLER

Brian Aylward knew what he was about to hear when he recognised Carl's car as it pulled up at the rear of the house. He went out to meet the two officers, his face rigid with apprehension. 'You've found her?'

'Can we go inside, Brian?'

Brian hesitated for a moment, then turned and went through into the kitchen. 'Drinks?'

'Janet will make them,' Carl said. 'Let's sit down. I have news.'

Brian slumped rather than sat. 'She's dead, isn't she? My Ella...'

Janet clicked on the kettle and broke the silence.

'I'm sorry, Brian, we have found Ella's body. The forensics team is with her now, so we have no details at all yet. We will need you to identify her, but I'll have to let you know when that can happen. I'm so sorry for your loss.'

He shook his head, in disbelief. 'How can everything go so wrong? We wouldn't have been here normally, we only came because of the break-in, which doesn't seem to be connected anyway. We were talking of decamping and heading back to our home until the warmer weather.'

'We haven't ignored the break-in, but off the record I suspect you're right. It was simply somebody looking for someplace to sleep in the warmth. These killings aren't random, they're linked in some way, and we will find what that link is.' His mind moved back a month to a previous case, to Tessa Marsden's way of finding potential links between victims. 'I need details of everyone on your Christmas card and birthday list, and Facebook friends of both you and your wife. Can you email them to me as soon as you have them?'

Brian's face was grey, but he nodded. 'She kept our Christmas card list in her phone. I can't really help with that because she had her phone with her. She had like a little holster

128

thing that she strapped to the top of her arm when she went running, so she didn't have to carry it.'

'You can access her Facebook account?'

'Yes, I'll sort that.'

Janet passed two mugs of tea onto the table, and Brian clasped his hands around his, as if it would offer some comfort to him.

'How do I tell the kids?' His face crumpled and he grabbed a tissue and held it to his eyes. 'It's so fucking unbelievable. She was determined to buy this house because she really liked the previous owner and look where it got her! Five years later, she's dead, and it's all because of this house.'

Carl felt lost for words, but Janet simply walked to stand by the distraught man and put her arms around him. 'I'm so sorry,' she whispered. 'You will find the words for your children because you're their dad, and they will be there for you. But you have to tell them now, because this will be on the news tonight. The village is full of media vans.'

He looked startled. 'On the news? I hadn't even thought about that. I have to get the kids out of school and to my parents. They'll be safe there. And they love their granny and grandpops. Can I go now, so that I can get back here tonight?'

'I'll get one of my men to take you,' Carl said. 'You're in no fit state to drive.'

Brian stared at Carl. 'Am I a suspect?'

'No, you're not. You arrived in Eyam after the first murder, so you're definitely not a suspect. It's simply that I want to make life a little easier for you and your children, by getting you to them quickly, and making sure you're not plagued by the press. How soon can you be ready?'

'Five minutes. I can ring Mum and Dad from the car, and they'll be ready for the kids arriving in an hour. Thank you, DI Heaton. Sorry if I snapped...'

'Snap all you like. It's understandable. I'll go outside and see who's available to take you. And I am sorry, Brian, this was the worst-case scenario. By tomorrow we should know a little more about it, and I'll be over to talk to you. If you decide to stay with the children tonight, let me know, and I won't come out here until I hear you're home.'

It didn't take long to find a volunteer to do the journey, and Carl stayed outside for a short while, mulling over the events of the day. He felt, knew, he was missing something that was blatantly obvious, and he couldn't pin down what it was. He needed to be back in his office reviewing everything they had. Everything. And he needed Tessa Marsden to talk to him, to help him see the invisible.

If nothing came to light over the weekend, come Monday morning he would be at Connection, following in the footsteps of Tessa and the late Hannah, talking things out, throwing ideas around. Simply being the Connection of old. Different characters, same routines, and definitely smart thoughts.

Cheryl drove up through the village on her way to pick up her kids from the school, and was shocked by the number of police at the top end of the village. Something must have happened, and she prayed they hadn't found yet another body.

She spotted Carl and acknowledged him with a lift of her hand, before driving carefully by the crowd of officers standing around. It was only when she saw the forensics van that she knew her fears were probably true.

She put her foot down once she was outside Eyam, and ten minutes later approached the school. Eleri and Tyler were waiting at the school gates, their faces set in grumpy mode.

They jumped in the car and immediately moaned. 'We could have been on the school late bus,' Eleri said. 'Everybody else was.'

'And how many were going to Eyam?'

'We were.'

'Exactly. Now I don't want to hear another word from you two for ten minutes, then I'll accept your apologies.'

She drove until she spotted the crowd she had already navigated her way through earlier, and both her children leaned forward.

'What's going on?'

'I'm only guessing because I haven't heard anything, but I reckon they've found the body of the missing lady, Ella Aylward. Still want to catch the bus?'

There was a moment of silence.

'Sorry, Mum.'

'Sorry, Mum.'

18

F red glanced at his watch every five minutes. He felt on edge, and recognised it was simply because he didn't know if his words in Brighton had been strong enough to get Julie Ann Needham to ring her estranged husband.

Until that happened, he couldn't count his mission as completed, and he knew he would feel he had let Ethan down. At 4:34 his phone rang.

'She rang.'

'Good.' Fred felt his shoulders slump. 'And?'

'They're travelling up on Monday and will ring before they come here. If there are issues with Ethan coming home, I'll contact them and tell them what's happening. They'll probably go to see him at the hospice, but to be honest I intend being there if that's the case. I don't want them seeing him without me, I don't want him panicking.'

'I can't tell you what a relief that is. If Ethan does come home tomorrow, can I pop round and meet him? I have a gift for him in the boot of my car, and I'd rather it not be there, but in his hands.'

'He'll be chuffed. And of course you're welcome anytime.

Definitely more welcome than my wife and my Judas friend. She kept the phone call very simple, made no mention of them sneaking away together fifteen years ago, and I didn't speak to Ivor at all. It'll be a difficult meeting on Monday, and on Tuesday I'll be instigating divorce proceedings.'

'Not hanging about then?'

'Nope. Would have done it years ago, to be honest, if I'd known where she was.'

'Then good luck, Cliff. Big changes over the next few months. I'll check in tomorrow with you and if Ethan is coming home, I'll see you in the afternoon.'

'Thanks, Fred, I'm so grateful.'

They disconnected and Fred sat back with a sigh and an overwhelming feeling of relief. So far so good. Tomorrow needed to go well, get Ethan home for a couple of days and prepare him for meeting his mother, albeit alongside the man he had thought was his father's friend, and wait for what was destined to happen on Monday.

It was Cheryl who rang him from home to fill him in on what was happening at the top end of the village, confirming she had called in next door to check Rosie, Imogen and Geraldine were all there and accounted for. 'Naomi is still at work, and she'll have heard bits from customers about another body having been found, but Geraldine says she's spoken to her to reassure her they're all safe. You're still able to pick her up?'

'I definitely am, and I would be anyway, even if I wasn't. I'd scrap what I was doing. These may all be opportunistic kills, but he certainly seems to know what he's doing. I'm closing down now, there's nobody else here, and I'll go and sit and wait for Naomi. Take care, Cheryl. Do not go out alone.' The last few words were said with a degree of force, and he heard her laugh.

'I promise. Now go and get Naomi.'

. . .

Jack Young was lifting in his suitcase when he heard footsteps. He turned around, spooked by the sound, and smiled as he saw Will Sandford.

'Jack, you don't have to go. I've nobody in the cottage till mid-April, so you're very welcome to stay.'

'I need to get home, Will. Our daughter's not handling losing her mum very well, and combined with recently giving birth, it's overwhelming her. I will have to come back to sort out collecting Faith's car but if I do I'll give you a ring and see if the cottage is still free. I hear they've found the third body. You take care, Will, because he's not necessarily only targeting women. I've let DI Heaton know what's happening and he's got my contact details.'

'I'll miss our sharing a four-pack, and I'd appreciate keeping in touch, Jack. Safe journey home, and my best wishes to your daughter and son-in-law and their new family. I'm sure Faith would have been very proud.'

'That's the worst part, Will. She would have been proud of the baby, and she never even got to see him. I'm going to make myself a coffee before I set off. Fancy one?'

'That's kind of you, Jack, I would.'

Jack locked the car and they walked up the front path and into Leaf Cottage. With the kettle on, Jack busied himself getting out two cups, knowing he was going to miss the cottage owner. They were of a similar age, enjoyed the same sort of films, and Jack appreciated how much Will had been there for him since the discovery of Faith's body.

Jack made the drinks and handed one to Will. 'I'll email you when I get home, but will you promise to email me if anything happens here? Like finding the damn killer?'

'I will, of course. DI Heaton seems like a smart chap, today's activities in the village were all down to him, so I hear. And it paid off.'

'He *is* smart. They were telling me down at Connection that his wife started off the detective agency with Beth Walters, but Kat's stopped now because she's pregnant.'

Will smiled. 'Let's hope he's read her the riot act about not going out on her own, because he's scared most of the village ladies witless.'

'I've learned a lot while I've been here, about this place,' Jack said. 'Unique history, hasn't it? I've walked everywhere, had a look at most of the stuff, the graves, the cottages, the stocks. No wonder Faith was so entrenched in it she had to come to see it for herself. I wish I hadn't persuaded her...'

'Jack, you can't blame yourself. She died three days before you even arrived! If anybody feels sorry about the way things turned out, it should be me. I knew she went out on that Monday, and I never checked in with her. I should have.'

'Why? Do you check in on any other guests when they stay in this cottage?'

'No, but...'

'Neither of us can blame ourselves for what happened to Faith. I'll regret persuading her to spend time in Eyam for the rest of my life, but what's done is done and I have to think of Helena now, who is absolutely falling apart. I also have to deal with Faith's publishers, her assorted social media stuff... and learn how to exist without her.'

'Ms Kingston?'

'It is.' The tone was velvety, and Carl imagined her to be attractive, short brown hair, brown eyes, a ready smile. He was correct on three counts.

'DI Carl Heaton, Derbyshire serious crimes unit.'

'Ah, I wondered if you'd contact me.'

'You did?'

'Well yes, Faith Young was our highest grossing author,

much-loved by all of us. On a personal level, she was also my friend, and I shall miss her. A lot.'

'I'm truly sorry for your loss,' Carl said, captivated by the genuine softness of her voice. 'Tell me a little about her. Did she ever get any threats? Any nastiness from any readers, or indeed other writers?'

'None that I'm aware of. The only nasty person in her life was Jack Young.'

'Her husband? Really?' Carl waited for her to continue.

'He wasn't abusive, not physically anyway, but he controlled her. As most authors have to do, Faith kept a diary that showed when her books needed to be emailed to us, what date she would get back her edits, when the edited manuscript should be back with us... that sort of thing. He took those dates, worked out her exact word count per day that she must do to be ready for submission day, and kept her to it. He controlled her finances, did her tax returns, did everything except write the books, and I suspect he felt aggrieved he couldn't do that. I was utterly gobsmacked that he booked her that cottage for a month, and she was so happy it was happening.'

'Are you in work tomorrow? I need a statement from you.'

'No, I'm painting our guest bedroom. You're very welcome to visit me at home though.' She gave him the address, and he disconnected saying he would be in Cambridge by around eleven.

Carl sat back in his chair, chewing on the end of his biro, deep in thought. Ringing Marianne Kingston had been almost an afterthought, and now he wished he had rung her before Jack Young had left Eyam.

Carl woke up his computer and began to read through statements they had already taken. He read twice through Jack Young's statement, becoming more and more aware that Jack had shown himself to be a caring, loving husband who would miss Faith for the rest of his life. Now it seemed everything he said might be one huge lie. Supposing... Carl dismissed the stray thought that Jack had been the killer, because there was no reason at all for him to kill Aileen Chatterton and Ella Aylward, and it had now been confirmed the same knife had been used on all three women.

Was it possible he had been in Eyam on the day of his wife's death? Carl had seen no reason to doubt Young's statement that he hadn't arrived in Eyam until the Thursday morning, three days after Faith Young disappeared. He made a note to double-check with Will Sandford exactly when Jack Young had arrived.

Mobile phones... he sat a little straighter in his chair and clicked on a different file. They had Aileen's personal phone, and against Faith's phone was the tag 'drying out'. The phone had apparently given one brief burst of tune when Jack Young had rung it as they searched for his wife, and then it had died, too sodden to work after three days in almost non-stop rain. It had to be dried before it was checked, and he rang the evidence clerk, explained what he wanted, and asked if the phone was now dry.

'Yes, sir, we've sent it through to the tech guys for them to have a look. It only came to life this morning so they may not have got to it yet. It was fully working though, which was a bit of a miracle.'

'Thank you. Have you received a mobile phone from the body that was found this afternoon in Eyam?'

'Yes, sir, that's been logged in and sent to the tech guys as well.'

'Do they work Saturday? Please say "yes, sir" again.'

The woman laughed. 'No, sir, they don't. You'll have to wait till Monday for that.'

For a brief moment Carl wanted to bang his head against his desk. Hard. Instead, he thanked her for her help, and asked her to send an urgent request through to tech for the phone breakdown of contents to be with him by Monday at midday, when he would be back in the office to collect the reports. He needed full reports on all three phones. Contact lists, text messages, Facebook friends, Messenger conversations, everything that would give them an idea of the life that the owners led as individuals, as opposed to the fiction perceived by friends and family, because the truth behind the scenes was never the same as the lie in front of the camera. He needed their secrets.

It gave him a small amount of pleasure that the killer had probably not realised Ella had a phone; with it in silent mode and the holster hidden by her hoodie sleeve, he wouldn't have heard Brian's increasingly frantic calls to his wife's phone.

Maybe, hopefully, there would be one single thing on each of the three phones that would link the three women, giving him the primary lead to a killer, someone Carl had no doubt hadn't finished yet. He knew with a sick feeling that this person was starting to enjoy it, was nurturing a feel for murder like no other, and wouldn't be stopping any time soon.

19

Carl had felt a sense of relief that Kat and Martha intended spending the day with his in-laws; Granddad would drive them around to various baby shops, and the new arrival would soon have a wardrobe all of his own. Finding out the baby was to be a boy had inspired Kat to almost stop being sick, and to begin bringing her plans for the nursery to life.

Kat and Martha waved goodbye to him as they drove out of the gates, and he climbed into his own car and set off for Cambridge. Checking out the publisher's website the previous evening had revealed the true image of Marianne Kingston, and his pre-conceived image of her differed from the truth only by her hair – it wasn't short and brown, it was long and very light grey. The picture on the website showed her with it in a bun that emphasised her professional status, and when he arrived to hear his satnav declare he was at his destination, she had already opened the front door, her hair tied into a ponytail with a scarf of bright in-your-face colours.

Her hands showed the colour of something newly decorated to be a sky-blue, and she waved him inside. 'Please go through to the kitchen, I don't want to risk sitting in the lounge with these clothes on. I never pretended to be an expert painter, but I do love doing it. I'll wash my hands, and then I can make us a drink.'

'You do all your own decorating?'

'I draw the line at the hall and stairs, but I'll tackle anything else. My job is very stressful, and I can choose to either switch off from it, or work out any issues that are bothering me, with a paintbrush in my hand.'

Carl sat at the table and waited for her to clean up.

She tutted as she inspected her nails. 'They might need a soak. Don't grumble if you find blue paint on your mug.'

'I wouldn't dare.'

She made the drinks and sat down opposite him. 'You've come a long way to see me. From that, can I deduce you're no nearer finding Faith's killer?'

'Every day takes us a little closer, and every day sees us following a different thought path. I wouldn't have travelled down to Cambridge if you hadn't mentioned Jack Young in the way that you did. My impression of him was completely the opposite to how you portrayed him. I figured you'd known him for some time, so your version was likely to be the most accurate. Hence, here I am. You have some blue paint on your cheek.'

'If it offends you, I'll remove it. If it doesn't, I'll leave it.'

Carl laughed. 'It doesn't offend me at all. In fact, it reminds me of Kat, my wife. She can't do anything without getting scruffed up to the eyes. Our daughter, Martha, who is currently learning to say I want before anything else is said, thinks she's a toddler artist. Kat encourages her, and the two of them seem to be permanently covered in paint. We'll be having a new baby in about three months, a boy. I shall steer him towards football. Do you have children?'

Marianne shuddered. 'Good lord, no. I've been with my

partner for twenty years now, and we did consider it at one time, but she's a doctor and I have not only a career but a business, and one day we simply decided not to bother. It's the two of us, and we have nephews and nieces so we use them occasionally if we want to do things like going to Harry Potter films and such like. Things that strictly speaking need kids. It's worked for us,' she finished with a laugh.

'So tell me about Faith Young.'

'Faith is our number one author. Her sales are phenomenal, and since she died she's gone straight back to the top of the charts with her latest book. All her others, right back to the beginning, are climbing healthily, and if you're looking for a suspect who's benefitted from her death, it's me. I'd swap all of these sales to have her back with us though. I can see her being at one, two and three by the end of the day, and she would be so proud. She lived for her writing. I think it was her escape from him.'

'Why did she stay with him?'

'All sorts of reasons. He was never violent, more controlling. And there was Helena, their daughter. She idolises her dad. He also took away the mundane side of being a woman – the cleaning, the cooking, that sort of stuff. Once she saw how high that first book climbed, her confidence grew, but it was only the confidence to write. He organised a cleaner, decided to do all the cooking, but only because he had tended to do it anyway, and managed her diary. Became a bit of an agent really.'

'He said he had an electrical business.'

'He does, employs people, doesn't do any of the physical day-to-day work. Jack's forte is paperwork and organisation. He's always available for her... sorry, was always available. I keep forgetting...' She stopped for a moment, then drew in a deep breath. 'She was my friend. I hated seeing how he was with her. She didn't like doing book signings and anything that involved meeting the public, but he insisted. I have never suggested to her that she does them, because I know how much she interacts on Facebook with her fans. It's a big part of her early morning work before she starts her writing, and she really enjoys... enjoyed... that side of being an author. My God, DI Heaton, I can't tell you how much I'm going to miss her.'

'It's Carl. Do you know anything about this trip to Eyam?'

'A little. Her new book is set there, and she wanted more information than she could find in books. I suggested to her that she take two or three days off and go and immerse herself in the place. She was a bit reluctant because Helena wasn't too far off giving birth, but I pointed out she still had two months to go, and if Faith took as long as a week to visit Eyam, it would be very unlucky if Helena went into labour during that week. She said she'd talk it over with Jack, and the next thing I knew he'd booked her a cottage for a month! The most surprising part was she was going on her own. No Jack, no interference. She said the plan was for her to check in with him each weekend, and she could write all day and every day if she felt so inclined. Or not. I think they were the telling words. Or not. Her decision.'

'Did Faith contact you at all?'

'She did, on the Sunday. Her plans were to cover a large part of the village on the Monday, and she mentioned the cottage owner as drawing her a map to cover the historical sites, and the journey back to the cottage via a different route. She was over the moon about the place. She said you had to be there to understand what the villagers did during the plague, to feel what they did. I rang her Monday night, as you've probably been able to see if you have her phone, but she didn't answer. Sometimes, if she's writing and it's a complicated section such as putting red herrings in, or hiding clues that will pop out later, she'll switch off her phone so she's not distracted by real life, and I assumed after her perambulations around the village that was why she didn't see my call. How wrong was I...'

Carl sensed the distress building in the publisher, and he hadn't a clue how to help. He needed the information she was giving him, even though he knew the man she was speaking about bore no relation to the man he had interviewed in Eyam. The caring husband, but did he simply care about the status afforded by his famous wife? Or did he genuinely care about her as a person. The impression Carl was getting from Marianne Kingston was that Jack was a manipulative, controlling man, and Carl knew he had to view Jack Young from a different angle. Did he gain from a dead wife, or would he have been better with a living one, able to earn vast amounts of money due to her not inconsiderable skills with a keyboard? Jack's life would bear further investigation, and he would make it a priority once he was back home with access to a computer.

They talked more about Faith the author, as opposed to Faith the mother and wife, and Carl felt he was getting a more rounded version of the woman he had last seen in an old wooden shed, the life drained out of her by a slash across her throat.

He took Marianne's statement and passed it across for signature, before leaving after shaking her blue-tipped fingers.

'Thank you, Marianne. It's been a pleasure talking to you. If there's anything at all that you think about after I've gone, please contact me. You have my card with my office and mobile number on, so ring either.'

She gave a slight nod of acknowledgement. 'Go and find the bastard. Safe journey home, Carl.' Marianne watched until his taillights disappeared before going back inside to pick up her paintbrush once more.

. . .

Tessa reached from the sofa for her mobile, the screen showing Carl as the caller.

'I know you're ill, but will you be in work Monday?'

Tessa laughed, which created a bout of coughing. 'I will. I may not be in all day, but I'll certainly be there for around nine. You want something?'

'I intend being you.'

'What, cough and all?'

'No, I mean when you were me. As DI Marsden you and Hannah used to go into Connection and talk, knowing it would stay in Connection. I need to do that. Things I thought were genuine seem to be a bit skewed, so I need to lay things in front of any of you, especially you, Luke and Fred, and see what shows up. You know what I mean?'

'I most certainly do. We always came away looking at things from a different angle, so unless I have a mighty relapse tomorrow, I'll be in Monday morning. I don't know whether I'm feeling better or not, or if it's the massive amounts of medication I'm taking that's masking the symptoms, but I don't feel as bad as I did yesterday.'

'Glad to hear it. It is a normal cold?'

'You mean is it Covid? I'm sure it isn't, I don't think Covid only lasts two days, and apparently you lose the senses of taste and smell. I can definitely taste this bloomin' awful cough medicine. It's a cold, don't worry. I'll let you know if I get worse though. If that happens, I won't risk the office on Monday.'

'You need anything bringing?'

'No, I'm fine. I make sure I've always got milk and bread in the freezer, so I can crawl into bed and not worry. Where are you?'

'I'll be home in about ten minutes. I've been to Cambridge this morning. Interesting outcome, it'll be part of the discussion

Monday morning. Rest, Tessa, and keep taking the tablets. I need you.'

She laughed. 'That's good to know. See you Monday, Superman.'

She disconnected, coughed, and laid her head back down on the cushion. Time to sleep.

20

———

Fred reached inside his car boot and lifted out the brown-paper-clad package. The front door opened and Ethan stood there.

'Are you my dad's friend?'

'I am. I'm Fred. Are you Ethan?'

'I am. I'm not very well. Have you come to watch football with us?'

'I hope so.'

There was the sound of footsteps clattering down the stairs and Cliff's face appeared from behind his son.

'I thought I told you to rest!'

'But I saw Fred's car pull up.'

'You think we should invite him in, then?'

Ethan smiled. 'Yes, he's come to watch football with us.' He turned and walked away, leaving his father to usher Fred through and into the lounge.

Ethan was lying on the sofa, following instructions, and Fred handed him the large package. 'This is for you. I hope you enjoy it, Ethan.'

Cliff helped him remove the string and the brown paper, and

both men watched as his face lit up when he saw the contents. 'It's Ronaldo.'

'It's Ronaldo's own shirt, one he's worn, and it's signed. I'm moving out of my house to live with my friend, and there's no room for it at her house. I can't think of anyone better than you to enjoy this.' Fred handed over an envelope to Cliff. 'These are the authentication documents.'

'When's he coming back to Manchester United?' Ethan was running his fingers over the glass-fronted picture. 'He's at Juventus now, you know, but he was at Real Madrid when he wore this shirt.'

'That's right. I don't think he'll be coming back to Manchester though. Rains all the time, doesn't it? And he's getting to be an old man, he's about thirty-five, isn't he? Bet they have a big party when he leaves Juventus though.'

Ethan laughed and laid his head back down on a cushion. 'You got something to say to Fred, Ethan?'

'Thank you very much, Dad's friend Fred. I'll get Dad to put it on the wall in my bedroom. It can stay in this room this afternoon though.'

It was after six when Fred pulled up outside Naomi's house. He hoped they weren't having a huge meal, he seemed to have spent the entire afternoon eating crisps, sausage rolls and chocolate, as well as watching football. He felt like a bloated football himself.

He opened the front door to silence. He had never opened this door to be met by silence. For a second, panic engulfed him but he moved quickly through into the lounge. Naomi was sat on the sofa, her legs tucked underneath her, with headphones in and an open book in her hands.

He walked around until he was facing her. 'Where's our family? Why is it this quiet?'

'They've all gone out. Luke and Maria have treated Mum and the girls to the cinema. You had a good afternoon?'

'The best. I'd like to keep in touch with Ethan, until we get to the point where I can't. He's a lovely lad, convinced Ronaldo is coming home to Manchester.'

Naomi closed her book and patted the seat at the side of her. 'You hungry?'

He shook his head. 'Not in the slightest. We've been nibbling on all sorts of stuff and I don't think I could face anything.'

'Then let's just sit. Is it still on for the Brighton couple to travel up on Monday?'

'It is. They were coming whether Ethan was in or out of hospital, and I think really Cliff would have preferred they didn't come to his home, but there's not much he can do about that. He's a very poorly young man. Dipped about four-ish, and had to have painkillers. He's a delight to chat with though. Amazingly knowledgeable about Man United.' Fred leaned his head back and groaned. 'My God, I ache. I think I must have kicked every ball on that pitch this afternoon.'

'Whisky?'

'Could be persuaded.'

'You want TV on?'

'Not really. It's Saturday. There's never anything on. We could have an early night...'

'Is that a euphemism?'

'Could be...'

'We'll take the whisky bottle and a couple of glasses with us.'

Luke wasn't particularly watching the film. It was enough for him that Maria's hand was curled inside his, and his thoughts drifted to the talks he had had with three different vets. It seemed that several dogs had died, poisoned. He had been dismayed to learn it wasn't uncommon, but all of the vets had said it had suddenly escalated.

Maria's practice vet had stepped in and made it an official request that Luke investigate it, after they had almost lost a tiny Yorkie that morning, and once again they had suspected poisoning. He had collected names of clients who had suffered at the hands of the dog-hater and had spent the afternoon on the phone talking to them. Two practices in Bakewell and the one in Eyam had been affected, and it seemed that the park in Bakewell was the spot the owners had visited with the dogs, to give them a good run.

His thoughts wouldn't leave it alone, and he decided he and Maria would talk it through when they got home and agree how to tackle it. It clearly needed to be immediate. He dipped his spare hand into the tub of popcorn, and tried to follow the film, wondering what on earth he had missed. It didn't seem to make any sense at all.

Luke delivered his nan and his two tired sisters safely home, and he and Maria drove down to their own place. Maria could sense that Luke hadn't been fully focused on the film, and knew it was the dogs case that was troubling him. He hadn't spoken much of what he had learned throughout his supposed Saturday off, but she had come to understand him; he preferred to think it through before he got to the discussion stage.

'Hot chocolate or something stronger?' she asked, heading for the kitchen.

'Hot chocolate, please. I want to talk, and I need a clear head.'

He leaned forward and pulled his notebook from the shelf

underneath the coffee table. He had written down everything he had garnered from the dog owners he had spoken to that afternoon, and the only link he could see between them all was that they walked their dogs in Bakewell Park. No two dogs were the same breed, but he did notice that the one who had survived was a Labrador, a much larger breed than all of the others affected. The vets hadn't had confirmation of the poison used but had promised to contact him as soon as it was available to them.

Maria carried the two mugs of chocolate through and sat down by Luke's side. 'Okay, let's talk.'

'You fancy some surveillance work?'

She laughed. 'You certainly know how to woo a girl. Where are we going to do this surveillance work?'

'Bakewell recreation ground. Apparently that's its proper name, but I've always called it Bakewell Park. All the dog owners go there to take them for walks. I've ruled out the River Wye as being contaminated, because if that was the source of whatever is killing the dogs, the ducks would be dead as well.'

'Do I need to pack a picnic?'

'Best do that, because we could be there for some time. We'll take our own chairs and some blankets.'

'We haven't got any blankets.'

'We'll pick a couple up when we get there. It's going to be cold just sitting around.'

'You don't think we'll stand out?'

'No, we're going to be sketching.'

She howled with laughter. 'You seen my drawing skills?'

'Look, I'll take two sketchpads, do a quick sketch in yours and you can sit there and look pretty with a pencil in your hand, and you can doodle around on the sketch. I'll do it properly in my sketch book.'

'What if it rains?'

'The paper will get wet.'

'Smart alec. I was more concerned about *us* getting wet.'

'Thickest coat you've got. Doris bought one for me after our first surveillance trip, because it was so cold. Plus we'll have a blanket for over our knees. Best take two flasks of coffee. Have we got two flasks?'

'We have. They were in that load of kitchenware Tessa brought to us. What time do you want to go?'

'About nine-ish. It's a Sunday, so hopefully the dog walkers won't be out too early.'

'And what will we be looking for?'

He sighed. 'I've asked myself that question a million times, and the answer is I don't know. I'm hoping we see something that's not right. Make sure your phone's fully charged, hopefully we can get some photographs. In fact, we keep snapping pics, because there may be something happening we don't see at the time, and we spot later.'

'Are these Doris's words?'

'Certainly are.'

Maria sipped at her hot chocolate, and took hold of his hand. 'She'll always be with you.'

He nodded but couldn't speak.

Tessa thought she might sleep soundly, but it proved not to be the case. Napping on and off most of the day had made her feel much better, but by the time she went to bed tiredness had deserted her. She read for an hour, put down her Kindle and was still wide awake half an hour later.

She let her thoughts drift to the three dead women, her brain ticking over between random deaths and planned deaths. The police officer's murder was seemingly out of sync with the others, but was it? Was there something in Aileen Chatterton's life that linked her to the other women, something nobody else knew about?

And was there some hidden connection between Faith Young and Ella Aylward? There had been no mention so far of a connection, and if that was the truth of the matter, then all three would probably prove to be random killings.

Her brain wouldn't leave it alone, so in the end she got up, took two paracetamol, made herself a cup of tea, and began to formulate ideas, ready for the promised talk on Monday morning with Carl Heaton.

She had questions. Who had known where the two women were going? When did Faith Young book the cottage? Did Jack Young find it for her? Did the author speak to anyone in the tea rooms before heading off to the woods? Was Amanda Gilchrist questioned about that? Was anybody seen to follow Faith into the woods? If not, didn't this suggest that the killer already knew she was going into the woods?

Tessa stared at the listing and knew that all of these questions would lead on to more of the same, but this time covering the murder of Ella Aylward. The difference was that Ella could have been followed at any time. Her route never varied, and she always wore a distinctive blue running outfit. An easy target for any killer wondering who to kill next.

Gut instinct told Tessa that she was looking at a serial killer who had no plan. Whoever it was, and she favoured it being a man, he was someone who simply wanted to kill. Preferably women who wouldn't have so much strength to fight back.

She finished her cup of tea, hoped the slight grittiness in her eyes indicated she was getting ready to sleep, and headed back upstairs. The medication was taking care of the aches and pains, the heaviness in her head, and she climbed back into bed, pulling the duvet up to her chin. With no heating on, the bedroom was cold, and she needed to drift off quickly.

An hour later she put down her Kindle and finally closed her eyes. Two more questions had been added to her brain list, not yet to the physical one. Who chose Faith Young's residence for the month of research, and had Jack Young's background been checked?

21

Sunday morning was fine, and when Luke checked his phone it said only a twenty per cent chance of rain, so he packed the car with the camping chairs and all his sketching equipment, then went back inside to help Maria finish making their picnic.

'If two flasks of coffee isn't enough to keep us warm, we can always go and buy a drink,' she said, putting the flasks into the bag first. Sandwiches followed, then she added biscuits and crisps. 'Want an apple or a banana or something?'

'Put them in, we might want them.'

'All done then. I've found my thickest coat, so we just need the throws. We don't want cold bums.'

'We'll call at the Edinburgh Woollen Mill shop as we go past it, they have nice tartan ones.'

She gave a brief nod and handed the bag to him. He pretended it was too heavy to carry and staggered towards the door.

'You're a wimp, Luke Taylor. Want me to carry it?'

He packed it in the boot and grinned at her. 'It's all those books on your Kindle that make it heavy. You sure that's your warmest coat?'

'It is, and I've brought a hat and gloves as well. I'm not anticipating it being proper picnic weather for our little jaunt. You certainly know how to treat a lady, Luke.'

'I know. You're a very lucky woman to have me.'

He closed the boot and walked round to the driver's side. 'Now we need to be serious. We're watching dog walkers, and anybody who gets close to the animals when they don't have a dog themselves. Somebody has clearly got it in for the pooches, and we don't know why. Yet.'

'You think we'll find somebody? Should I have packed a baseball bat?'

'You want arresting?'

He started the engine and drove down their drive, heading in the direction of Bakewell.

Luke took out the newly-bought tartan throws and folded them so they would be on the seat, but also wrapped around their legs. Maria stashed the picnic bag between the two chairs to keep it upright and settled back in her chair with a sigh. 'This actually is quite nice. Those trees are sheltering us, and it's not as cold as I thought it would be.'

'Plenty of dogs around though. Can't warnings be posted in vets advising people to steer clear of this rec ground?'

'Who would see them? Visits to vets are pretty rare for most animal owners; pets aren't like humans, you know, running to the doctors at the first sign of a cold or a headache. We could put up a notice, but we maybe would get one or two dogs in at the most, the rest are made up of cats, snakes, rats, hamsters and suchlike.'

'Snakes? You deal with snakes?'

She laughed at his face. 'Of course. We deal with everything as a rural practice. You want to pass me a sketchpad then?'

'You don't want me to start you a drawing?'

'Nope. I can do this. And if I can't I'll read my Kindle.' She took out her phone and wedged it down the side of her leg. 'I'll keep that there, then it's handy.'

'There's been no toxicology yet on the dead dogs?'

'Expecting it tomorrow. We can make an educated guess, but that's not the way we work. However, I will say, because of this educated guess, we should be looking at anybody feeding dogs with human food containing sweeteners. Things like peanut butter – a peanut butter sandwich can kill a small dog and make a larger dog very poorly for the rest of its days. There's an ingredient called Xylitol that's an absolute killer with dogs. It's present in many different things, things that unfortunately the dogs help themselves to when they stick their noses in their owners' handbags and suchlike.'

'Peanut butter can kill a dog? What about cats?'

'Cats aren't like dogs, they don't particularly want human food, but most dogs think they are humans. My Buddy definitely thinks he's human. He dictates when he wants a walk, makes it very clear when he doesn't, and he has a passion for green beans.'

'Yuck, he can have mine,' Luke said, pulling his sketchpad onto his knee. 'It's a long time since I did any outdoor sketching, I'm quite looking forward to this. Do we look like casual sketchers? We don't look like people who are here on surveillance duties?'

'We look far too young to be on surveillance, so don't worry about that. Just start drawing, and I'll kind of follow what you do.'

They sat in silence for a few minutes, Luke making swift, practised movements across the page, Maria attempting to keep up with what he was doing.

'This is hard,' she said eventually. 'The scene keeps changing for a start. There's an ice-cream van just pulled up and it's stopped right in the middle of my view.'

'You want one?'

'An ice cream? That would be nice.'

'I'll go get us one. In the meantime, take a photo of the scene you want to draw, then use that picture to draw from. You can control things a lot better by doing that. Plus it helps capture what's going on.'

He stood and walked across the green, his eyes constantly moving, watching everything. He could hear Doris speaking to him. *'Keep looking. If you have to go for a pee, move your head all the time you're heading for the gents. Don't waste a second of surveillance, Luke.'*

He carried the ninety-nines back to Maria, and they sat still for a few minutes, enjoying the ice cream, and simply looking around them.

'Who'd have thought this would be such a hot spot for canines?' Maria said, mopping her chin to remove the ice cream that had missed her mouth. 'In that little section to the right of the van there are six that I can see. We had a discussion the other day at work about how many people now prefer to have more than one, they feel as though it's necessary for dogs to have a companion. I'm not convinced by that. I don't think Buddy would appreciate another dog arriving on the scene. He would have to share us with the newcomer, and I'm certain that wouldn't go down well at all.'

She finished her cone with a deeply satisfied sigh. 'That was delicious.' She ferreted around in her bag for the baby wipes and handed one to Luke before wiping her own hands. 'Don't want ice cream marks all over this masterpiece.'

'I'll show you how to watercolour when we get home. That's when it really will turn into a magnum opus.'

She picked up her phone and moved it around to get the shot she wanted, wondering how on earth John Constable had managed without a camera when painting Flatford Mill. Would he have gone day after day after day to the same spot, painting a section at a time? Or did he have some other magic system for capturing what he wanted on his canvas?

Maria settled on the image she wanted and took four more of the areas either side of it. She scrolled through them, then went back to the first one. It was definitely the best.

Glancing across at Luke's sketchpad made her feel like a complete amateur. He had chosen to draw the point where the river could be seen as well as the grassed area, which in itself was a work of art dominated by tall oak trees.

'That's wonderful,' she breathed. 'Will you be painting it or leaving it as a sketch?'

'Not made my mind up yet. Probably painting it. Why?'

'I'd like it on the wall. It'll be a memory for us, and it will always remind me of the day I became a private investigator, albeit a part-time one.' She laughed. 'You're totally amazing, Luke Taylor.'

'I'm no Constable, but I do enjoy drawing.'

'I was thinking of Constable a minute or two ago. Mum took me into Sheffield, to the Millennium Gallery, to see an exhibition of Constable's work. I was so close to one, about a foot away, and there was nothing between me and it, no glass, no screen of any sort, and it suddenly occurred to me I was standing in exactly the same spot that he must have stood in front of that picture, when he was painting it. I burst out crying. I felt overwhelmed, and Mum had no idea what to do with me. I couldn't explain what was wrong, because nothing was wrong, it was right. Very strange, powerful feeling. I'll never forget it.'

He reached across to squeeze her hand. 'I completely understand. I stood like an utter fool in front of the Mona Lisa when we went on that trip to Paris with school. I daren't dry the tears in case my mates saw me. That was a memorable moment for me.'

She turned and smiled at him. 'I know.'

He began darkening the tree trunks, and then turned to her. 'What do you mean?'

'I know. I was there. I saw. I wanted to dry your tears, but I knew it would draw attention to you. I think I saw a very special Luke Taylor back then.'

He couldn't speak, wanted the moment to last for ever, but a teenager on a bike took his attention back to the present. He watched him cycle up towards the ice-cream van, but he didn't approach, simply stayed astride his bike watching what was happening.

Maria had already snapped a picture of him when Luke turned towards her. 'He's probably perfectly innocent, but that's the sort of thing we have to be aware of.' *'Everything, every little thing, Luke,'* he heard Doris say.

The boy rode off, and Maria took one more picture. 'He did nothing,' she said. 'I'm going for a little walk, take some more pictures. You stay here with our stuff and carry on drawing. We'll have a sandwich and a hot drink when I get back.'

He nodded. 'Don't go out of my sight though. There's somebody killing women not a million miles from here.'

She gave him a swift kiss and headed towards the river.

Luke continued to draw, his eyes constantly watching for anything out of the ordinary. He pondered the issue of the Xylitol and realised just how easy it was to poison a dog. Accidental poisoning where the dog had literally helped himself to food that its human had left accessible was one thing, but to deliberately lace food with something that contained the product was another thing altogether.

Luke went into mild panic when he realised he couldn't see Maria, but she reappeared after a few seconds. She waved at him, and he acknowledged it by raising his thumb.

He had also been taking pictures – the ice-cream van had attracted quite large numbers of people, and anyone who had wandered away from the van and not carried on walking had been photographed. He stood and did a complete video of what could be seen from where they had set up camp, rotating three hundred and sixty degrees to capture it all.

Maria rejoined him and began to unpack their food. She handed him a cup of coffee. 'It's turning cooler. Get this down you, and we'll soon feel the benefit.'

'I've really enjoyed today. We'll do it again one day when we're not looking for dog-killers and such. When we get home we'll look at all these pictures we've taken on a bigger screen than our phones, and see if there's anything there we didn't spot earlier.'

'It's a lovely place. It was chilly by the river, but enjoyable. I did feel a bit spooked by you saying about the women being killed, but I took this.' She slipped the knife back into the picnic bag and grinned at him. 'You only said don't take a baseball bat.'

22

The ice-cream van drove away shortly after two, and Luke and Maria decided to pack everything away and walk back to the car.

'I'm just going to where the van's been all day, and have a walk round there before we head back, so don't fold your chair up yet.'

Maria nodded, sat down and opened her Kindle. 'Don't rush,' she said, and smiled at him.

Luke walked across the grass, and stopped when he reached the spot where the van had been. The grass was flattened all around the rectangular shape, and he simply stood and surveyed the area for a moment. It was peaceful; the morning dog walkers had all gone home, and the evening ones hadn't started. A hundred yards away a family had organised a game of football and there was lots of cheering and laughter, but even that was faint.

He stood and slowly turned his body around, just looking, taking note of anything that seemed to be not quite right. The rubbish bin was full to overflowing, and he had been watching earlier when the ice cream seller had gone over and squashed the mound of rubbish further into the bin. He walked across to it, picking up bits of litter as he walked. He thought it strange that there were several pieces of rectangular silver paper scattered around – at least a dozen.

'Why would anybody need so much chewing gum at once?' he said out loud, then looked guiltily around hoping nobody had heard him. On a whim, he gathered up the papers. What did Tessa call it? Gut instinct? He was feeling it by the bucketload.

He sprinted across to Maria, who closed her Kindle quickly. 'Is it in chewing gum? Xylitol?'

'It is. The sugar-free variety.'

Luke held out the one empty packet he had found. 'Like this one?'

'Yes. You've found the gum itself? Tell me you have.'

'Not yet. Let's get all our stuff over near where the van was so we can keep an eye on it, then we'll go look around. I found all of these.' He delved into his coat pocket and produced the silver wrappers.

She picked up their belongings and they placed everything by a large tree.

'We can see it all there. Okay, I found all these about six feet from the waste bin. It's really full, so it looks as though chucking them on the ground was the easy option. And it's deliberate – nobody throws fresh chewing gum around. Chewed, yes, but not fresh.'

Maria nodded, not sure where to look first. 'This stuff is our biggest problem. Owners keep it in their bags, but dogs love it. They dig in to see what goodies are there, and this stuff smells particularly nice to dogs, so they help themselves. One won't do much damage, but to a little dog three or four of them are enough to kill. And it's not an easy death. There's vomiting, lethargy, difficulty with walking, liver failure, seizures, and then death.' She bent down and picked up two small white tablets of gum. 'Whoever it is doing this is dropping the small tablets as well as the strips. We have to find as much as we can, Luke.'

They found very little, dropping what they had found into an empty sandwich bag. Once back at the car Luke sat deep in thought. 'I have to tell somebody.' He took out his phone, and scrolled down until he found Ray Charlton's name.

Ray listened carefully, then said he'd be there in five minutes.

'No, you've had a hell of a week,' Luke said. 'I was more ringing you to get some advice.'

'Luke, I live five minutes from where you are. You in the riverside car park?'

'We are.'

'Give me ten minutes max. Then I'll need you to take me to where you've found the wrappers. I'm going to ring a park ranger now, they need to be brought in on this. See you in ten.'

Hugh Ellerman, the park ranger, stared at the contents of Luke's sandwich bag. 'Damn, we had a spate of this sort of stuff a couple of years ago. Not here, over in Baslow. We stopped it then, and I haven't come across it since. If this lot's been put down today, then the vets could be busy tomorrow.'

'We've been sitting close by all day, and we've seen nothing obvious,' Luke said. 'And that's why we've been here, to watch. We had sketch books, but that was just for cover. Neither of us saw anything that made us look again. It was just instinct that made me come and have a look round. It's been busy all day in this little area with the ice-cream van being here.'

'We've loads of photos and little video clips,' Maria said. 'I'm sure Luke's smart enough to forward them all on to you if you'd like them.'

'Certainly would,' Ray said. He handed his card to Luke. 'Send them to that email address, and if there's anything we want a closer view of, I'll send it on to the tech lads. You got time to do a bit more searching?'

'We have. But really this part needs some sort of cordon on it to stop any more dogs and owners from using this part of the rec ground before we can guarantee it's clear.' Maria spoke firmly.

Luke smiled. 'Maria's training to be a vet,' he explained. 'The dogs come first.'

'She's quite right,' Hugh said. 'I'll get some reinforcements down here, they'll bring some temporary fencing. The ice-cream van will have to find a different spot for a while, although I'm not sure he comes during the week unless it turns sunny. Give me a minute.' Hugh turned away and spoke into his radio.

'Luke, I know it's your job but thanks for this. Don't feel disheartened that you didn't spot somebody actually throwing this on the ground – I bet you didn't see them drop that apple core either, did you? Dropping this poisonous stuff would take a simple flick of the hand, as if swatting a fly away or something. Anybody walking past this well-populated part of the park could have just casually opened their fist and dropped out several of those little mints, or a couple of sticks and nobody would have thought anything of it. How many people know about this Xylitol anyway? It's probably something you read about once, and don't ever think about again. Until your eleven-year-old Shih Tzu dies and the vet says it's been poisoned.'

Hugh rejoined them. 'Okay, that's sorted. Two of the lads are bringing a truck down and we'll get a fair bit of the area cordoned off in the next half hour. I'll have a team down here tomorrow and we'll comb it for anything that looks remotely like gum, and it will all be passed on to you, Ray. I'm increasing park patrols initially for a week, but hopefully there'll be some results before then.'

'Can't you put up some signs?' Maria asked. 'Dog walkers need to be warned. Tell them dogs must be on leads at all times. I know they'll grumble, but that's better than a spate of very poorly or dying pets.'

'I'll make sure there's something at certain points around the park. Let's have another walk round this section while we're waiting for the fencing, and tomorrow I'll organise a fingertip search. It'll be going dark soon, so there's no point pulling in a team now.'

They split up and, eyes glued to the ground, found five more small white tablets of gum.

Ray walked towards Carl, his face grim. 'Young Luke rang me this afternoon.'

Carl Heaton laughed. 'Young Luke? You mean the Luke who is living with a woman, who is a partner in a thriving business, and is definitely no longer the kid who started life as a junior at Connection? That Luke?'

'That's the one. Young Luke. Anyway he's working on a case the local Eyam vets have asked him to look at – dogs are dying from what they believe is Xylitol poisoning. There's a link between the dead animals and that link is the owners took them for walkies on the recreation ground in Bakewell. Anyway, him and his lass took themselves off down there for the day, sat and sketched, took lots of photos, kept a close eye on the busiest area, which was around the ice-cream van, and after the van had gone Luke walked over for a look around. He found a lot of evidence of chewing gum wrappers, all the same make, so gathered them all up, along with any chewing gum he could find, then he rang me. Said you'd got enough on your plate with dead bodies, without having dead dogs as well. The long and short of it is that I'm reporting in to you because I've had a busy afternoon.'

'I'll put in for a medal for you. Apart from that, you need me to do anything?'

'No, I kind of left it in the hands of Hugh Ellerman, he leads the Park Ranger team. He's taking it very seriously. I wanted to give you a heads-up because Luke is going to forward all the photos and videos they took, so if you can spare somebody tomorrow to look through them...'

'You do it, Ray. Might as well see this through. If there's anything you feel not happy about, send it through to tech. Rejoin us at the church hall when you're ready. And thanks for responding this afternoon. Today was a day off.'

'I've got two dogs, sir. We walk them in that park.'

Maria helped Luke empty the boot, then sank into the sofa, clutching one of the new throws they had bought earlier that day. She sank her face into it. 'They're so soft. I could be asleep in two minutes flat if I were to do something stupid like lay down with my head on this cushion and pull the cover over me.' Her head dropped to the cushion.

Luke looked at her, his face wreathed in a huge smile. 'You've been an absolute star today, Maria London, and I love you very much, but we've got work to do.'

'You do it,' she mumbled.

'I'll make you a cup of coffee, that'll wake you up.'

She struggled up to a sitting position. 'Slave driver. You're our technical guru, can't you do it?'

'I can, but I want us to look at the pics first, together. You took lots when you went off for your little walkabout, and I haven't seen any of them. I need you awake. Apart from that, if you sleep now, you won't sleep tonight, and you've to be up for six. Big op day tomorrow, isn't it?'

She groaned. 'Okay I give in. But you're making the coffee, aren't you?'

'I'm doing it now, then I'll set the TV up to take our photos. Don't put that beautiful head anywhere near a cushion while I'm gone.'

They sat side by side on the sofa, the tartan throws shared between them, mugs of coffee on the coffee table. The first picture came onto the TV screen and they stared intently at it. The ice-cream van was in place, and a short queue had formed. At the front of the queue a father had lifted his young daughter up for her to point to a picture on the van window, and behind them stood a woman with two children. The boy was holding a lead attached to a small dog. Everything looked to be normal, nothing to make anybody's hair stand on the back of their necks, and Maria said, 'Next.'

23

Luke sat with his notebook open, creating a timeline of events that unfolded from the many pictures they had taken. What became very obvious very quickly was that a lot of dog walkers used the park. Luke and Maria had no way of knowing if that was because it was a Sunday, or if it was like that every day of the week, but there were too many to count.

'If we drew a ten-mile radius around this ice-cream van, would you be able to find out how many veterinarian practices there are?'

'I could probably find out.'

'I think we should. I think there needs to be some co-ordination in this. It may be that some little vet somewhere doesn't know about this happening right now, and we miss something. Check with...' He hesitated.

She laughed. 'Trefor. Trefor Griffiths. You kind of need to remember that – he's my boss.'

'He's the one! It's his first name I struggle with. I've always known him as Mr Griffiths. Trefor, Trefor. I'll remember it now. Anyway, ask him about the possibility of emailing as many as you can find and asking them to contact him with information about suspected Xylitol poisoning over the last... two weeks shall we say?'

'I'll talk to him first thing tomorrow. Once the operation is over, I'll get on to it. I'm sure he'll agree, he's the one that's pushed for your help. There's an awful lot of these photos – think we should send out for a pizza?'

'I do. Now I've warmed up I don't want to move from here, never mind attempt to cook a meal.'

'Pity they don't do shop-to-sofa deliveries. I'll order, you sort us a can of Coke or something, and let's have ten minutes away from watching photos.'

It was the initial picture, post-pizza, that grabbed their attention. For the first time there appeared to be no queue at the ice-cream van. This had been the point when Luke had offered to get them an ice cream, and the picture clearly showed the vendor in his white overall outside the van, having a cigarette. The next picture showed Luke walking across to the van, with the ice-cream man seemingly tossing his cigarette in the general direction of the already-full waste basket. The picture that followed showed Luke standing at the van window, and the ice-cream man dropping his cigarette on the ground and stamping on it to put it out.

'Hang on,' Luke said, almost at the same time as Maria said, 'Just a minute...'

He looked at her. 'What did he throw at the waste bin if he then stubbed out his cigarette? Have we got any other photos of him taking a walk away from the van?'

He picked up his own phone and quickly scrolled through the dozens of snaps. He passed it to Maria. 'Look at this one. He's walking back to the van from the other side of the waste bin. It doesn't show him doing anything other than smoking, but what's he already done prior to our catching him on this picture? You know what, I feel almost as if I should apologise to that young lad on the bike, I concentrated on him. He just seemed to hover around the area, and I took several shots of him. Got that wrong, didn't I? He simply rode away after probably resting.'

Maria touched his hand. 'Don't beat yourself up about it. We can't tell what that ice-cream man is throwing, the picture will have to be enlarged a lot, and we could be completely wrong about this as well. Let's make a note for Ray, when we send him these photos, tell him what we've spotted, and I'm sure he'll know what to do about it. Now let's carry on, see what we can, and get them emailed. I really do need an early night.'

Monday morning was grey, colder than the day before, and an ever-present threat of rain cast a pall over Eyam. Interviews with residents continued, and Carl made his way down to Connection clutching a box of buttered scones, with instructions to bring the plastic container back with him as it belonged to Nora.

Fred, Tessa and Luke were already in Luke's office when Carl arrived. 'I bring gifts, hand-baked by the ladies at the church.'

'Really? Well that beats Luke's biscuits.' Tessa took the box from him and placed a pile of napkins on the table. 'Coffees for everybody?'

They all nodded, and Carl turned to Luke. 'Hear you had an exciting day in Bakewell.'

'Yes. You could call it that. Did I do the right thing by ringing Ray Charlton? I thought it was a bit trivial for you, and I know what sort of a week you've had.'

'You did. He's just turned up at the church, he's passed the photos on to the tech team, and he's looked carefully at the ones you've earmarked. He said to tell you he shares your concerns. Something about an ice-cream man?'

'Good. Let's hope it leads to something. An email has been sent a few minutes ago to many vets in the area affected, asking for notification of suspected Xylitol poisoning over the next few days. What I don't understand is why? Why would anybody want to deliberately do it? I understand it happening accidentally, dogs will eat anything, but this is deliberate.'

They sat down, and helped themselves to a scone. 'You have information, Carl?'

He shrugged. 'No idea. It's a bit like the dogs situation really. Why? I simply need to talk. I have three dead women, no link between them, killed by the same person. We're finally having their phones checked, and I think we're very lucky to actually have Ella Aylward's phone. I don't believe he saw it. It was strapped to her upper arm and was on silent, effectively hidden by her jacket. It's taken us a while to dry out the phone that was outside for three days, but now it's being worked on by our tech team, so if there is anything that links these three women, it should show up on their phones.'

'Then let's talk through Faith Young. As far as you're aware, she's the first victim?'

Carl nodded. 'Yes. We've checked for similar attacks, similar deaths, but nothing is jumping out and saying these could be linked. Nothing at all.'

Tessa frowned. 'So do we think it began with Faith because she upset him in some way? Some fan of hers who she's upset, maybe?'

'I could have followed that, if she'd been killed at home, but what fan knew she would be in Eyam for a month? Nobody did, other than her husband, her daughter and son-in-law, and her publisher. She came here to write, to research, to capture the soul of Eyam. I believe she was stalked until he got her on her own, but what I can't work out is did he stalk her as Faith Young or as a woman? Without the other two deaths thrown into the mix, I would have thought it was because she was Faith Young, but that doesn't hold up when Aileen Chatterton and Ella Aylward are added to her murder.'

'She arrived here on the Saturday?' Fred joined in. He was fascinated by the interaction, felt quite proud of the fact that Carl trusted this small group of civilian individuals enough to give them details of such a complex case.

'Yes. Soon settled in. According to the cottage owner she asked where the nearest supermarket was, he told her it was two minutes away, the Co-op, so she drove down to pick up a few supplies. He walked down later, and her car was still in the Co-op car park.'

'Why did it take her so long?'

'She told Will Sandford she'd walked around the village centre before going in the shop, so she'd ended up coming out at the same time as he was there. He offered to draw her a map of different walking routes that would give her an overall feel of the place and he said she was really pleased when he did just that. He didn't see her again until Sunday afternoon, when he went up to drop the map through her letterbox. She picked it up immediately and came out and thanked him. That was the last time Will saw her.'

'Did fingerprints in the car reveal anything?' Tessa asked. She coughed and picked up her coffee. 'Apologies if I'm infecting all of you.'

'Fingerprints in the car? After her Saturday jaunt to the shops, she didn't use her car. We haven't sent it to forensics. I believe it's still parked up outside Leaf Cottage. Jack Young is making arrangements to come up with somebody else, so he can drive it back home.'

Tessa stared at him. 'And supposing Aileen Chatterton's or Ella Aylward's prints are found inside it? Wouldn't that give you the link you're looking for?'

'But Ella Aylward wasn't in Eyam then, and Aileen was working out of Chesterfield.' He paused for a moment, sensing he was being illogical. He took out his phone. 'Get Faith Young's car into forensics. I want everything you can get from it.'

Carl took a second scone and bit into it. 'I knew I needed to come here. Not only for the decent coffee you make, but also because you think outside the box all the time. We're too law-abiding in the police. Too strait-laced. It stiffens up your thoughts as well as your actions.'

Tessa grinned. 'It's why I used to call in here when I was doing what you're doing. They always seemed to make sense, but it was always one step removed from my thinking. I'm that one step removed now, and happy to help.'

'Then maybe I need to find where this box is that you all think outside. Let's see where your thoughts go about the tea rooms.'

'Excellent afternoon tea, Amanda Gilchrist is lovely, and can't wait for it to open as a bistro. And if the killer was in the tea rooms with a sudden desire to kill a woman, he had the perfect one with Faith Young. If he overheard the conversation between Amanda and Faith, he would know exactly who the smart woman dressed in green was. Who doesn't know the name Faith Young? Has something happened in his life that has given him this urge to kill? Is it only women, or will anybody do?' Tessa coughed once again, and stood up to get a bottle of water. 'Sorry, time for some tablets I think.'

'Oh God, I'm so sorry, Tess. I should have left this till tomorrow. You shouldn't be back at work yet.'

'I should. I was going doolally at home. I'm not a good patient. And you've set my brain back into thinking mode. Having the car checked was more or less a ticking off the list exercise, I don't expect anything to come from it, but once Jack Young has removed it from Leaf Cottage it becomes worthless anyway. I used to find that being the SIO on a case tended to put you too far into it, and when I was struggling, Hannah used to say shall we go and have a coffee at Connection. Sometimes the slightest little thing triggered something in my brain, and sent me in a different, more accurate direction. And, of course, you know we won't repeat anything that's said in here.'

24

'Okay,' Luke said, 'let's go back to basics. Who knew where she was going? As far as I can see, the only two who knew for definite were Will Sandford because he drew her the map, and Amanda Gilchrist, who had the conversation with her. To me, it looks as though the innocent chat with Amanda is the weak link. Anybody in that café could have overheard what they were saying, especially as it appears Amanda got a bit giddy about getting her books signed. So it's not narrowed down to only two people, it's narrowed down to maybe a dozen. Did anyone come forward following your appeal for people to contact you who had been in the tea rooms that lunchtime?'

'Two. And they don't remember seeing or hearing Faith and Amanda talking.'

'You've presumably checked out debit and credit card payments?'

'First thing we did really. Unfortunately most people used cash. No help there at all.'

'And Jack Young?'

'Ah – Jack Young. It turns out he wasn't quite the affable author's husband we'd originally thought him to be. I went to

Cambridge on Saturday to meet with Faith's publisher. It seems our Mr Young was a controlling, interfering busybody, who even monitored the number of words his wife wrote per day. You met him – did he come across like that to you?'

Luke shook his head. 'I thought he was okay. Does this make you rethink things with him? Did his alibi hold up?'

'To a certain extent. He definitely didn't travel here with Faith, Will said she was on her own. He didn't meet Jack until the Thursday when he came here looking for his wife. Jack's alibi for the Monday, which is when Faith was killed, is that he stayed home doing paperwork for Faith, tax stuff and so on, and then Monday evening his daughter rang to say her waters had broken and she was on her way to hospital. He said he didn't rush to be with her, he knew her husband was by her side, and she had been optimistic that they could hold back on delivery. By Wednesday it was clear that wasn't going to happen, and he tried contacting Faith, to no avail. He turned up here on Thursday.'

'He has no alibi for Monday at all? He gave you no name to confirm he was at home? Life insurance? Is she insured by her publisher? They're going to lose big time by her death, aren't they?' Luke looked at Carl. 'I'm sorry, I'm probably teaching you to suck eggs, aren't I.'

Carl laughed. 'Not at all, this is what I appreciate about all of you. As it happens, I am aware he has no alibi for Monday, and he only lives a couple of hours drive away. I just don't see what he would gain by her death. Yes, she has life insurance, but it's for a trifling amount in comparison to what she earns, so he needs her alive to continue with the lifestyle he lives. He's basically her agent, packed his job in as soon as she became a best-selling author. This is why I can't relate her death to him, he gains nothing. But that's only with the facts that are available to us. We're checking her laptop, but so far nothing untoward on it.

With them working on all three phones we should see if there's any connection by the end of the day.'

'And Brian Aylward?' Tessa asked.

'Alibied for two of them, and as it's the same killer for all three, that means he's alibied for all three of them. We still haven't found out who was staying in their holiday home while they weren't there, but it did occur to me that you can see from that house to the bottom of the hill where you leave the village to enter the woodland. Faith Young would have been visible all the way up that hill.'

'So the killer could have been patiently waiting in there for a few days, ready for a woman entering the woods.' Luke pursed his lips as he thought things through. 'That's creepy. He'd be sitting on that bed in the main bedroom, comfy because he'd helped himself to their pillows and duvets, eating pizza and waiting for a lone woman to walk up that hill.' He shivered. 'This was planned in advance, wasn't it?'

'I think so. It doesn't feel random. Maybe the woman was random, but I'm also not convinced about that. This man wants to kill, and for some reason it has to be a woman. Could he be of small or slight stature? Not strong enough to take on a man? I don't know, but he got into that house without breaking any windows, or bashing in any doors.'

'So did I,' said Tessa.

'But you genuinely thought there might be a key under the plant pot, didn't you? What if there was? What if our killer checked it as well?' Carl once again picked up his phone. This time his call was to Brian Aylward. 'Mr Aylward? Sorry to trouble you, but can you tell me if you kept a spare key anywhere outside your property, in case one of you came back without the other?'

Carl listened to the response, then thanked Brian before disconnecting.

'Definitely not. They considered having a key safe on the wall, but decided against it, feeling that wasn't secure enough as they were away from the property for such long periods of time.'

Luke frowned. 'So that needs some thinking about. If it was the killer using that bedroom for observational purposes and not just a squatter, it's leading me to think the killer is from Eyam. That house is in the middle of nowhere and unless you knew it was there, you wouldn't know it was there. Sorry if that sounds particularly stupid, but you can probably work out what I mean. Didn't get much sleep last night, and it might just be catching up with me.'

'Too much information,' Fred said.

'If only. Nope, it was all about dead dogs yesterday. A killer of a different kind. Couldn't stop thinking about it, daren't move in case I woke Maria because she had to be up for six, and in the end I got up when she did, and sent the email to Ray Charlton with all the pictures on it. My head's buzzing.'

'It might be buzzing, but I can't help thinking you're right. I think it's somebody local, and maybe somebody amongst our army of officers going round this village will feel that tingle you get when you know something's amiss.'

Luke stood. 'I need another coffee. Shall I make four?'

They all said yes, and Luke added a little extra coffee and a little less milk into his in the hope it would shock him awake.

Carl thanked them all and promised them he would keep them informed about the contents of the phones if anything stood out. He had received an email from the tech department with the results of the three phone inspections, and so he headed back up to the church hall where he had access to computers.

Being so close to lunchtime, officers drifted in and out for sustenance and several spoke to him. They had very little to report, but most homes had the leaflet, and they were reaching the end of interviewing the residents. It seemed that Eyam hibernated in the cold months, and nobody had seen anything of significance. Ella Aylward's body had appeared by magic behind that shed, no vehicles had been seen, and even the late-night dog walkers hadn't spotted anything out of the ordinary.

Carl made a point of thanking his colleagues; he knew it was a soul-destroying job, especially on cold March days, and he truly did appreciate the job they were doing. He commandeered a laptop and headed off to a quiet corner next to a radiator. One of the ladies brought him a cup of tea and he thanked her.

'It's a pleasure. This is the most excitement we've had in this village for years.'

She walked away and he shook his head. She called three murders excitement? He sipped at his tea, warming his icy cold hands on the cup. He wasn't the best typist in the world, and having cold hands didn't help at all.

Slowly the feeling in his fingers returned, and he called up his emails, opening the one from the tech team. They had sent an assortment of headings, and so he took Faith's phone first, and looked at her pictures, selecting the date of her arrival in Eyam as a starting point.

Her pictures mirrored the route Will Sandford had mapped out for her, and he smiled as he recognised the so-familiar landmarks. He too had treated the village like the tourism hotspot it was when he had first moved in with Kat, but eventually it had morphed into home. Now he was seeing it afresh from a newcomer's eyes, and Faith Young had taken lots and lots of pictures.

She had continued to be snap happy inside the tea rooms, clearly trying to get a feel for the place that could be later transcribed into a book. She had caught most of the customers, and he dragged those pictures into a separate folder for further inspection. There followed a couple of shots as she had stood outside the tea rooms, waiting to cross the road to head towards the woods. She had photographed cars on these pictures, so he dragged them across as well.

The pictures taken as she began her ascent up towards the top of the village via the woods were spectacular. She had captured the moodiness, the bleakness of the weather, probably without even thinking about it. It was simply there. The trees formed a dark green canopy all the way up the hill.

There was a picture of Woodlands off into the distance, then several more of trees and a hedgerow as she climbed the incline, followed by a final two photos of Woodlands. One was a distance shot, the other was a zoomed shot. He frowned. What had made her zoom in? Something she had spotted? He dragged all of the Woodlands shots into the extra folder.

He opened up the pictures on Ella Aylward's phone, but it consisted mainly of interior shots of the house where the intruder had been. The bedroom was extensively photographed, the log fire in the lounge, the family bathroom and the en suite leading from the main bedroom, all had been snapped possibly for sending to their insurance company. Carl opened yet another folder and labelled it Woodlands, before transferring Ella's most recent pictures.

Aileen's photographs held no relevance at all. The last one taken had been of a child's birthday party some seven days earlier. Carl picked up his drink, and sipped at it thoughtfully. He'd leave the photographs for a few minutes, then come back at them with an open mind.

Ray walked over to him and sat down. 'Everything okay?'

'We've had the results of the mobile phones from the tech guys. I've only checked the pictures so far, pulled some out to look at closely, but I'm leaving them for a couple of minutes. You heard anything from the Park Rangers?'

'They've found pockets of where the chewing gum has been thrown around, so there's a massive clean-up going on right now. I don't know if we've any issues with poorly dogs, but Maria will probably be the first one to hear about that. We've tried to enlarge the photo they were most concerned about, with that ice-cream vendor throwing something on the ground that wasn't his cigarette, but it won't give us the detail of what he's thrown. He's due back in the park on Wednesday according to the bookings clerk, so I think we should have a couple of us in there with a decent camera, filming him every time he steps out of that van. If it is him, we arrest him there and then.'

'You want to do it?'

'If you can spare me from this. I'd like to take Luke, if that's okay. This is his baby really.'

'That's fine. Keep him out of the way if you do make an arrest, and get somebody from the tech team with a decent camera to go with you, somebody who knows what they're doing with a camera. Let's hope that clears up that issue.'

25

Julie and Ivor Needham spoke very little on their journey north. They both felt all talked out, unsure what their future now held. Seeing Ethan for the first time in fifteen years was daunting, but it was seeing him for whatever was left of his life that was even scarier. Each time they saw him from this point onwards he would have deteriorated a little more, and Julie knew it would be hard to handle that.

She leaned forward and switched on the radio, pressing the button for Classic FM. She wasn't sure she could handle singing, she needed soothing. She tried closing her eyes, and was suddenly aware of the engine sound changing. She gazed around, noticing they were pulling into a services, and breathed a sigh of relief.

She felt as if she'd been sitting down for ever, and quickly opened her door as soon as the handbrake went on.

'We're having a toilet break, or a drinks break?' she asked.

'Drinks break. Food as well if you need some. I could eat a cheeseburger or something.' He slipped his arm around her shoulder, and they walked across to the main building. She went to the restroom while he stood in the queue, and they finally sat down on plastic chairs that scraped along the floor. She looked around. 'Why do they have to keep it so dark in these places?'

'It's so you can't see the muck in the corners.' He grinned at her. 'I need you to cheer up a bit, sweetheart. We can't show our true feelings around Ethan; he doesn't need to know how hard this has hit us, so we have to be really careful how we go in.'

Julie sighed. 'I know, but it's so bloody difficult. Since that Fred bloke came on Friday I've hardly slept.'

'Think I don't know? We always knew that one day there was a possibility you would be needed for Ethan, and I know neither of us thought it would be at this young age, so we have to act. We have to pretend there is no cancer, this is an arranged visit so you can get to know your son as the man he's become. Are you with me?'

'Of course I know what you're saying, but knowing it and doing it are two different things. I thought I was scared stupid on the day we left Bakewell, but it was nothing compared to this. The life I've known for the last fifteen years is being ripped apart and...'

Ivor grabbed hold of her hand. 'We can weather this together. We've lived the last fifteen years knowing we were meant for each other, and today isn't going to change that. Eat up, and let's get this first meeting over with. We can discuss with Cliff what happens after that, but this week is to get to know your son, my stepson, again. When we head off back to Brighton on Friday, we need a plan in place for you to see as much of him as possible, or as much of him as Ethan wants. It seems he's the one who's asked to see you, this isn't about Cliff dragging you back into their lives, so let's keep that at the front of our minds.'

A brief smile crossed her face. 'You always make me feel so much better. Come on, let's escape this dungeon and finish our food in the car. Are we still on course for getting there about two?'

Ivor glanced at his watch. 'We are. Might be a bit earlier, it all depends on traffic.'

They headed back to the car, seeing sunshine trying to break through the cloud cover. 'You want me to drive for this next stretch?' Julie asked.

'Nope. I want you to put the seat back and close your eyes for a bit. You're knackered, my love, and the best thing for you is sleep.'

'Can I finish my cheeseburger first?'

'You can indeed. And your milkshake if you really feel the need.'

She gave him a quick kiss and walked round to her side of the car. A minute later he was reversing out, and preparing to rejoin the motorway.

'Can I wear my Manchester United shirt?' Ethan asked.

'You can, but don't you want a smart shirt?'

'My Manchester United shirt is a smart shirt.'

'I know,' his father said with a sigh. 'But you've not worn any other top since Saturday, and I have to wash it every night.'

'The machine washes it.'

Cliff wondered if he would ever get used to his son's logical mind. He guessed not – it had never been any different since he learned to speak his first words.

'Okay, I give in. Wear the Man U shirt.'

'Manchester United, not Man U. When Ronaldo comes home, I shall have his name put on the back.'

'Of course.' Cliff smiled. 'And I shall take you to have it done.'

'I wish I could meet him.'

Dear gods, Cliff thought, *and I thought it was a hard enough task when he wanted to see his mother.*

'Not going to happen, pal, he's at Juventus.'

'I mean when he comes to Manchester.'

Cliff stared at the back of Ethan's head. His son was so utterly convinced that such a move could be on the cards, and yet he must be the only one in the whole world apart from possibly Sir Alex Ferguson who thought it was a possibility.

'Then let's keep our fingers crossed, Ethan, that it does happen sometime in the future, and if it does, I'll make sure you meet him. How's that for a promise?'

'It's good, Dad. A good promise. Thank you.'

Ivor and Julie arrived quarter of an hour early, and Ethan insisted on going to the door.

'Hello, Ivor. Thank you for bringing this lady. Are you my mother?'

Julie, unused to the abrupt form of speech employed by her son, almost flinched, and Ivor slipped his arm around her waist. 'I am, Ethan, and it's lovely to see you.'

Cliff appeared behind him. 'Ethan, let your mother and her partner come in.'

Ethan stepped to one side, and Ivor and Julie shuffled by him.

Cliff showed them into the lounge. 'Welcome home, Pippa.'

'It's Julie now, Cliff.'

'I'll try to remember.'

Ethan moved into the centre of the room. 'You two can sit on the sofa. Me and my dad have the armchairs. We like the armchairs.'

The Needhams did as instructed.

'Can I offer you a cup of tea? Coffee?' Cliff asked.

'Tea for both of us, thanks, mate.' Ivor squeezed Julie's hand, he could sense the turmoil escalating inside her.

'I'm not your mate. Sugar?'

'Milk no sugar in both.'

Cliff left them sitting close together with Ethan staring at them, and he hid the grin. He knew exactly how unnerving Ethan's stare could be, and it usually meant he was working something out in his head that, by the time it left his lips, would be mind-blowing.

'How are you feeling, Ethan?' Cliff heard the soft tones of his wife as she tried to communicate with her son.

'I'm okay. I have good medicine now that stops my stomach ache.'

'That's wonderful. You've been in hospital?'

'In the hospice, not the hospital. Nurse Sammy looks after me, she's lovely. I'm going back again in four weeks to let them see if I need a new tablet.'

'Of course.'

There was an awkward silence, and Cliff appeared with a tray of drinks. He placed it on the coffee table. 'I've brought you milk, Ethan,' he said.

'Thank you, Dad. My dad bought me my new shirt.'

'You still support Man U then?' Ivor said.

'It's Manchester United.'

'Sorry, of course it is.'

'We watched the match on Saturday with Fred. He brought me a picture of Ronaldo.'

Julie looked at Cliff in query.

'Fred, the chap who found you, came to bring a gift for Ethan and stayed to watch the match with us. It was a good afternoon, wasn't it, Ethan?'

'Very good. I like Fred. Ronaldo wore the shirt.'

Cliff explained. 'It was a signed shirt, authenticated, one

from his Real Madrid time. Maybe Ethan will show you his room before you leave, I've put it on his wall.'

'That's brilliant, Ethan,' Ivor said.

Again there was an uncomfortable silence, and they all sipped at their drinks.

'Ethan has to have a nap in the afternoon, it's part of his treatment, so he'll be going to his bedroom after he's had this drink. We can talk more then. He only naps for about an hour, but they found in the hospice he benefitted from it.'

Julie responded quickly to his words. 'That's fine. We can go, and come back tomorrow, we're booked in at the hotel until Friday, so we can see Ethan every day until we go home.'

Cliff watched the sudden downward turn of Ethan's mouth with some trepidation. Something wasn't suiting him, but he had no idea what it was. He watched as his son slowly sipped at his milk, then he tilted the glass and drained it.

'Bed now, Dad.'

'That's fine, Ethan. I'll wake you in an hour. Try to sleep, but if you can't, make sure you rest. Okay?'

Ethan held up a thumb. 'Okay, Dad.'

'He seems good,' Julie said.

'He's also on medication strong enough to fell a horse.' Cliff felt no responsibility towards being nice towards this woman. 'He's lost his... enthusiasm for life, his joie de vivre. He's not good, and every day he seems to lose a little more of himself, so don't presume anything, Pippa or Julia or whatever you're called. Our son is dying, no platitudes from you are going to change that.'

'That's enough, mate,' Ivor said, standing up.

'No, it's not enough, and don't call me mate. You lost that

fucking right when you ran off with my wife fifteen years ago, and didn't have the balls to tell me.'

Ivor sat back on the sofa with a thud. This wasn't how he'd envisaged the meeting going, he'd thought they would talk it through like responsible adults faced with an impossible situation. Obviously that wasn't the way Cliff was seeing it.

'You two are here under sufferance. In one way I was hoping Fred wouldn't be smart enough to track you down, but he was, and now we have to live with the consequences. But I don't have to be polite to you when Ethan isn't here.'

There was the sound of a bedroom door being forcibly closed and Ethan clumped his way down the stairs.

'You okay, Ethan?' his father asked.

'No. I've been thinking. The cancer isn't in my brain yet and I can still think, can't I, Dad?'

'Of course. You can always think, Ethan.'

'Then my thinking is that I don't want her for a mother. I thought I did, but now I have seen her, I do not. You are my mother, Dad, my mother and my father. So can you go home now, you two, and do not come back again because I do not want to see you. I was wrong. I will tell Fred I was wrong as well, and he will know I am sorry for making him do so much work. I am going back to bed now for my resting nap. Close the door behind you.'

Cliff had never been prouder of his son.

26

Tuesday morning saw the residents of Eyam wake to bright sunshine and horrific coronavirus updates. It was getting clearer by the day that changes were coming to their lifestyles, and in many cases residents of the village had already implemented their own adjustments by isolating indoors with shopping being delivered by relatives, and standing well back when anyone came to the door.

The police officers had accepted it as normal that they stood halfway down the path when visiting the houses, and Carl noted that they were down to only two unvisited households. According to neighbours one was on holiday, due back any time, and the other one was working abroad, they thought Dubai. Leaflets had been left, and Carl transferred the absentee villagers onto a back burner in his mind. They couldn't have been killing anybody in Eyam if they were out of the country, was his way of thinking.

He gathered everybody together to discuss where to go next, and there was a concerted groan when he said he wanted all statements in report form and uploaded by that evening. 'I want you all to double-check everything carefully, and if there's anything, anything at all, that requires a second look, then take that second look yourselves, or highlight it for me to make the decision. We don't want to have done all of this work, then go and miss something. On the plus side, if you're working in here it will be a lot warmer for you.'

There was a general cheer from most of them – it had been a cold few days. 'And don't expect these ladies to wait on you – you want a coffee, you go and make it. Now get on with the reports. Ray? Can I see you for a moment?'

Ray held up a hand in acknowledgement and weaved his way through the assorted desks and tables scattered around the hall. He stopped briefly to answer a query and eventually reached Carl's desk by the radiator.

'Boss?'

Carl held out his hand, Ray looked at it for a moment and then shook it.

'Congratulations, DS Charlton. And it's about time. You don't regret taking the exam?'

Ray's smile was huge. 'Not for one minute, sir. I just had to wait till the time was right, and now it is. Well, this has brightened my day.'

Carl banged on his desk to get the attention of his officers. 'Can I introduce our new Detective Sergeant, Ray Charlton? I'm sure you'll all want to join me in offering our congratulations.'

There was a loud burst of applause and wolf-whistles, and Ray's face turned red. 'That's enough,' he said. 'And thank you, everybody. Let's get on with the job now, shall we?'

He looked down at his feet, then at the smile on Carl's face. 'Well, that wasn't embarrassing at all, DI Heaton. I can't wait for the day you get your next promotion.'

. . .

Fred was standing chatting to Cheryl, his coat on and ready to head out to speak to a new client when the call came through. He checked his screen and saw 'Baines'.

'I'll be in my office for a bit,' he said to Cheryl, and said, 'Hi, Cliff,' into his phone.

They exchanged the usual pleasantries, until the point that Cliff said, 'They're on their way back to Brighton, and I've already started divorce proceedings.'

'Well,' Fred said, surprise evident in his voice. 'They came all this way for one afternoon?'

'No, it seems the plan was to stay until Friday, and visit Ethan every day. Get to know the man he's become, as opposed to the boy they remember. Unfortunately, the man he has become has decided he doesn't like the mother she's become, so he's told them he doesn't want to see them again.'

'He's sure?'

'Oh, he's sure all right. Quite firm about it, did all but throw them out of the door. I spoke to Pippa last night, told them not to bother coming round again because I didn't want Ethan upsetting, and she rang this morning to say they'd already set off for Brighton. I told her I'd spoken to my solicitor about the divorce, and she disconnected. You know what Ethan said, Fred? He brought a lump to my throat, I can tell you. He said he didn't need her, because I was his mother as well as his dad. He also said he wants to apologise to you for sending you all that way to find her.'

Fred laughed. 'He's priceless. And smart. You can tell him the pleasure was all mine, heading off to Brighton. I took Naomi, my new partner, with me, and we had a wonderful night in a really posh hotel, so it seems everything turned out for the best.'

'It did. Pippa's out of our lives now, he's satisfied with the outcome, and I don't have to have further contact with her until... well, until I have to. So can you send me your final bill,

Fred? I'll get it paid and we can write Pippa Baines out of our lives.'

'Of course, but I won't email it. I'll bring it round if that's okay. I'd like to keep in touch...'

'You can come anytime, Fred. I'm under instructions to ask you if you'd like to come over Sunday afternoon because Manchester United are on TV again. That's Manchester United, you understand, not Man U. He says we can have pizza and crisps.'

'Oh my God, I'd love to. Can I bring Naomi?'

'Of course. Bring anybody you want to bring. Let's have a party for my lad, he's bloody amazing.'

'I know he is. I'll only bring Naomi, we'll be escaping for a couple of hours from our lot. And I'll bring the bill then, no need to settle it straight away.'

'Thanks, Fred, for everything. See you Sunday.'

Luke was surprised to see no traffic, so strolled across the road towards the vets. The text from Maria simply said they had received a report of a poorly dog, with poisoning suspected, and did he have time to nip over the road. He did.

'Hi, Luke.' Trefor Griffiths' Welsh accent greeted him as he walked through the door. 'Can you just drop the lock, we're closed for lunch. Maria's through here.'

Luke followed him through to a back room, and Maria was stroking the head of a tiny dog, a bichon frise, Luke presumed.

Maria looked up. 'He's very poorly. He's been brought in by a dog sitter who has been looking after him since his owner went on holiday on Saturday. She took him in Bakewell Park yesterday evening, but didn't let him off the lead as she wasn't convinced he would return to her call. She did have him on an extending lead, so he was some distance away from her at times, and she says she didn't see him eat anything. That, as we all know, doesn't mean a thing with dogs. They eat anything, and they eat it fast. We're waiting for blood test results.'

Luke pointed to the drip. 'What's that?'

'Just saline. We need to keep him hydrated, but we can't treat him until we know what's wrong. If we treat him for Xylitol poisoning, we could do more harm than good if it isn't that.'

'Have you heard any reports from the other vets you contacted?'

'Not a thing.'

'I'm going down to Bakewell again tomorrow. Ray Charlton rang about an hour ago to see if I wanted to go with him. There'll be a member of the tech team with him who has a long-distance camera, should pick things up much more clearly than our camera phones. The ice-cream man is due in so I think he said a female officer will be with him, because he will arrest him if they get proof it is him who's throwing this chewing gum about.'

The little dog gave a brief moan, and Maria stroked his head again. 'Sssh,' she said, 'we'll know what's wrong soon.'

'Is he in pain?'

'Hopefully not,' Trefor said. 'Again it's knowing the right balance, and while we can't treat the problem yet, we can manage his pain.'

'Does the owner know?'

'She does. But she's with the whole family in Greece, so can't get back. She's authorised us to do whatever is necessary, but then broke down in tears and said just save him. It's not as easy as that. If this is Xylitol poisoning and they manage to survive it, it leaves them with long-term health problems like liver damage, difficulty with mobility, things that can't be resolved. Why on earth anybody would want to inflict this sort of damage on a dog, I have no idea.'

'I imagine that's pretty much how the police are feeling at the moment. There doesn't seem to be any logic behind the killing of the three women, no motive, precious few clues, and even when they get to court, sometimes the perpetrators still haven't said why. If this does prove to be the ice-cream man, or the lad on the bike, let's hope we get some answers.'

'The lad on the bike?' Trefor looked round from checking the fluid drip.

'Yes, he kind of took my eye, but I thought after that I was probably stereotyping him because he looked to be about thirteen or fourteen, and on a bike, ergo up to no good. I took a lot of photos of him, but he did nothing wrong and eventually rode off. He was at the side of the ice-cream van for ages though.'

Luke leaned down to stroke the dog. 'Come on, pal. You can do this. We're all rooting for you.' The dog didn't respond, and Luke stepped back. He looked at Maria. 'You'll let me know...?'

'I will. I may be late tonight.'

'Okay. I'll walk back down to meet you, so don't set off on your own. Promise?'

'Promise.'

Vinnie Wainwright waited until his dad set off for the pub, then slipped outside to the shed to get his bike. He had things to do, and he didn't want folks knowing about it, especially his dad. It hurt when he walloped him.

He put a knife and a screwdriver into his small backpack, shuffled it onto his back and walked the bike round the side of the house and onto the road outside. He'd hung around long enough in Bakewell Park on Sunday to follow the ice-cream van home, and he knew exactly where he was going. He'd wanted to go the night before, but his bloody dad hadn't gone to the pub, he'd watched the match on the telly instead. So, tonight was the night.

Vinnie mounted the bike and rode off into the dark.

Fifteen minutes later he saw the van, parked where he had last seen it, on a drive down the side of a house. He rode a little further on until he saw the bush he had seen on Sunday, and pushed the bike as far in as he could get it, then he jogged back to the van.

He slipped the bag off, took out both the knife and the screwdriver, and jabbed at the front tyre with the knife first. He'd not been sure which implement would be most effective. The knife did it. He could hear the air gushing out. He slipped the screwdriver back in his bag and stabbed once more with the knife. He stood up to move around to the other front tyre when suddenly the piercing sound of the van alarm stopped his breath. The movement of the tyre collapsing had triggered the alarm, and Vinnie grabbed the knife and the bag and ran.

He reached home twenty minutes later, the house still empty, and a huge grin on his face. Part one of his plan completed.

27

Luke heard his phone ping, read the message that said **I'm coming home** and set off immediately to walk down to the village centre. Everywhere was deserted, and it occurred to him that a combination of murder and coronavirus was all that was needed for quiet streets. He saw nobody on the five-minute walk, and Maria was waiting outside the vets when he arrived.

His heart lurched when he saw Maria's face. 'He didn't make it?'

'No, we battled all afternoon. We had the blood test results back and it was Xylitol, but he was too badly affected. He went peacefully, not in pain, but his owner is devastated. As is the dog sitter, who's already said she'll never take any dogs in her care into Bakewell Park again.' She wiped away a tear. 'It's been a rubbish day...'

He tilted her head and kissed her. 'You wouldn't be you if you didn't feel like this. These animals are your life, and I love you for that. Come on, let's go home and talk, try to make you feel a little better.'

She nodded and slipped her hand in his.

· · ·

Fred and Naomi were on their own. Rosie and Imogen had gone to Rosie's room to watch television, and Geraldine had asked Naomi to ferry her to bingo, as she expected it to be closed down shortly. 'This bloody virus thing,' she had grumbled, 'it's even affecting my bingo now!' Naomi had laughed and driven her down; as a result it was quiet in the lounge of the Taylor home.

Fred was, quite unsuccessfully, working on a crossword, and Naomi was reading. He glanced at his watch. 'What time does Geraldine need picking up?'

'She doesn't. She's texted to say her friend has turned up, so she's got a lift home.'

'You reckon she'll be okay looking after the girls Sunday afternoon?'

'No problem. Why?'

'We've been invited out for pizza and crisps, and to watch Manchester United on the TV.'

'We have? If I'd known my life was going to be this exciting, Fred Iveson, I'd have stalked you six months ago.'

He laughed. 'You should have. Ethan asked his dad to invite us. Just one rule – it's Manchester United, not Man U.'

'Then I can't wait. Do I need to take anything?'

'You could bake a cake, or some scones or something. That would be good. I like your cakes. What's a seven-letter word for a drop in blood pressure?'

'Anything in it?'

'It ends with E.'

'Syncope.'

'Smart arse. Why would anybody know that?'

'I read dictionaries,' she said, returning to her book.

Kat Heaton leaned her large stomach over the back of the sofa and kissed her husband on the top of his head. 'I'm taking

Martha up now, and going to read her *Bear Hunt*. Again. Then I'm going to bed, it's been a long day.'

'I'll be following you shortly. Before you go, just look at these pictures. Spot the difference?'

Carl placed the two A4 sheets of paper side by side, and waited.

'It's Woodlands. In the woods. Shutters open on first one in the upstairs room, and closed on the second one.'

'Ten out of ten. You want a job?'

'No thanks. So what's the issue?'

'Faith Young took the picture of the house with the shutters open as she walked up through the woods, and virtually from the bottom of the hill. The second one was taken around ten to fifteen minutes later from the spot where we believe she was abducted.'

'So the killer was waiting for her? Looking out for her?'

'We thought it was a possibility, but these pictures prove it.'

'Well don't stay up too late thinking about it, there's nothing you can do tonight. Martha, give Daddy a kiss, and let's go on a bear hunt.'

Carl smiled as he heard his two favourite girls clomp upstairs, both saying the all-too-familiar words *we're going on a bear hunt, we're not scared...*

He gathered up the pictures he'd been going through, and slipped them in his folder. Time to stop thinking for tonight. He walked around the house checking everything was secure, made two hot chocolates before switching off the lights, and headed upstairs. He met Kat as she came out of Martha's room and waved the mugs at her. 'Our treat for tonight,' he said.

'It's more of a treat that we're actually in bed together, after heading there at the same time.' She laughed.

· · ·

Just before three, when the night was so black it was like thick treacle, Joel and Beth shuffled wearily from the plane and headed for baggage reclaim. They didn't have long to wait, and walked outside to an icy blast of air, fuelled by raindrops.

'Bloody hell,' Joel said, 'that's a bit of a shock. Come on, can you run and drag that suitcase that cost us an extra fifty dollars to bring through customs, Mrs Masters?'

'You're not used to calling me that yet then?'

'I'm still trying to believe we did it.'

They ran across the road to airport parking, and quickly found Joel's car. He pretended to groan as he lifted Beth's suitcase into the back, and she grinned. 'I married a proper wimp, didn't I?'

'We'll see if you're still saying that when I let you lift it back out.'

They sat quietly for a moment while they waited for the windscreen to clear. 'They're all going to be surprised to see us, but I daren't risk staying there any longer and being stuck in some mind-blowing lockdown situation in the States.'

'I fully understand,' Beth said, 'and let's face it, we have enough wonderful memories of our time there to last us a lifetime. We'll go back, maybe for our first anniversary, surely they'll have sorted this Covid thing out by then.'

He shrugged. 'Who knows. It can take years to produce a vaccine. I think staying in this country for the foreseeable future is definitely on the cards. You're not going to the office tomorrow, are you?'

'I'll see how I feel when we wake up. May leave it till... Thursday? Are we on Wednesday now?'

Joel laughed. 'We are. And I can only say that with confidence because I worked it out while we were on the plane, trying to decide when I would go back into work.'

'Okay decision made. When I wake up tomorrow... today...

I'll give Tessa a call and tell her we're back, make sure they've not blown up the place or anything, and I'll go back on Thursday.'

'Good plan, Mrs Masters. You going to mention the name change?'

'Might do.'

'Should do.'

'Why?'

'Because I want everybody to know we did it. We got married! We must remember to cancel Kat though. Don't want the celebrant turning up at church in April, and we've already done the deed. And we need to organise a big party to celebrate our foreign nuptials, yes?'

'Let's wait and see what Mr Johnson says first.'

Joel nodded, put the car into drive, and began the long journey back to Bradwell. He'd never felt happier than he did at that moment, and knew beyond any doubt that Doris would have approved of what they had done.

Tessa hugged Hannah's pyjamas to her, and chewed on the end of the pencil. She had bought a notebook that declared Muggles Keep Out, and she was sketching the changes she wanted to make in her cottage, when she finally took possession of it. She intended knocking down a wall to give her an open-plan kitchen and diner instead of the two separate rooms it currently had, but she felt torn between getting the shiny white kitchen she craved, or going for a more cottagey feel, and preserving the history of the place.

Apart from decorating, the lounge was perfect. The previous owners had installed a log burner, and it appeared to be a fairly recent addition. She would need a chimney sweep – or a very small child to nip up to the top with a sweeping brush. She wrote chimney sweep on her to do list.

Her thoughts drifted towards Little Mouse Cottage, and the serenity and peace Doris had managed to weave into the very walls of the place and knew that was what she wanted, her ultimate aim for what she knew would be her forever home. And Doris hadn't opted for a white kitchen...

You want a white kitchen, you get a white kitchen. It was almost as if Hannah was in the room with her, and Tessa turned her head round. Nothing. But the words had been so clear, and while she recognised they were only in her head, she also acknowledged that Hannah would have said them if she had been there.

'Thanks, lovely,' she murmured, and left the words white kitchen on the list.

Her thoughts drifted to all the changes that seemed to be happening at Connection and wondered what the next few weeks would bring. Fred moving in with Naomi was good, and not only for him. Naomi's family would benefit from having him in their lives; even Luke seemed to have come round to the situation.

Luke and Maria seemed settled and happy, Joel and Beth would take time to adjust to a world without Doris, and even Simon, although quiet, had taken to life at Connection in a positive way. He seemed to get on well with Luke in particular, and it seemed Beth was happy that she had chosen him to add to their team. But they needed her back. Beth was their captain, whether she realised it or not. Just a few more days and they would be flying home, and that caused a feeling of relief.

She put the notebook down, switched off the iPad and picked up her Kindle. *Just one more chapter*, she thought, and was asleep within minutes, the Kindle laid on the bed at the side of her.

. . .

And slowly the NHS filled up its hospital beds, plans were made to open Nightingale Hospitals to take the overflow patients, and everybody asked where the extra staff would come from to man them. Daily Covid reports were on television, with a Prime Minister saying it was okay to shake hands as long as you washed them whilst singing happy birthday to you, and masks wouldn't be mandatory.

But that night, that St Patrick's Day like no other, the team from Connection slumbered on, unaware of the changes that would happen in the very near future. With a complete lockdown only days away, with a village with a largely elderly population already repeating history and locking themselves inside their homes without waiting for the government to get its head in gear and issue the command, the young and the old did what they knew they had to do. They prepared.

Eyam had done it once in 1665, and it would rise once more to face similar issues, albeit three hundred and fifty-five years later.

28

Luke felt a sense of relief when he woke to sunshine. They needed good weather to entice the mums and children into the park, to get the ice-cream van there, and to observe his actions.

His conversation with Ray the previous evening had led to an agreement for Luke to go in his own car, and act in exactly the same way as he had the previous Sunday, sketching and surveillance. He loaded up the car, dropped Maria off at the vets and headed over to Bakewell.

He knew he was early, so didn't go directly to the recreation ground following the side of the river, but walked through the town centre. He collected a takeaway coffee and a bacon sandwich, then set up camp a little nearer to where the van had parked three days earlier. The cordon had been removed the night before, opening up the entire area once again, and already there were dog walkers everywhere. The grass was immaculate, a credit to the groundsmen, and he made himself comfortable. The sun was out but it wasn't very warm with quite a cool breeze blowing.

He saw Ray about fifteen minutes later, sitting on a bench

with a woman by his side who Luke assumed was a police officer. They were chatting, and Luke acknowledged he had seen them with a slight nod. Two benches away was a man with an impressive-looking camera around his neck; Luke guessed he was the forensic cameraman.

Luke sketched quickly, getting down the main layers of his drawing before adding shading and definition. He became immersed in the scene, and felt as though his heart had stopped when he heard a voice behind him.

'Saw you t'other day.'

Luke pivoted his head and saw the bike before the owner.

'Yeah?'

'Yeah. With your girlfriend. She not here today?'

'No, she's at work.'

'It's good that drawing.'

'Thanks. Do you draw?'

'A bit. Not got a proper sketchpad like that though. I draw on cardboard, cornflake boxes and stuff. I like cartoon strip drawing. I've got felt tips. Found 'em in here, somebody had left them.'

'What's your name?'

'Vinnie. Why?'

'No reason. You not at school then?'

'Going this afternoon.'

Luke nodded. 'Supposed to go every day, in a morning, aren't you?'

Vinnie shrugged. 'Come in here on a Wednesday and make sure he sees me.'

'Who?'

'Ice-cream man. He killed my dog. He sees me and he knows I know. He'll be late this morning.'

'He will?'

'Yep.' He swung his leg over his bike. 'I slashed his front tyre last night,' he said as he rode off.

Luke took out his phone and texted a garbled message to Ray, giving him details of the conversation with the young boy, then sat back and waited to see what Ray would do.

Ray looked at his phone and relayed Luke's message to Janet Grayson, who shielded her eyes as she looked around to see if they could still see Vinnie. He had disappeared.

'If this bloody ice-cream van isn't here by one, we'll call it a day. Best laid plans and all that. You agree?'

Janet nodded.

Luke carried on sketching, detailing the stone wall. He was immersed in it but spotted the return of the bike. Vinnie jumped off, took a small folding stool out of his backpack and sat down beside Luke.

'Okay if I watch for a bit?'

'You can, 'course you can, but I'm no expert.'

Vinnie fished around in his bag again. 'This is what I do.'

He handed Luke a small piece cut from a Cornflakes box – the drawing was manga, and Luke stared at it. 'This copied, or from your head?'

'I started out by copying, so I could get it right, but now it's from my head. I was working on that one last night. I've a mate at school who saw mine, and he does it now as well. Nipped home to get it so I could show you.'

Luke reached into his backpack and took out the sketchpad Maria had attempted to draw in the previous Sunday. He carefully removed her sketch, and handed the pad to Vinnie. 'Here, I've a spare one. Want it?'

It was clear the lad didn't know what to say, so Luke thrust it towards him. 'It's okay, take it. I brought it for my girlfriend to have a go, but it's not for her, so I'm more than happy to give it to a fellow artist. And don't let anybody ever knock you for drawing, this is brilliant.' He waved the small piece of cardboard.

'Tell you what, we'll swap. You have my picture, I'll have your sketch book. That okay?'

'You sure? Maria's gonna love this.'

They looked up at the sound of an engine, and the ice-cream van pulled on to the pathway. It stopped in the same place it had been on Sunday, and they both stared at it.

'You want to fetch us an ice cream? I'll watch your bike,' Luke said, aware he was testing the waters with the lad. If he had indeed slashed a tyre on the van, there was clearly no love lost between him and the ice-cream man.

'Not likely. I'll wait here if you want to go and get one, but I'll never have one from him again. He killed my dog.'

'So you said earlier. What do you mean? He ran over him?'

'No, at least that would have been quick. I had a smallish cross breed, bit of staff, bit of Jack Russell, called him Shandy. My dad brought him home one day, his mate didn't want him anymore, so Dad said as long as I looked after him, paid for his food, I could have him. I got a paper round to buy his food, and he stayed. He didn't like this feller though, the one in the ice-cream van. Snapped at his ankles one day, and he kicked him. Shandy was laid on the grass whimpering, so I stayed with him and stroked him until he recovered a bit, then the man came over with a dish of ice cream for him. "This'll make him feel better," he said.'

Vinnie gazed into the distance, clearly remembering every second. 'That night he started to shake, and be sick, then went into a sort of collapse. Dad wouldn't let me take him to a vet, said it cost too much money, and I had to watch Shandy die. He died next morning. I know it was something he put in that ice cream, that evil bastard. I buried Shandy in a black plastic bag, in the back garden.'

'When was this?'

'Last September. Just before we started back at school.'

'You said you slashed his tyre...'

Vinnie smiled. 'Don't go blabbing that out. I went to do both front ones, but after I did the first one it set off the van alarm, so I legged it. That's why he's late this morning. I've been putting dog shit through his letterbox, broke the windscreen wipers on the van... he'll wish he'd never hurt my Shandy.'

Luke handed him a pencil and a rubber. 'Draw him. Draw Shandy for me.'

Luke sent a quick text to Ray saying not to approach him, he was information gathering, at the same time telling Vinnie he was texting Maria. Seeing the cameraman stand up and move towards the van, Luke tracked his movements as he walked across the green. The ice-cream man was outside his van having a cigarette, and the cameraman was snapping pictures of the stone wall that surrounded the entire park. With the camera switched to video mode, he swung it around, following his target as he moved towards the waste bin, casually dropping things as he walked.

The cameraman, who turned out to be called Dave, spoke into a collar microphone, and Ray and Janet stood.

'Look, Vinnie, you up for a secret?'

Vinnie looked at Luke, a frown on his face. 'Might be.'

'Don't kick off or take off, and you're in absolutely no bother about slashing tyres or anything else you may have done, but I think you're about to get justice for Shandy. My name's Luke Taylor, and I'm a partner in the Connection Detective Agency as well as being a very amateur artist. I believe our ice-cream vendor is about to be arrested for poisoning dogs. How's that sound?'

Vinnie sat immobile. 'That straight up?'

'It is. I couldn't tell you before anything happened, but now it seems it is. I can't force you, but I'm asking you to stay with me, because I think DS Charlton may need a statement about what happened to Shandy. Do the right thing by your little dog, and let's enjoy this next bit. Okay?'

'Bloody hell,' Vinnie said, his eyes huge. 'I hope they hang him.'

It was over very quickly. Monty Latham was arrested on suspicion of killing dogs by poison, and Ray took Vinnie's statement with Luke acting as responsible adult. He said nothing about the tyre or the windscreen wipers, simply told the story of his little dog who had first been kicked, then fed a bowl of ice cream, then died within hours.

Ray and Janet returned to the station to question and charge Latham, but Luke stayed on in Bakewell for a while. Police activity supported by Hugh Ellerman was an evidence-gathering exercise, and once again small squares and sticks of chewing gum were removed from the scene, and bagged for forensic testing.

Luke and Vinnie stayed to watch the unfolding activities, until Luke asked him if he wanted some lunch. They found a sandwich shop, bought three different assorted ones because they couldn't decide which they fancied the most, two cans of Coke and headed for the river.

'This is mag,' Vinnie said. 'Dad needs all his money for the pub, so if I have a sandwich I make it myself, and it never has prawns on it.'

Luke laughed. 'Then make the most of it. Delicious, isn't it. My favourite sandwich.' He handed Vinnie his business card. 'Look, if you ever need any help, or just want a chat if something's bothering you, this is me. I had you down as a suspect last Sunday, but that was only because you're a teenager on a bike. I'm sorry about that. I shouldn't have judged you. Keep up with the drawing, and I'm going to frame this little manga and give it to Maria tonight. She'll absolutely love it, and I'll get brownie points for doing it. Would your dad let you have another dog, or was that a one-off?'

'Probably a one-off 'cos it was his mate's dog.' He shrugged. 'One day I'll have left home, and then I'll get another.'

'Then no more days off school. Get a good job, you don't need a father who treats you like shit.'

Vinnie took a second sandwich, then stared at him. 'You had the same?'

'Walked out when I was eight. A couple of birthday cards over the years and that's been it. Mum's recently met a new feller who means more to me in the short time I've known him than my real father ever did. If they don't treat you right, they're not proper dads. Okay?'

Vinnie held up his thumb, unable to speak for the ham salad sandwich in his mouth.

'And I heard DS Charlton say you might have to give evidence in court if Latham doesn't plead guilty. I'd like to go with you, if that happens. I think you have to tell your dad what's happened today, to cover your back if the police turn up at your address, but play it down, say you gave a statement and that's it. I honestly think he'll plead guilty, we have him on video scattering the gum. Then it's all over.'

'Thanks, Luke. And thanks for lunch. I've got to go now to make afternoon registration, it's art today and I'm not missing that. It's been a banging morning.' He stood and put his backpack on his shoulders, then climbed on his bike.

'We'll keep in touch?'

Luke nodded. 'We will. I've got your number now, and I'll let you know next time we're in the park. Take care, Vinnie.'

29

Carl finished the briefing and his meeting with senior officers, then headed to the tea rooms. Amanda welcomed him with a smile, and gave him a corner table. 'It'll be quieter here,' she said, 'a bit further away from Stefan and his hammer.'

'How's it going?'

'He's tentatively suggesting one week, then done. We're all keeping our fingers crossed, believe me. Now, what can I get you?'

'Pot of tea, and a cherry scone, please.'

'Jam and cream?'

'Naturally. I could do with a chat as well if you can spare five minutes.'

'No problem. We're not busy.'

She went to prepare his order, and he sat looking out of the window, staring at the spot where Aileen Chatterton had been so brutally attacked. She had been such a lovely girl, always polite, helpful, and hadn't moaned at all at pulling the overnight protection of the crime scene.

Amanda carried over his order, and pulled out a chair. 'Okay, what do you want to know?'

'I have absolutely no idea.' He sighed. 'Somebody must have seen something, if not that day, then some other day. We believe whoever the killer is was planning this for some time, and must have been around this area, because you're bang opposite the entrance to the beginning of that steep climb up into the woods.'

'I do see people using that path, of course I do, but they're mainly people who live here in Eyam.'

'And what if the killer is somebody who lives in Eyam?'

He watched her eyes widen. 'You're serious?'

He nodded. 'I want you to think about it. If anything occurs to you. Please get in touch.' He handed her his card and she slipped it into her top pocket.

He finished his scone and drink and sat for a moment deep in thought, before crossing the road and through the opening leading to the path. It was looking much more trampled than it had been two weeks earlier, and he walked a few yards in, waiting for the first time he could see the view of the house that Faith had seen when she had taken that first picture.

He took out his own phone and snapped it when he judged he was in the right place, then checked his watch before beginning the climb up the hill. He didn't rush; he knew Faith was on a research trip and would have been absorbing the scene, not dashing up the hill to get out of the rain.

Carl reached the point from where she had to have taken the second picture, and he paused, unknowingly leaning against the same tree Faith had rested against.

He snapped the second picture, noticing that the shutters were open with smoke rising from the chimney. There was now a definite pathway leading across to Woodlands, and he trekked across to see how Brian Aylward was holding up. The sun was flickering intermittently in and out, cloud cover ruling out the potential of a full day of sun, but the walk across to the house was a pleasant one.

Brian was outside on the back patio, sitting on a folding chair. He held a mug of tea in his hand, and waved it at Carl. 'Want one?'

'No thanks, Brian. I've had one at the tea rooms. I'm just walking the route Faith Young would have taken, then I'm going up towards the one your wife took. Don't ask me why because I've no idea. I needed to do it on my own, seeing it as they would have seen it before they were attacked. How are the kids?'

'They're okay. In shock, but I've persuaded them to go back to school until the funeral. With the ongoing investigation I thought it was best they weren't here. The school has been brilliant, as have their friends, so that's about the only thing that's right at the moment. I can't tell you how much I miss her, my Ella. We've been together since we were kids really, we were still at school, and it's so hard without her.'

Carl nodded, and looked around. 'You got another of those chairs?'

'In the shed.'

'I've time for a cuppa if that's okay.'

Brian put his own mug on the upturned plant pot he'd been using as a coffee table, and stood. 'No problem.' He handed him a small sweeping brush. 'Best brush it down to get rid of any spiders though.'

The two men sat, aware that when the sun did manage to evade a cloud it was warm. And pleasant.

Brian took out a cigarette and offered the pack to Carl, who shook his head. 'No thanks. Never done it. Tried it once and I choked on the smoke, so decided there and then it wasn't for me.'

'I'd stopped. Been stopped five years now, but I walked down to the Co-op for some milk and bread, and came back with cigarettes as well. It's been so easy to slip back into it. Have you brought me any good news at all?'

'Not really. The team have completed what I think of as the grunt work, going door to door interviewing the entire village. All the reports are being added to the database as we speak so the next job is to go through them all, glean anything different from them, then do any revisits that might crop up from the reports. I'm expecting forensics to have completed any checks on Faith Young's car today, so there'll be that report to go through, but nobody seems to have seen anything.'

'There's a lot of them isolating in the village, so I understand. This virus is keeping them indoors. I suppose it's good for killers.'

Carl smiled. 'That's an odd way of looking at it, but you're right. If you walk through the village at night, it's deserted. The pubs are almost empty, just the die-hard drinkers in there, and they'll soon get fed up with the miserable atmosphere.'

'Think Johnson will close it all down?'

'I don't think he'll have a choice. The hospitals are already bursting at the seams, he'll have to try to contain it somehow, and only a complete lockdown will do that. God knows how I'll do my job then. I'll be interviewing people while standing in their front gardens talking through the window to them.'

They sipped at their drinks and eventually Carl stood. 'I'm going up towards where Ella started her run, then following it through as far as where the second set of dogs found traces of blood. Then I'll head back up towards the church hall, and computer land. I'm hoping results will be filtering in by then, after all this work. One thing I do believe is that the killer was in this house until he saw Faith Young at the bottom of the hill. Then he left to be in place for where he guessed she might pause, on that levelling out section. She did, and that was her fate sealed. If she hadn't stopped there, he would simply have followed her until she did stop.'

'And he carried her? All the way up the woods to that shed? He's not a weakling then, is he? With Ella he would have been close to a car, she wasn't too far from a road, but with the author lady he had a heck of a trek with her, always running the risk of meeting up with somebody. Or did he bring her here? He could have done, surely, then brought a car down into the courtyard to transport her body to where it was found.'

'I'd also considered that, and when we find him, it'll be the first thing I ask. I could always see how he would transport Ella, but Faith wasn't near the road. There is also the possibility that he made her walk if she wasn't unconscious. She was killed in the shed, not out here. And motive is absolutely absent as far as I can see. I'll keep in touch, Brian, and I'm always at the end of a phone if you need to talk, or ask anything.'

Carl left Brian lighting up another cigarette, and climbed the short pathway to where Ella began her run. He walked as far as the point where the dogs had found the blood that had been hidden by the winter leaves carefully scraped over it, but he felt nothing. He looked around, then continued with his own journey up to the road and back to the church hall.

Carl walked around having a few words with everyone who was tapping away inputting the data collected from the door-to-door visits, relishing the warmth of the building.

He eventually wandered over to his own desk, a plate with an iced bun on it in his hand, and sat down. He opened his emails and swiftly scanned them all, opening up the one from the forensic team.

He quickly read through it, then repeated the process a little more slowly.

He saw Ray at the far side of the room, and waved him over. He stood to let his new DS sit down, and Ray repeated Carl's actions of double-reading the email.

'Shit,' he said. 'What does this mean?'

'It means that Faith must have known her killer. They've eliminated all fingerprints – only hers and Jack Young's were present, with three fingers and a partial palm print found on the door handle the exception.'

'And they're not on our database,' Ray said thoughtfully, 'but they do match fingerprints taken from the bedroom at Woodlands, fingerprints presumed to belong to the stranger who was squatting there as they didn't belong to either of the Aylwards.'

'That's right. This confirms that the killer was in Faith's Aygo, and also in that bedroom.' He sat back. 'Unfortunately we have no idea who he is.'

Ray stood, allowing Carl to retake his seat, then went to fetch a chair. 'Let's talk it through and see what we can do about this. This is a massive step, the most information we've had really. I can remember a case years ago where they asked the entire male population of a village to have fingerprints taken for elimination purposes. I can't remember what case it was, or even if it did any good. Is that a possibility?'

'It might have been if we hadn't been on the verge of having the entire country shut down. It takes time to organise something like that, and I don't think we have time. Look, we have the knowledge of the prints now. I don't want to call a halt to the massive amount of work going on in this hall because we need it completing as soon as possible, but I want everybody back in here for eight tomorrow morning for a briefing, before the church ladies come in. Can you let everybody know? In the meantime, keep those brain cells moving. Let's work out what this means.'

. . .

Carl rang Tessa as he was driving home.

'Hi, Carl. Everything okay?'

'Kind of. You feeling any better?'

'If I don't breathe, I'm good. You need something?'

'Not really, I wanted to thank you for jolting me into getting Faith Young's car forensically examined. It's kind of come up trumps. It seems there's a set of prints on the door handle that aren't on our database, so we can't ID them, but the same prints were in that bedroom at Woodlands. I'm briefing everyone in the morning, didn't want anything to distract them from getting all these interviews logged on, but I'm feeling as though we're battling against time. Or is that only me? I think next week we'll be in total lockdown, and I don't know where that leaves us.'

'I agree. I'm hoping Joel and Beth manage to get back from Florida, we need to have a meeting to discuss what we do. I don't want to disturb them by asking when they're due back, but I'm praying they're seeing the British news while they're over there. But it's good news that the forensic team found something in the car. When you do find the killer it'll help put him away for life.'

30

Luke leaned over the back of the sofa where Maria was sitting, her legs curled under her, reading her Kindle. He picked up the empty plate and juice glass she had used for her breakfast, and handed her a wrapped gift.

'This isn't really from me, it's from Vinnie, the young lad who's going to be instrumental in keeping the dogs safe in Bakewell Park. I swapped it for your sketch book. I was actually giving him the sketch book anyway, but he insisted I have this, so I've framed it for you.'

Maria put down the Kindle and took the little package from him. 'It's for me?'

'You'll love it as much as I do.'

She tugged at the string surrounding it, and removed the paper. She stared at the framed picture, then looked up. 'That's awesome. Did he copy it?'

'No. He started out by copying, said it gave him a feel for them, but he draws his own now. I've had a message from Ray Charlton to say Latham admitted to deliberately harming the dogs, said it was because a German shepherd had bitten him, and made a mess of his leg. He's now banned from Bakewell

Park, him and his van. That means Vinnie won't have to attend court, which is good. I'll finalise our bill later, and have a walk across with it.'

The early morning briefing in the church hall was interesting if unproductive. Carl explained about the prints that had been found which were a definite link between the squatter and Faith Young, he congratulated all of them on the excellent way they had covered the entire village and the mammoth input-of-data day. When he asked for thoughts, there was silence.

It made him smile. He had had exactly the same reaction from Tessa Marsden, and also Kat the previous evening. There was literally nothing to say about the valuable fingerprint information, and he dismissed them all by saying they were all rubbish if they couldn't work out the name of the killer from the information he had just given them. Somebody called out that it was Professor Plum in the library with a hammer, and the meeting broke up.

Carl returned to his desk and brought up the door-to-door results on screen. His mind wasn't on them, it kept drifting to the words *he doesn't have an alibi for Monday,* with reference to Jack Young. Surely the first thing a killer would do would be to sort out an alibi? And it didn't really make sense that he would kill three women – or maybe this was his way of steering the investigation away from him having killed his wife. Kill two more unrelated females, and attention is diverted from the husband?

Carl was missing something, something he needed to take back to the beginning and look at again.

.   .   .

The call from the tech team was unusual. Communication from them was always via email, and Carl answered with a flutter of hope.

'DI Heaton? I'm sending you an email that contains a large file. This is the new book that Faith Young was writing. I finished going through her emails and other messages, found nothing that merited further checks, and just because the book was on the laptop and I'm a fan, I decided to treat myself to reading the first chapter. The first strange thing is it was passworded, but I've removed that now. The rest of her stuff wasn't passworded. There's a sort of notation at the end of the first chapter I think you should see, and you may need to check the rest of the manuscript out. It's disturbing.'

'Thanks, Pete. Send it now.'

He waited until the email arrived, then opened it.

Ray Charlton appeared at his elbow. 'I've got to go for a bit, boss. Latham's in court at eleven, and we're hoping to keep him locked up. He'll be a danger to dogs if they let him out on bail, so I need to go and plead our case, tell them what he did. I'm hoping the magistrate is a dog-lover.'

'That's fine, Ray. Good luck with it, hope you get a woman magistrate. They're always soft about dogs.'

'You doing anything interesting?' Ray could see the writing on the screen.

'Reading a book.'

Ray paused for a moment. 'That's good. The Bible, is it?'

'Had a phone call from Pete in tech. They've checked Faith Young's laptop and it's clean. Nothing helpful at all. He's a bit of a fan of her books, so decided to read the first chapter of her new one, because I think he knows it will never be published unless Marianne can work miracles with it. Apparently there's some sort of notation at the end of chapter one, and if that does say anything to concern me, I'm going to have to read through the rest to find what she's trying to tell us. Why would she put a password on the manuscript, when there was no password to keep you out of anything else?'

'She's written something she doesn't want Jack to see? Surely he's the only one who would have access to her computer?'

'My thoughts exactly. So it's pipe and slippers and armchair time for me, I love a good book. Go and do your court stuff, and hopefully we'll have something enlightening when you come back.'

The working title for the new manuscript was Eyam Book, and it made Carl smile. He hoped the real title would have been more inspirational.

He read the first chapter carefully, noting that she had spelt acknowledge as acknowlege, and reached the end. There was a small section typed in italics. He highlighted it, copied and pasted it to a Word document, then reread it. Even at this early stage he felt this was important.

I know something's going on. He's seeing somebody else. I'm not emotionally bothered, but I'm not giving him half my earnings in any divorce. How do I tackle this? Follow him? Get a private investigator to follow him? Who the hell is she? I could always kill her. I know a million ways. Fuck you, Jack Young.

So Jack Young was indeed a man of mystery. Carl had felt it when the man's alibi was so airy-fairy, no real alibi, simply pottering around the house, watching television, doing admin stuff for Faith. Or seeing another woman? Cat being away and mouse playing sprang into Carl's mind.

The story was good, and already he was hooked and wanting to know more. He would have liked to have met this woman, spoken to her, got a glimpse into the mind that could produce twisted endings, flowing narrative and characters who would live inside you for a long time.

He strolled over to get a coffee, and walked around for a few moments geeing on the troops. They were all reading the reports, and he had told them not to read the ones they had personally taken, but to read through everybody else's. At the end of it he wanted a list of everybody who didn't have an alibi for Monday afternoon.

Chapter two carried the story further, and he knew that when Marianne Kingston got her eyes on this, she would move heaven and earth to have it as a full manuscript, and because of the tragic circumstances surrounding it and it having to be finished by someone else, it would become a best seller.

At the end of chapter two was a second italic notation.

Am I being paranoid? He went out last night, said he was meeting a golfing friend at the pub, and he wouldn't be late. He wasn't! He was home for nine. If he is seeing somebody else, does this suggest she's married as well? Or was he telling the truth?

Carl once again copied and pasted the section, then sat back to think. She was clearly using her manuscript chapter endings as some sort of diary to let out her feelings, and was a tormented woman. He was getting the impression she didn't love her husband, but wasn't prepared to let him go. The personal nature of her italicised endings made the password protection much clearer; she didn't want anybody else, especially Jack Young, reading her thoughts. Was she scared of him? Afraid he would do her harm?

There was nothing at the end of chapter three but chapter four revealed more of her feelings.

He's booked a weekend away. A golfing break with Giles and Tony, he says. Well, two can play at that game, Jack Young. I can take the weekend off as well, and believe me, I won't be on my own.

Carl saved it, and reread it. Had she made good on her threat, and who with?

He carried on reading the book, becoming immersed in the storyline despite him telling himself he mustn't do that, but he had no choice other than to read it. For the first time he felt he was seeing the real Faith Young, the one who used words to control or vent her emotions, and he knew he needed to pick up on any tiny out of place comment, especially if it was italicised.

His one wish was that he could tie in the author's written words to a date, but he wasn't that smart. He stuck to chapter numbers to tell him where the copy and pasted pieces could be located. It was chapter eight when he began to feel uneasy.

All at once I don't care what Jack is doing. My number one fan has made me happy. How soon can I get to spend more time with him? What a joy it is to talk to him, and now I have seen him I know I will have decisions to make. Eyam, my beautiful book location, no longer seems so far away. And neither does he.

Had Faith being dicing with death from this point onwards? And who the hell was her number one fan?

Carl was trying to guess who the fictional killer was as the book progressed, and Faith had written her last words in chapter twenty-six, but her last comment had been at the end of chapter twenty-five.

Will I really see him this weekend? Will I? I'm sure as sure that Jack has somebody else, but does it matter? He can go. I feel so happy at what is to come next, but full of trepidation. I haven't slept with anyone else for many, many years, but my fan has said he is a patient man. When I am ready, I have only to let him know. Tomorrow I am travelling to Eyam, and the irony is that Jack has paid for the cottage. My love nest. I feel I know him so well, my fan. My number one fan.

Carl gave a huge sigh. Despite the security of the manuscript being passworded, she hadn't had the courage to name him. Carl was more convinced than ever that the killer lived in Eyam. Carl transferred the last section to the Word document, printed it, and sat studying it, rereading every one of the italicised sections created by Faith Young.

He was sure Marianne Kingston hadn't known about this fledgling affair of Faith's, or indeed about any affair that Jack Young might or might not be having, because she would have said.

Carl's undrunk coffee had gone cold, so he walked down the room towards where the ladies, still a presence amongst them, were washing pots and making fresh drinks. He collected another coffee after apologising for wasting the first one, and Nora remarked he seemed to have been deep in thought. 'We decided not to disturb you,' she said.

'Thank you, it was a difficult job. I'm going outside for a bit to clear my head.'

He took his cup and sat on the steps. He thought about this new direction the book was sending them in, and wondered what would come of it. Had she slept with this new man, or had things taken a much more sinister direction?

31

Latham was remanded into custody pending his full appearance, and Ray felt a happy man. He returned to Eyam with a smile on his face, and was handed the transcript of what Carl had gleaned from Faith Young's manuscript.

'This puts a different light on things, doesn't it? Am I correct in remembering she found the cottage, but Jack Young paid for it? We need to talk to Will Sandford, find out if he knows anything about how she came across his cottage. Was it a recommendation from somebody, somebody she was tentatively hedging towards spending a month with?'

'Let's have a walk there now, see if he's in.'

The two men arrived at Will Sandford's home, and had to knock twice before he answered. He looked bleary-eyed.

'Sorry, I'd nodded off. Could have sworn the knock on the door was in my dream...'

'No problem,' Carl said. 'Can we ask you a couple of questions, Will, to try to clear up something that's arisen from information we've received?'

'Sure. Come in. Drink?'

'No, we're good thanks. The ladies in the church take care of us very well.'

He led them into his lounge. Ray took out his notebook and waited for Carl to speak.

'When Faith Young booked the cottage did she happen to mention how she had come across it?'

Will closed his eyes, as he tried to remember. 'Don't think so. I advertise in quite a few places, so she could have seen it anywhere. She rang to see if it was free for a month, explained why she wanted it, then paid for it. I seem to remember it was her husband's card she used, not hers. She said she would be here on her own, and that was it. She rang the day before she arrived to confirm her arrival time, and I told her the cottage was ready for her. The next time I spoke to her was when she arrived at Leaf Cottage.'

'She was alone?'

'She was.'

'Did she have a visitor at any point over the Saturday or Sunday?'

'Not that I'm aware of. As I said before, she went shopping on the Saturday, and on the Sunday I gave her that map. Monday she disappeared. I wish I could be more help.'

The two officers stood up. 'Thanks anyway, Will, it was a bit of a long shot, but it's got it out of the way. We'll see ourselves out.'

The two officers returned to the church hall, the biting wind seemingly cutting through their clothes.

'Bloody cold,' Ray said. 'It was nice earlier, but it's freezing now. I don't like him.' His last few words came out abruptly, and Carl turned to him.

'Who? Will Sandford? Or are we back with this Latham feller?'

'Will Sandford. Too clever by half. Every time we've seen him or spoken with him, it's like he's laughing at us, at our... uselessness.'

'I think it's just his personality. I haven't known him long, haven't really known anybody else in the village for that long, because I'm definitely an incomer. It's a couple of years now since I moved in with Kat, and I met him for the first time in Connection. He was chatting to Doris, I believe. We spoke about the insularity of living in Eyam, and he said he'd lived here most of his life, and I'd many years to go before I could count myself as accepted. He seemed friendly enough.'

'He's not helped though. And he wasn't asleep. His cup of tea was still hot. He'd rubbed his eyes to make him look half asleep, I reckon. He didn't want to talk to us, clearly. I wonder why not?'

Carl laughed. 'Have we reached the stage where everybody's a killer? It could simply be that he's part of the majority of our population who wouldn't help the police, no matter what. It's maybe time to bring back torture.'

'Maybe. Time to stop being nice and polite to the riff-raff of this world. I'm all for it.'

'Well I reckon you'd be sick the first time you held an electric prong to somebody's balls.'

'You could be right.' Ray sounded disgruntled. 'Worth a try though.'

Carl banged on his desk, and everyone swivelled their chairs.

'Only need you for a minute. I'm sending round a few copies of some annotations made by Faith Young, at the end of certain chapters in the manuscript she was working on at the time of her death. They are in no way connected to the chapters, she appeared to be using this manuscript as a sort of way of keeping a diary, where she could put down her thoughts. She password protected it, and from the tone of the paragraphs I think you'll see why she did that. I want you all to have sight of this document, and if you have thoughts on any of it, come and talk to me.' He waved a sheaf of papers. 'There's twenty copies, so grab one when you can. Okay, on to the door-to-door reports. Has anything occurred to anyone, while you've been going through them?'

'Only that everybody seems to have seen the same dog walkers, going out and coming back. All of them are Eyam residents, no strangers.' The voice came from the back of the room.

'That was my impression as well.' Carl raised his voice to acknowledge the speaker. 'Okay, early night tonight, you've earned it. Go home at five, and unless DS Charlton's torture policy is put in place overnight, you don't need to be back here till half past eight. We'll have a briefing first, then back to these reports.'

Carl knew he was missing something. He felt he was concentrating too much on the Faith Young death and not enough on the other two victims, so he left his team to finish off, got in his car and drove around to Woodlands. He hoped that maybe a chat with Brian Aylward, not an official visit, may bring something out of the woodwork that wouldn't have appeared under normal circumstances.

The kitchen was warm, and the two men sat facing each other across the table, each nursing a coffee. A packet of custard creams lay between them, and Brian gave a rueful laugh. 'Ella would have gone mad, the biscuits should be on a plate, but I reckon we'll manage out of the packet, don't you?'

'Certainly do. But stop me after two, I've got a bit of an addiction to these and every so often Kat throws a wobbly and bans them, says they're not good for me. I'm not telling her I've had these. You're coping okay?'

'Hanging on by a thread is the term I'd use. I'd be better if the kids were with me, but I don't think it's right for them to be here. I speak to them every night and we've left them in school to try to keep some normality in their lives. They're going to Mum and Dad's for Easter, but I've reached some decisions about this place. I'm bringing the decorators in for inside and out, then it's going back on the market. We can't be here, it will always be a reminder of the awful way Ella left us, so it will be goodbye Eyam.'

'I'm sorry to hear that. But don't do anything in a rush, it's a big decision.'

Brian stared into his coffee. 'It's the not knowing. I could be saying hi to anyone in the street, and it could be the feller who killed my wife. You still have no leads?'

'Different avenues of investigation are opening up all the time. We will find him, I can promise you that, but as yet I can't say too much. One thing I can tell you is that my team have put a hundred per cent effort into this. I've told them all to go home at five today, but I know if I go back up to that hall at six, there'll still be officers there beavering away. They're currently working on the doorstep questionnaires, analysing them, making sure they check the ones the others did and not their own. It'll cost me a fortune in the pub when we solve this one, and it'll be worth every penny.'

'I keep going over and over what happened that morning, and it's killing me knowing I let her go off on her own. I could maybe understand some crazy fan bumping off Faith Young, somebody who'd maybe stalked her because she'd put something in a book he'd disagreed with, but Ella? She wouldn't have harmed anybody, and everybody loved her.' He paused. '*I* loved her, more than life itself. It's hard, Carl. Very hard.'

'I can understand you wanting to stay in the village, but maybe you'd be better in a B&B until we find him. You must feel very isolated out here, it's so cut off from the rest of the village. That, of course, is why it was so ideal for your unpaying guest to stay here unobserved. We do have his fingerprints by the way, and have matched them to prints taken from a different location, but unfortunately he's not on our system – a proper goody two shoes who's turned to murder. When we do catch him, we'll be able to prove it was him, but we can't do it in the normal way, prints equals identification.'

'You know, Carl, I've thought and thought about everyone we know, trying to remember if Ella – or me, for that matter – have ever upset anyone that could have escalated to this, and I can't. We're not that sort of couple. We have a family, we have good jobs where we work from home most of the time, our kids are at boarding school where they're happy and settled, we had a near-perfect life. Who could hate us enough to do something like this?'

'Let's go way back. How long is it since you moved here?'

'Five years or so. This was our long-term project. It was in a bit of a sorry state and I know Will didn't want to sell, he loved the house, but it needed too much doing to it. He'd found that cottage in the village, and it came with Leaf Cottage in the selling price. He took that and we bought Woodlands from him.'

Carl felt as though the earth stood still. He almost stopped breathing, and the cup that had been on its way to his mouth paused in mid-action. 'You bought this house from Will Sandford?'

'We did. It was a bit touch and go because Ella... didn't...

like... him...' His words trailed away as he realised what he was saying.

'Why? Why didn't she like him, Brian?'

'He came on to her, tried to kiss her, and she walloped him. She laughed about it after, but it upset her at the time. We let it go because we were about to complete on the house. I gave him a bit of a warning, and there's been no bother since.'

Carl thought back to the time when he had asked Will Sandford if he knew the Aylwards. *I know the owners as Brian and Ella, had a chat with them one night in the pub, and they did tell me their surname, but I can't remember it.* He had glossed over just how well he had known the purchasers of his property, and Carl gave him ten out of ten for his acting. Now, it seemed, he had known them, and known them well enough to make a pass at Ella, a pass that had been rejected emphatically by what her husband described as a wallop.

32

'We'll need you to amend your statement, Brian. I'll get somebody out here to sort it, but I need this information about the previous owner adding to it.'

'No problem, Carl. Another cuppa?'

'Why not. So he didn't want to sell?'

'No. I think he liked being away from it all, but it's a big old house for one person to rattle around in. Believe me, I know. He bought Oak Cottage which came with a pretty derelict cottage as a freebie, did up the smaller Leaf Cottage for a holiday let and now has an income from that. I have nothing to do with him, didn't from the day we moved in here, but he got the warning about staying away from Ella. He never bothered her again. He apologised – to me, not to her – saying he'd had a bit too much to drink. He's a strange one, didn't seem to have too much respect for women.'

Alarm bells were ringing wildly in Carl's head, and he quickly downed his second drink, along with a third biscuit, and took his leave of the man he felt was walking around in a lost world of his own, unable to understand what had gone so dramatically wrong in such a short space of time.

He drove home, kissed Kat and Martha, and headed upstairs to his study, where he opened up his laptop, logged in using his work access and pulled up the statement taken from Will Sandford.

It told him nothing. Sandford knew nothing, had seen nothing, and had spoken of nothing.

Carl leaned back in his chair, and knew Friday would be an interesting day. He picked up his phone and rang headquarters to give his daily report on progress and actions.

After some polite queries from his DCI about how the investigation was progressing, Carl requested a search warrant. He outlined his reasons succinctly, and it was agreed the paperwork would be available from seven the following morning.

'You think this is him?'

'Ninety per cent yes. And above all else I'm looking for that one item that will lock him away for a long time. And it's something he doesn't know we're looking for.'

'Keep me informed.'

'Of course. You'll hear me cheer.'

They disconnected, and Carl stared at his screen. He needed a van there for seven o'clock to transport Sandford to Chesterfield for questioning, and he needed a six-member team to turn the house upside down looking for anything that could possibly link him to the murders.

Could Will Sandford possibly be fan number one? Carl thought back to the notations at the end of Faith Young's chapters, to the woman who had been excited to meet this man, who was considering starting an affair with him... could that person be Sandford? They only needed to link him to one of the women and he would be charged with the murders of all three as the same knife had been used. A sharp, non-serrated knife that had been honed until it sliced through

ANITA WALLER

flesh as if it was butter. And then there were the two sets of prints.

Carl rang headquarters once again and organised a team of four to join him and Ray Charlton at the church hall for six thirty the following morning. He would brief them and lead them down to the cottage, where Sandford would be woken and arrested, then despatched to Chesterfield.

Carl left the organisation of the prisoner transport vehicle to the duty sergeant as well, and it was only when he was satisfied that everything was good to go the following day, did Carl venture back downstairs.

Kat was on the sofa reading to Martha, but the little girl's eyes were almost closed.

'You want to take her up?' Kat whispered, and he nodded. He leaned forward and gathered the sleeping child into his arms. He carried her to her bedroom and tucked her in, before heading back down.

'Fast asleep,' he said.

'Good, it's been a long day. Everything okay?'

'Ask me tomorrow. I'll talk to you while we're eating, but hopefully after tomorrow it will be safe for you to venture outside again.'

'Oh good.' She moved towards the kitchen. 'Steak and chips okay?'

'Definitely. They'll go down well with the custard creams.'

'What custard creams?'

'I might have had one this afternoon.'

'Carl Heaton! That little bit of a paunch will get bigger and bigger until you start to resemble an elephant, and then eventually you will explode, and your entrails will be scattered far and wide across the Peak District...'

'After three custard creams?'

'Three? You said one.'

'That could have been a little untruth.'

He grinned as she stomped off into the kitchen. 'Slippery slope,' she was muttering, 'all this lying. It's the beginning of the end.'

'Hi, Ray, it's Carl.'

'Oh, hi, boss.'

'You're eating? Sorry to disturb you–'

'That's okay. I've finished the main meal, this is only a bit of tiramisu.'

'I've just had a lecture on my entrails being cast far and wide across Derbyshire for eating three custard creams. God knows what's likely to happen to you after tiramisu. Anyway, tomorrow I need you at the church hall for half past six, we're bringing Will Sandford in for questioning, and I've arranged a search warrant. After the search warrant, the two of us will question this feller.'

There was a period of silence, and Ray said, 'What the fuck...'

'One little bit of information that appeared almost by accident this afternoon and it's steered me to this. I'll brief everybody in the morning, but we're looking for one thing in particular in that house. I'll not keep you now, but don't have much more of that tiramisu. See you in the morning, Ray.'

'Night, boss.'

They disconnected, with the bewilderment in Ray's voice hanging between them. Carl tried not to laugh, but knew Ray would be first there the following day, desperate to know what the hell was going on, and why were they heading off to arrest a man who had helped them several times in the searches for the two missing women.

.   .   .

Kat was in bed for nine after warning him to keep away from the biscuit tin, and he settled down with a book. He had read three pages before he realised he had no idea what he had just read.

He closed the book with a sigh, and went back to thinking about the following day. He would need to get the forensic team out to transport Sandford's car, and if he was right, certain fingerprints already recovered and not matched would start to come together.

But why? Was it simply a case of not being able to understand no means no? Had Faith realised he wasn't quite so amenable in the flesh, and she didn't want what he was expecting from her? And he knew Ella Aylward's wallop had said a very definite no. Did this mean at some point he'd tried it on with Aileen Chatterton and she'd dealt with it? Had he approached her during the searches in the woods?

Carl's mind was reeling with his thoughts, and his ninety per cent gut feeling suddenly escalated to ninety-five per cent. He took out his phone.

'Danny. It's DI Heaton.'

The moment of hesitation was hardly noticeable. 'Sir?'

'Only a question. Did Aileen have any problems with anybody when we were doing the searches in the woods for Faith Young.'

'Nothing me and Blackie didn't handle, sir. Sorry – PC Blackstone.'

'Handle?'

'That creepy feller tried to push her against a tree. I was close, but didn't see it, he'd waited till she was on the opposite side of the tree away from me. So she brought her knee up. When I got to her she was staring down at him on the floor. I went to help him, thinking he was in trouble, but she stopped me. She simply looked down at him and said "pervert". We joined the others, and when we got to the church hall she told us about it. The next day we had a word with him, me and Blackie. Didn't hurt him, like, but we told him we would do if he touched anybody again.'

'Creepy feller? Define creepy feller.'

'The bloke who rented out the holiday let to Mrs Young. Am I in trouble?'

'Not at all. Might organise a commendation for you. See you at half past six, Danny.'

Ninety-seven per cent.

His text to Tessa was succinct. **Tomorrow. Search warrant for Will Sandford's place. Will keep you informed.**

Thought he was one of the good guys! Don't judge a book by its cover.

He grinned at her reply, and picked up his book. He flipped back three pages and reread what he'd already tried to understand; he was working his way through Kat's Stephen King collection and was now at *The Stand*.

After ten minutes he put it down, his thoughts once more drifting to his own horror story that hopefully would be resolved the following day. He'd locate Danny and Blackie out at the rear of the cottage, they were the youngest and presumably the fittest. After all, he had a three-custard-cream paunch now. Whoever had had the training with the Enforcer would be at the front door just in case Sandford didn't respond to the hammering on the door, and the transport van would be positioned at the end of the front garden.

Carl wanted it to be over, he almost ached to be in that interview room with a man he believed to be a murderer, and he craved to blow all his alibis to smithereens, and to confront him with fingerprint and DNA evidence eventually.

And he also needed quite desperately to be able to say to

Brian Aylward, 'Go and spend time with your children when they go to your parents for Easter. I've found Ella's killer, go and learn how to be both Mum and Dad to your children.'

Carl poured a glass of milk and walked out into the back garden. It was bitterly cold, and the brightness of the moon added to the chilling effect. He loved their back garden; no matter where you stood you could hear the tinkle of the brook that ran down the back of the property, and he headed over towards it, to the summer house. There was a chair on the tiny wooden patio, and he sat. He didn't fancy going inside the wooden construction, you couldn't see spiders in the dark.

He listened to the gentle sound of the running water, sipped at his milk and contemplated the events that would unfold. Whatever happened on his fateful Friday, he would spend this weekend with his family, show them the love he felt for them. Kat was six months pregnant with their son, and it seemed every day she produced something new for him.

Over their steak, she had handed Carl two babygros, one in navy and one a Sheffield Wednesday babygro. He had queried if they had a frequent delivery reward system on Amazon, and she had said glibly she had been to the Sheffield Wednesday shop at Hillsborough for that one. She was, she said, safer at Hillsborough than walking down into Eyam village, and if he didn't catch this damn murderer soon, she was going to shout at him.

He couldn't stop the smile as he remembered her words. He couldn't remember how his life had been before he had met Kat; it had been a life of numbers with the fraud squad, and one easily forgotten. Keeping his family safe was now his priority, and that meant keeping crime away from Eyam, their forever home village.

Tomorrow would be a good day, he decided, standing and heading towards the back door.

Tomorrow Will Sandford would really discover what rejection was all about.

33

The briefing was exactly that – brief. After putting Stephen King back on the bookshelf the previous evening, Carl had made detailed notes about the raid, and by half past six the following morning was going through them step by step with the men and women gathered around him.

Danny and Blackstone would be at the back door, and when Carl spotted the burly frame of PC Pete Plant already there, he knew the door would give way with one swing if it became necessary.

Janet Grayson and Stella Rainworth would go inside, accompanying him and Ray Charlton, leaving the transport team to ferry Will Sandford to Chesterfield. Danny and Blackstone would join the search team inside the property once the transport team had left the house.

The men picked to ferry Sandford to Chesterfield joined them and sat down with their colleagues, listening to the softly spoken DI, following every word. Their job wouldn't last as long as the search team, but they had to get it right.

Carl filled everybody in on the talk he had had with Brian Aylward the previous evening, and they mirrored his reaction.

Everybody's head lifted a little higher. He followed that by describing the actions of Sandford towards their colleague, Aileen, in the woods, and this caused muttering amongst the small group of police officers.

'This doesn't mean you can go in that house and trip him up, or even knee him in the balls,' he warned. 'We'll get him for everything he's done, don't worry about that. However, there is one item I want you to look for in that house. If we find it, it will solve everything.'

He talked to them for fifteen minutes, listened to their questions and answered them with as much as he knew, then they stood.

'It's time to move out. Let's put this bugger away for good.'

The transport van parked fifty yards away, waiting for the signal to move closer. The search team took two cars and parked on the main road just below Sandford's cottage, then quietly dispersed to their designated points. Nobody spoke until Danny confirmed they were in place, then Carl hammered on the front door.

'Police! Open up, Mr Sandford! Police!' Gone was the softly spoken DI, and in his place was a man who was totally pissed off with another man who had killed three women. 'Sandford! Open this door! You have thirty seconds to comply.'

He began to count to thirty in his head, as did Janet and Stella standing just behind him. Ray was busy watching the gentle swing of the Enforcer as Pete geared up for the blow.

'Five, four, three, two, one... Pete, your turn now.'

Pete didn't rush. He had a reputation to maintain as One-bash Pete. He hit the door in exactly the right place and the lock and half the door disintegrated. He stepped back and allowed his colleagues to enter, then turned to take the ferocious implement back to the car.

Carl, Janet and Stella were in the hallway when Will Sandford stumbled down the stairs, and Carl recalled Danny and Blackstone to join them. 'We have him. Best come round to the front.'

Sandford looked dazed. His hair was all over the place, his pyjamas held up by his right hand as he clearly believed they were about to fall down, and he stared at the people standing in his hallway.

'What the fuck... and what's happened to my door? You'll pay for this, Heaton!'

Carl was reading him his rights as Danny and Blackstone came through the battered front door, and Carl asked Danny to go upstairs with Sandford and to stay with him at all times while he found some clothes. 'Check the clothes before he puts them on, Danny. We don't want him taking anything out of this house.'

Danny went up three stairs, but Sandford didn't move. The police officer gave him a push and the man stumbled.

'Careful, Danny,' Carl said with a smile. 'We don't want him too injured, do we? Mr Sandford, we have here a warrant to search the premises, and to have your car taken in for forensic examination. We need your keys, please.'

'Find them,' Will Sandford snarled. 'You've got a fucking search warrant, haven't you?' He headed upstairs, followed by Danny, and Carl went outside to beckon the transport team. They drove down and joined everyone else crowded into the hallway.

'We should get started, but I need the keys found first.' He grinned at everybody. 'We're going to have a helluva job locking that front door when we go.'

Pete held up his hand. 'My bad. Sorry.'

The keys proved to be hanging on a hook in the understairs cupboard, and when Danny brought Sandford back down, fully dressed, Carl waved the bunch of keys at him. 'Found them, thanks. You will now be taken to Chesterfield, where you will be held securely until I arrive. You will need a solicitor, this is a triple murder charge, and if you don't have one of your own we have a duty solicitor we can ask to step in. Turn around, Mr Sandford, and put your hands behind your back.' He nodded to the transport team who handcuffed him and escorted him outside.

He was helped into the van, and driven off quickly.

Eyam was waking up, and Nora stood outside watching in disbelief. *Oh my,* she thought, *this was something to tell the church ladies.*

Carl looked through the set of keys, and separated the car key from the rest of the bunch, ready to hand it over to the forensics team when they arrived for the Sportage. He resisted the urge to check out the car, and hoped he could resist the urge to harass the forensics people for the results of their intensive scrutiny of the vehicle. He wondered if Kia would ever include it in their advertising that a Sportage was good for the disposal of bodies...

His search team was busy; Danny, Blackstone and Janet had taken the upstairs, with Stella and Pete currently working downstairs. Carl moved into the lounge. It was a small room with a bookcase built the full length of one wall. Carl glanced at it and decided to leave that till last, he would work his way through everything else first.

The room held two armchairs, a small coffee table, a television on the wall and a small sideboard. His first impression was that he liked the room, it felt cosy, and he imagined with the two small Tiffany lamps lit at night, it would be a place of solace.

A place of solace for anybody who didn't go around killing, anyway.

He tackled the sideboard first, obviously antique and although it had a slight whiff of camphor it was clearly cherished and polished frequently. It was also very tidy. It consisted of a right-hand cupboard and three drawers, and Carl worked his way through everything. There were many photographs of Woodlands and its surrounds, but family-style pictures consisted of two that simply said Dad on the back, and one of a lady who he presumed to be his mother, that said Bitch on the back. Carl slipped all three into an evidence bag.

After pulling out the empty drawers to check there was nothing attached either to the undersides or on to the carcass of the piece of furniture, he put it all back together. He paused for a moment to wonder at the significance of the word Bitch; questions would be asked about that, Carl decided.

He checked both armchairs and didn't even find so much as a five-pence piece, so glanced briefly behind the television, turned the coffee table upside down, switched on both lamps, then turned them off again, and finally moved to the bookcase.

At first glance it seemed to Carl that Will Sandford collected collections. Even just thinking the words made him smile. *Do you have a hobby? Yes, I collect collections.* Like Kat, Will had a vast set, taking up two shelves, of Stephen Kings; he seemed to have a full set of Patricia Cornwell's and all the alphabet series of Sue Grafton. Carl was impressed. There were many others, and he knew the only way to tackle it was to pull each novel out individually, check it and put it back in the same place. Back-breaking and time-consuming. When he reached the Faith Young series of thirteen books he paused.

He looked at the books, and wondered just how many other people were sickened by the loss of a favourite author. Many thousands, he guessed. He took the thirteenth book off the shelf and flicked through it before shaking it. As with all the other books he had already treated in this fashion, nothing fell out of it. There was, however, a hand-written dedication on the front page.

To Will, our time will come. With love, Faith. xxx

Had Faith seen Will Sandford as her escape from a controlling husband? Or was it just somebody on the side to give her some light relief from a life of everything being about books? At forty-three had she still wanted a life with some pleasure in it?

He moved on to the next book, and discovered eight to thirteen all carried a dedication that got increasingly warmer in the words used by Faith. He took pictures of each dedication before putting them back on the shelf. It was as he replaced the eighth one that he caught a glimpse of something behind book seven.

Carl removed the three books in front of it and carefully pulled out the small notebook.

The first page was headed *Eyam Book Notes,* and he read through, almost following the route she had walked on that Monday morning. And then he saw the part that he hoped would send Will Sandford to prison for the rest of his life.

House. White – grey in rain. Smoke dark grey. Shutters closed. Why? Open earlier. Ivy black not green. No obv people.

These two lines of Faith Young's observations reflected the point when Will Sandford left his observation post in Woodlands, and headed for the spot where he knew Faith Young would have to pass. And he knew about that point because he'd given her a map to get to it. And Amanda Gilchrist in the tea rooms had seen Faith writing in the little notebook while having her lunch, just prior to entering the woods, so it had been about her person, probably in her coat pocket, as she began the climb to meet her killer.

Carl dropped the booklet into an evidence bag, then left to go upstairs. There was a cheer as they saw what he was holding up. 'This is what I wanted. I knew if we found this, we had him. Has anybody found anything?'

'Only a confession, sir,' Janet said, trying to keep her face straight.

'Smart arse,' he said and headed down to the kitchen and dining room.

He chatted to the other two, then said he was nipping out for ten minutes to see Brian Aylward. 'I rang him last night to warn him there would be action in the village today, but now I need to tell him what that action is. I also need to see Aileen's parents, and Jack Young will have to have a phone call. It's important I do that before they're inundated with press, so Ray, can you finish off the bookshelves please? Come with me and I'll show you where I'm at.'

Ray followed him through to the lounge. 'I've almost finished the kitchen. He's very tidy, isn't he?'

'Certainly is. Look at these.' Carl pointed out the various series of books, and said he would finish off the Faith Young set, then go and see Brian.

'No problem, boss. Give him my best, won't you.'

'I will, Ray. I'll not be too long, then we'll get off to Chesterfield. Let's see what he's got to say. You found the murder weapon?'

Ray hesitated. 'Could have. There's a brand-new set on the side, six knives in a block, and I reckon any one of three of them could have cut throats. I've bagged the whole set, but I can't say anything for definite. There's no visible blood on any of them. I've asked Pete to go through the shed in the garden next, because he's just about finished the dining room.'

34

Carl pulled into the courtyard at Woodlands, and Brian came out of the back door to meet him.

'You've something to tell me?'

'I have. But first I need to check something.' He walked towards the back door, took the set of Will Sandford's keys out of the evidence bag, and studied the door for a moment before inserting one of the keys. The lock clicked backwards and forwards.

'I guess Sandford took copies before he signed the house over to you,' he said quietly.

'You've arrested him?'

'The jungle drums are working then.'

'Nora saw you.'

'We have arrested him, and I'll be interviewing him this afternoon.'

Brian shook his hand. 'Thank you, Carl.'

'Don't presume anything, Brian. He'll be lawyered up by the time I get there, and he'll be saying *no comment* to everything.'

.   .   .

Fred was filling Cheryl in on his plans for the following week when Beth walked through the door.

'Good grief,' he said. 'You're a surprise. I didn't expect you back until the middle of next week.'

'We had to come back. We could have ended up being stuck in Florida, not able to get home, so here we are. Am I hearing right that Will Sandford has been arrested for the murders?'

'Seems like it. Carl rang Tessa to tell her, but I think Nosey Nora has told the rest of the village. So you had a good time?' Fred gave her a quick kiss on the cheek. 'Welcome back.'

'It's been amazing. Here.' She fished around in a capacious bag that proclaimed Minnie Mouse rules, and pulled out a stuffed Mickey. She handed it to Fred.

'Just what I've always wanted. Thank you, Beth...'

She handed a Minnie to Cheryl. 'You crack me up, Beth,' Cheryl said, 'but thank you, it will share this desk with me.'

'There's something else I need to share with you.' Beth turned around and walked towards her office door. She slid the brass name plate out of the slider that contained it and handed it to Cheryl. 'Can you organise getting another one of these, please?'

'Somebody new starting?' Cheryl looked and sounded puzzled.

'No, just a different name. It needs to be Beth Masters, instead of Beth Walters.'

There was silence for a few seconds then Cheryl screamed. 'Oh my God! You're married!'

Tessa and Luke came close to falling down the stairs, thinking Cheryl was being attacked. Beth calmly handed Luke a Mickey, and Tessa a Minnie, and grinned. 'Don't panic, it's just Cheryl being a wuss.'

'She's seen a spider?' Luke asked.

'No, I told her my new name. Beth Masters.'

Simon joined them as she spoke, and she handed him a Mickey. Tessa hugged her and whispered her congratulations, but it took Luke a little longer to catch on to what was happening. When he did, his face lit up.

'You got married? In Florida? Was that the plan all along?'

'Not for me.' She laughed, waggling her ring finger around as if showing proof of her words. 'But it was for Joel, apparently. While I was sorting you lot out with some information, he was sorting out our wedding day. It was amazing and so special, but now we've had to come home. And we have to organise how we're going to keep this business running, because we're not going to be able to meet up after next week. It seems it's full lockdown, to try to control this virus. All the time we've been in the States we've avoided everybody. And if I'm being honest, I was glad to come home.'

'Kat knows?'

Beth smiled. 'She does. I've taken her and Carl a Mickey and a Minnie, but Martha got one of each and a suitcase full of Mickey and Minnie clothes. I had a whale of a time shopping for her. Speaking of whales... let me tell you about manatees.'

'They're not whales,' Luke pointed out.

'I know they're not, but it just kind of led on to it. I am now an expert on them, so expect a PowerPoint presentation arriving in your inbox.'

Fred smiled at his boss. 'I'm sure we'll all look forward to it. Congratulations, Beth, from all of us. I know Doris would have approved. I'll put the kettle on, shall I?'

Carl called in at Connection; his visit home to check his girls were okay had seen him receive the news of the Beth and Joel partnership, and he threw his arms around the girl he considered his sister-in-law, and gave her a huge kiss on the cheek.

'Congratulations, lovely,' he said. 'We having a party?'

'We are as soon as we can. Don't hold your breath for a date for it though. Anyway, it's you who needs the congratulations, so I hear?'

'He's a long way from being locked up for the rest of his life, but we'll get there. He's made mistakes along the way, and we'll be capitalising on them. I'm interviewing him this afternoon, so it could be a long day. I'm calling to see Aileen Chatterton's parents after this, because I've no doubt they've heard rumours already. Brian Aylward knows, as does Jack Young. It's strange, but he was number one on my list, once I'd found what he was really like behind this Mr Nice Guy façade he has.'

Carl accepted the cup of tea Fred handed to him, and sipped at it almost without realising what he was doing. 'Have you decided what will happen if this lockdown does start next week?'

'I don't think there's any *if* about it.' Beth spoke quietly. 'We can, in quite a few cases, work from home. Surveillance is a thing done while alone, so we can manage certain issues, and I'm going to place an advert in trade papers and on Facebook, plus our website of course, that spells out we are still available for Zoom and telephone consultations, so we'll see what happens. What will happen with you?'

'Precisely nothing. The police can't stop, even if the rest of the country does. That's the scary part, I have a six-month pregnant wife. If I catch it, it's almost certain she will. Right, thanks for the tea. I'll keep in touch, no matter what happens. I'm off to see Mr and Mrs Chatterton now, and I'm dreading it. It's so hard when it's a serving officer, but at least I'm not there to tell them we're getting nowhere.'

· · ·

Carl was back behind his desk before two, and switched on his computer. The email at the top of a long list was from Forensics, saying they had delivered a small bag of car contents for him to check, that luminol had revealed blood in the boot and it had been sent for testing.

He punched the air, and then looked around the desk for the bag of items removed from the car. Ray stepped through the door holding them.

'They handed them to me, so I hung on to them till you got here. We found nothing else at the house, so his phone and his laptop are with the tech lads, you've got this,' he waved the bag around, 'and all we have to do now is prove he did it.'

'Easy,' was Carl's dry response.

'What time do you need me?'

'About three? I'll sort the emails, have a sandwich so my stomach isn't growling all through the interview, and we'll make a start. He got a solicitor?'

'He did. Barclay Wright.'

'His choice or as duty solicitor?'

'Duty. He was totally uninterested in getting one apparently, says he's done nothing wrong. We asked Wright to talk to Sandford, and he's agreed a solicitor can sit in but say nothing.' Ray shook his head. 'Some people are so stupid.'

Carl opened the bag of items from the car, and began to go through them. It seemed Will Sandford's tidiness extended beyond his home and into the car. A pack of baby wipes, a small pack of tissues, an A5-sized book of maps and a case containing a tool for removing the locking wheel nuts. 'Is that it?'

'Unless you want the spare tyre as well, it is. The chap who brought this up, and if I could remember his name I'd tell you, said it had been recently cleaned, the boot reeked of bleach and the car interior was spotless. They have found miniscule amounts of blood, but enough to test, so they'll send the results through as soon as they've got them.'

'Thanks, Ray. Take a break now, it could be a late night.'

'Just nipping out for some decent coffee. You want one?'

'Thanks. Latte.' He handed his sergeant a ten-pound note. 'My treat, we've earned this.'

35

Will Sandford's head lifted as he heard the door open. 'About time. What the hell's going on?'

Carl stared at him without responding to the aggression oozing out of him. He sat down and switched on the recording machine. 'DI Carl Heaton, DS Raymond Charlton, Barclay Wright, solicitor and William Sandford. Friday, twentieth March, twenty-twenty.' He glanced at his watch. 'Three fifteen pm.'

He placed his file on the desk and slowly opened it. 'For the record, your address is Oak Cottage, Eyam, Derbyshire. Is that correct?'

'It is. Do you want my postcode?' The cockiness was evident in his voice and Carl's face retained its impassivity.

'No thank you, we have it already. Mr Sandford, we are here to discuss three murders: Faith Young, PC Aileen Chatterton and Ella Aylward. I'm going to speak of them in turn, hear your side of the events that led up to their deaths, and then we'll move on to what happens next.'

'What happens next is I bloody go home.'

'That's not very likely, Mr Sandford,' Ray said quietly. 'Not for forty years anyway.'

'Does your monkey have to be here?' Will snapped.

'Afraid so.' Carl smiled. 'He's the one who's found most of the evidence against you. Did the gorilla work, you might say. Now, let's start with Faith Young. She rented Leaf Cottage for one month from you?'

'She did.'

'And how much did she pay for the month?'

'She didn't.'

'She rented for free?'

'No, as you already know, her husband paid for it, and he paid two thousand pounds.'

'Why did she need it?'

'Faith was an author, and needed to be in Eyam for research for her new book. She rang to enquire about Leaf Cottage, and then booked it with her husband's credit card.'

'And that was the first time you encountered her?'

He touched his thumbs together. 'Yes.'

'I do have to tell you that we believe you did know her. Number one fan? We have just searched your home and seen the collection of Faith Young books, with the dedications handwritten by her. We have also seen additional confirmation of the intention to have an affair with you, so what went wrong? What did you do to her that caused her to back off?'

He linked his thumbs this time. 'No comment.'

Carl smiled. 'Well. That didn't take long. We'll leave that for a moment and move on to Aileen Chatterton. PC Aileen Chatterton. This might get you some kudos inside, killing a copper, but it won't while you're in this building. Let's talk through your attempt to assault her, shall we?'

'What?'

'You pushed her against a tree. She took aim with her knee,

and you ended up on the ground. Would that be a reasonable explanation of what happened?'

'She was coming on to me... and those thugs of yours had a go at me when she twisted it all and told them her version later.'

'Coming on to you? She was twenty-two, you're forty-eight. And if she'd been coming on to you, she certainly wouldn't have kneed you in the balls. So was that why she died? Another rejection straight after Faith giving you the push?'

'No comment.'

'Okay, let's move swiftly on. We've a fair number of murders to get through here, haven't we?'

Once more Sandford pressed his thumbs together.

'Ella Aylward. Did you think it would be nicely significant leaving her body round the back of a shed in an ex-copper's rear garden? You knew DCI Mitchell lived in that cottage, he was close enough to you to be a neighbour of yours. Did it give you an added kick to leave it there?'

'No comment.'

'And of course, Ella was another lady who rejected your advances, wasn't she? See the pattern developing here? Will Sandford fancies somebody, Will Sandford gets rejected, Will Sandford kills them. This is not the behaviour of normal people, Will.'

'No comment.'

Ray leaned forward. Once again he used his gentler voice. 'Saying no comment isn't going to help you, Will. You see, we have proof that you were the last person to see Faith Young. We collected something from your house this morning that only the killer could have got, because it was in Faith Young's coat pocket.' He reached down to a box file, and removed the evidence bag holding the small notebook.

'For the tape, I am showing Mr Sandford a small A6-sized notebook, with a few annotations in made by Faith Young to be used as research material for her forthcoming novel. Do you recognise this, Mr Sandford? We found it at the back of your Faith Young collection.'

'I found it on the floor outside her cottage.'

'It was with her when she was abducted. Her notes tell us that. And it isn't wet at all, it hasn't been left out in the rain. It was removed from her pocket either before or after her death, and we believe it was kept as a souvenir by the killer.'

'No comment.'

'So you didn't find it on the floor outside her cottage?'

'No comment.'

Janet Grayson knocked and entered, handed Carl a printout and just as quickly left.

Carl touched Ray's foot to indicate he would take over, and Ray sat back in his chair.

'We took your car in for forensic examination this morning, Will. Can you confirm you are the owner of this Kia Sportage?' He passed a photograph provided by the forensic team across to the man, who was starting to have beads of sweat on his forehead.

'It is mine, and you'd better not have damaged it.'

'We haven't damaged it, but we have cleaned up the blood a bit better than you did, despite you using bleach. It seems we've managed to find two lots of blood inside the car, one matching Faith Young and one matching Ella Aylward. Do you have an explanation for that?'

'I cleaned the car boot with bleach because I put my walking boots in it after I'd been in the woods with you lot, looking for Faith.'

'Did I say it was the boot? I thought I said the car.'

He watched as Sandford again forced his thumbs together. 'But that's not all we have.'

He located the evidence bag holding one of the knives from

the knife block lifted from the kitchen of Oak Cottage, and placed it in front of him.

'Do you recognise this knife?'

'No.'

'It's one of a set of six that normally stands on the work surface of your kitchen.'

'You sure?'

'Definitely. It also has been tested for blood, and guess what, we've linked the minutest amount trapped between the blade and the handle, and Ella Aylward. You see, the thing is, Will, we only need to match something of yours, like a murder weapon, to one of the women, and we can charge you with all three murders, because you've not been the smartest cookie in the biscuit barrel. You used the same knife for all three women, according to the autopsies.' He held up the bag. 'This knife. And you washed it and put it back in its proper place, in that knife block. I would suggest you need a new dishwasher, your old one doesn't remove blood.'

For the first time, Barclay Wright spoke. 'I'd like a few minutes with my client, if that's okay, officers.'

'Certainly. We'll go and grab a coffee, and I'll have two sent in here. That okay?'

Wright nodded his thanks, and Carl and Ray stood, gathering up everything they had before leaving.

'You think we've done enough?' Ray asked Carl as they looked through the one-way glass. Wright and his client were deep in conversation, their drinks still untouched on the table. They had been talking for twenty minutes.

'This coffee's a crime in itself. Can we lock somebody up for this?' Ray said, taking a small sip out of the cardboard container.

'A vending machine? You want to lock up a vending machine?'

'Whatever and whoever. That latte we had earlier was ace, but this tripe is horrible.' He tipped the dregs back into the drip catcher tray, and rejoined Carl at the window.

'They're still talking. Think they're cooking something up to explain all this away?'

'No idea, but there'll be no explaining anything away. He had the notebook, he's got the blood in his car and on his knife, what's to explain away?'

'Then let's hope he's admitting everything.'

'And we didn't even have to question him about the photograph with *Bitch* written on the back.'

The mood in the briefing room was one of jubilation. None of them had dared to hope for a confession, but after an hour and a half of being closeted with Barclay Wright, Will Sandford had capitulated.

Carl and Ray were convinced that the dreary solicitor had bored Will into making the confession, but it seemed that whatever he had said to his client had worked.

Will Sandford had been charged with three counts of murder, and was scheduled to appear in court the following day.

Telephone calls had been made to Jack Young, the Chattertons and Brian Aylward, and now Carl emptied his wallet of all his cash and was persuading Ray to take everybody to the pub after work, and get them drunk.

'Thank you, everybody. You've been a brilliant team throughout this investigation, enjoy yourselves tonight. We'll probably be in lockdown by next week, so make tonight a good one!'

They cheered, and tidied their desks, leaving the room in

silence within about ten minutes. Carl headed back to his own adjoining office, and sat back with a sigh. He hadn't even had to introduce the fingerprint evidence, but he felt satisfied that the proof was there – Will Sandford had been the man who had used the Aylwards' bedroom for observation of the path through the woods, but Carl was now equally convinced that the dead women were all targets and not random females out for a walk.

Sandford didn't like rejection; he had tolerated Ella's 'wallop', but the threat from her husband to back off probably saved her life five years earlier. However, he didn't forget... the successful killings of two further women who had rejected him effectively sealed Ella Aylward's fate. And Carl strongly suspected that the *Bitch* had rejected him just as emphatically at some point in his life, all of which would be in their discovery package by the time he appeared before a judge for sentencing.

Carl felt saddened. Three lovely women with many years in front of them, all dead because one man couldn't take rejection.

The news from Carl certainly livened up the staff at Connection, and they toasted their friend in his absence with coffee and doughnuts.

'Wonderful result,' Fred said. 'A full confession makes life so much easier for all concerned, takes away the stress, and definitely helps victims' families, so I'm pleased for him. And Eyam's safe once again. Mind you, it's a safe place anyway with Nosey Nora on the lookout.'

He stepped back into his office, and came out with several small boxes. 'I've got everybody a box of these. I know our erstwhile leader, Boris, has said they don't do much good, but if we've to see any clients face to face, I think we should afford them the courtesy of wearing a mask.' He handed the boxes around, and saw trepidation in their eyes.

Beth smiled at him. 'Thank you, Fred. I don't quite know how we're going to handle this, but I don't doubt we will. I want us to have a Zoom meeting every Wednesday at ten, and we'll judge for ourselves if that is enough. Cheryl, I think the best thing to do is transfer all calls to your home number if that's okay with you, and you work from home. You'll be our point of stability. I too can work from home because I can keep in touch with my clients by Zoom, as can Simon, but the rest of you, our out-based workers, are going to have to play it by ear every day. It will depend on the case as to how you handle it. If you need help, shout up. Tessa, I hope everything goes smoothly with your house purchase, and again, if you need help we're all here for you.'

Beth was the last to leave that Friday, and she closed and secured the shutters with a heavy heart. Oliver had gone home with Luke and Maria, to take up permanent residence in their home instead of the office, Cheryl had switched the landline number through to her own phone at home, Fred had waited in the Co-op for Naomi to finish, then walked her home, and Tessa had given Beth a huge hug, saying they would get through it, and come back stronger than ever.

She climbed into her car, and headed for Little Mouse Cottage. It was time to set up an office space for her and Joel, working from home would become the new normal for them.

And Eyam slipped slowly into lockdown, melding seamlessly into its history, replaying the actions of September 1665 all over again, some three hundred and fifty-five years further down its own historical timeline. Eyam's second plague had arrived.

EPILOGUE

JULY 2020

C arl Heaton sat in his back garden nursing his tiny son, Jacob. He couldn't believe how much love could be inside him for such a small scrap of a thing, but love him he did. With every bone in his body.

Kat and her mum Enid were busy sorting out food in the kitchen, looking forward to welcoming their guests who were due any time. The sun was shining, and all was right with the world, in an odd sort of way. Lockdown was slowly being eased, but very slowly, and they had decided to have a barbecue to get everybody back together.

Fred and Naomi were the first to arrive, followed shortly after by Luke and Maria. Luke immediately helped in the kitchen, and Maria took charge of the baby while Carl disappeared to start the barbecue. Tessa arrived on foot – now she was living in Eyam she intended walking more, and she figured there would be wine at Kat's house, so maybe it was a good idea to walk rather than drive.

Beth and Joel arrived with several bottles of wine, and Cheryl appeared last, accompanied by Cliff Baines. Fred immediately crossed the lawn towards them, and shook Cliff's hand.

'Good to see you, Cliff. You okay?'

'Getting there, Fred. Since Ethan went time goes so slowly, but Cheryl has been wonderful. She doesn't let me get too maudlin, as she puts it, and we've had several trips out, as best you can in a lockdown situation. And I'm pleased to say my divorce is now final, so I don't have to have anything to do with the Brighton duo anymore.'

'Good. Time to move on.'

Cliff looked towards Cheryl, where she was helping to bring food out into the garden, under the shade of the gazebo. 'I hope so, Fred, I hope so. I miss Ethan so much, but the pain became intolerable, so they had to let him slip away. I wouldn't want him back with me to go through any of it again. When I start to dip, Cheryl lends me her kids. That soon stops the spiral, I can tell you. Lovely kids.'

Carl walked towards the group holding cans of lager. 'These okay?'

'Certainly are. Good to see you, Carl. And this is Cliff Baines, the estate agent who sold Tessa her cottage.'

'So I understand.' Carl smiled. 'The cottage that came with its own corpse in the shed.'

'Sorry about that,' Cliff said, stifling a laugh. 'I check them all now, just in case.'

The afternoon passed by in a blur, and after Martha and baby Jacob had been put to bed, the guests sat around, drinking and eating. They began to drift away between nine and ten, and as darkness fell Kat and Carl sat back with a deep sigh of contentment. The brook trickled lethargically in the background, and Carl reached for her hand.

'I love you, Kat Heaton.'

'And I love you,' she responded.

'I spoke to Beth tonight. It seems this lockdown has made very little difference to Connection. They've all worked the whole way through it, the only thing missing from their lives that was there before is doughnuts.'

Kat thought for a moment. 'Yeah, I can understand that. It was always a large part of our working life, the doughnut break.'

'I did get the impression they'd all like to be back at the office, but it's worked for them having to be at home. They're upbeat about the future, and looking forward to extending even more.'

Kat smiled at him. 'Carl, my love, it'll take more than a triple murderer and a virus to put Connection down. Long may it survive!'

THE END

ACKNOWLEDGEMENTS

As always, my gratitude goes to the entire team at Bloodhound who have supported and encouraged me with every book I have written. This one was no exception, and I am truly 'Yorkshire chuffed' about the excellent covers designed by Betsy for all three of the Connection Trilogy books. The matching set look amazing side by side.

Amanda Gilchrist and Cheryl Dodd both feature once more in this final book, so thank you, ladies, for lending me your names! I hope you're pleased with the end result.

To my beta reading team (Marnie Harrison, Tina Jackson, Denise Cutler, Sarah Hodgson and Alyson Read) and my ARC group – words can't say how much I appreciate all your efforts on my behalf. The arrival of so many reviews by launch day is amazing, and I bless you all every time I bring out a new book.

Morgen Bailey – my super-hero editor – thank you. I have discovered so much through your comments and thoughts, and

I am so sorry you have to keep correcting POV. I can't even promise one day to understand it!

My friends in my literary world, you make life in front of a computer screen so much better: Susan Hunter, Judith Baker, Tara Lyons, Mandy James, Valerie Keogh, Patricia Dixon, Livia Sbarbaro, Claudia Hopkins and Leigh Russell, with you I smile.

And finally, my love and thanks go to my family. Dave, for listening, my little lot at Kirkheaton, my other little lot at no.19, my other little lot at no.151, and all the assorted animals at these homes, I love you.

Anita Waller
October 2021

A NOTE FROM THE PUBLISHER

Thank you for reading this book. If you enjoyed it please do consider leaving a review on Amazon to help others find it too.

We hate typos. All of our books have been rigorously edited and proofread, but sometimes mistakes do slip through. If you have spotted a typo, please do let us know and we can get it amended within hours.

info@bloodhoundbooks.com

Printed in Great Britain
by Amazon

77942323R00159